KARL J. MORGAN

Heartstone:
Sentinels of Far Sun

Contents

Chapter 1

The night was too quiet. Bill Marshall was accustomed to the sounds of crickets chirping outside his ranch house. The occasional hoot of a passing owl would normally remind him that nature is hard at work even in the middle of the night. Even while asleep, his ears were focused on the sounds of the local coyotes. He had lost more than one lamb to the intruders who were brazen enough to make their way into the barn. Tonight though, there was no sound outside. He could only hear Bonnie breathing deeply as she slept next to him.

Bill rolled over and looked at his alarm clock, which read 3:30 a.m. He climbed out of bed and walked over to the small window overlooking the front of the house. The few security lights showed no signs of motion or life. He couldn't remember the last time he saw those lights without a cloud of insects around them. It seemed surreal, as though all life on Earth had disappeared, leaving just he and his wife on their small ranch in rural San Diego County. Bill walked toward the bathroom to get a drink of water. He stubbed his toe on Bonnie's shoe that lay in his path. He hopped on his other foot and held back a shout of pain.

"Bill, what's going on?" Bonnie asked dreamily. "Why are you out of bed?"

"I was just getting a drink of water, sweetheart," he replied. "I'm sorry I woke you. Please go back to sleep." Bonnie rolled over and fell back to sleep almost immediately. Bill was jealous of her ability to sleep almost anywhere. If Bill wasn't in his own bed, he always had a hard time getting any rest. Even here, he often woke at any unusual sound, or even the lack of sound. He filled a glass with water and drank deeply. The throbbing in his toe had stopped. Being refreshed by the water, he climbed back into bed. He rolled over to look at Bonnie's face. She had a small smile on her face. Believing she was having a good dream, Bill relaxed and soon was asleep himself.

Shortly after four o'clock, a sound woke Bill again. The sliding doors of their closet were banging against each other. The first tremor shook the entire room. Bonnie sat up straight in bed, wide awake. "What's going on, Bill?" she cried.

"It's an earthquake, sweetheart," he replied. "Just stay in bed. It'll stop in a few seconds." A second tremor rolled through the house, causing their bed to move a few inches across the floor. Bill heard the water glass in the bathroom fall to the floor and shatter. Bonnie was in his arms now, with her face buried in his chest. The third tremor was the strongest yet. Pictures fell from the walls. Bill could hear glass breaking downstairs. Their bed slid over toward the window, crashing into the wall.

An eerie quiet took over. Time seemed to stand still as they clung to each other awaiting the next tremor. After a minute, Bill said, "I think it's over, Bonnie. Let me go check on the damage." Bill quickly changed into jeans and a tee shirt and pulled on his boots. He looked in the bathroom and saw the broken glass as well as shampoo and other bottles littering the floor. "Be careful, Bonnie, there's broken glass all over in here." He ran over to the window and opened it. Insects were buzzing around the security lights now. He could also hear his sheep braying in the barn. "Honey, please see what happened downstairs. I've got to check the animals." Bill ran down the stairs and out the front door.

It had started to rain as Bill sloshed through the new puddles toward the barn. He opened the man-door and stepped inside. His German shepherd Zelda ran right past him and headed out into the dark. He called after the dog, but she was long gone. Bill looked at his flock and all the animals seemed to be fine. The tremors had shaken all the water out of the trough, so he refilled it and walked out of the barn, being careful to latch the door behind him. Bill checked on his other buildings and found the feed shed had shaken itself to pieces. Bags of feed were strewn around. The wreckage was too dangerous to work on in the dark, so he left it and returned to the house.

As he stepped up on the porch, he felt a mosquito land on his shoulder. He slapped it with his hand, but immediately knew something was wrong. He looked down and saw the insect still moving, although it was injured. It did look like a mosquito, but was too big to be real. He stomped it with his boot to make certain it was dead. He picked it up and dropped it in a glass jar that his granddaughter had left on the porch after her last search for lightning bugs. He screwed on the lid as tight as he could, and then went inside. He found Bonnie in the kitchen making a pot of coffee. She had already swept the broken plates and glasses into a pile in a corner. She had turned on the small television she always watched while cooking.

Carl Dennis, a local reporter was talking to the camera. "We've had a major earthquake in San Diego County, centered about twenty miles northeast of the city. There are no reports of damage yet, but the quake occurred only a few minutes ago. The preliminary report shows the strength at 8.9 on the Richter Scale, which will make this the most powerful earthquake ever to hit this area. All citizens are urged to stay at home until morning if it is safe to do so. Report any damage to your local police or the Highway Patrol."

"Bill, I'm scared," Bonnie said. "We're twenty miles northeast of San Diego. How was everything outside?"

"The sheep are fine. That damn dog ran out into the woods when I opened the barn. She must have been more scared than you!" Bill laughed. "One of the sheds collapsed, but it was that old one I use for feed bags. Everything else seems okay. If that was really an 8.9, we are very lucky to still have this house standing."

There was a knock at the door and Bill went to see who it was. He returned in a minute with their son Frank, his wife Cindy, and their daughter Cybil. After saying hello, everyone sat at the table to have coffee. Bonnie brought milk and cookies for Cybil. "Dad, we need to stay with you guys tonight," Frank said. "Our house took a big hit and half the roof collapsed. We're lucky it wasn't worse than that."

"Of course! You guys have your coffee. Cindy and I will make up the guest rooms for you," Bonnie said. The two women left the kitchen.

"What the hell is that?" Frank said when he saw the bug in the glass jar. He picked up the jar and turned it in every direction to examine the creature.

"I think it's some kind of mosquito, Frank," Bill said. "It landed on me when I was checking for damage outside. I slapped it, and it fell off but was still moving around. Finally, I had to stomp on it to make sure it was dead."

"It does look like a mosquito, but it's the size of a hummingbird. I've never seen one that big. Did it bite you?" Frank asked.

Bill pulled the arm up on the sleeve of his shirt, but there was no mark. "I guess I got it first. I'll take it to the vet tomorrow. Maybe he'll know what it is. By the way, where's Chachis?"

"When the quake hit, our bedroom window fell out of the frame. That dog jumped off the bed and out through the window. I looked around a long time but never saw a sign of her," Frank replied. "Cybil was crying and crying for that dog. But it was just too dangerous at the house for us to stay and wait for her to come back. Another tremor could hit anytime, and we could be dead."

"You're right, son," Bill replied. "It's odd that Zelda did the same thing when I went to the barn to check on the sheep. She practically knocked me down trying to get out that door. She ran straight into the woods. I'm sure she'll be back in the morning."

"Grandpa, do you want some cookies?" Cybil said holding out a handful of cookies.

"I sure do, sweetheart," Bill replied as he kissed her on the forehead. "You probably shouldn't eat too many or you won't be able to get any sleep."

"Do you think Zelda ran out to find Chachis for me?" Cybil asked.

"I hope so, sweetheart," Bill smiled. "They can take care of each other until they come back to us."

"It definitely looks like a mosquito, Bill," Doc Watson said. It was eight in the morning the day after the earthquake and Bill arrived at the veterinarian's office before anyone else. Now he sat in the office with Doc Harry Watson who turned the jar over and over examining the insect inside. "I've never seen one that size before. I might drive down to the UCSD campus this afternoon and show it to a couple professors I know there. Perhaps they can tell us where it came from."

"I'd appreciate that Harry," Bill replied. "I only saw one, thankfully. I can imagine what a group of these things could do if they attacked. My son Frank googled big mosquitoes today and couldn't find anything remotely like this."

"Did you have any other damage from the quake last night?" Harry asked.

"We had lots of glasses and dishes break. My feed shed collapsed, but that thing was decades old, so I'm not surprised. Frank had a lot of damage to his house. He lost most of the roof. His family has moved in with us for now," Bill said. "There was on odd thing. Both my dog and Frank's ran away after the quake. It was the strangest thing. I'm not sure how I'm going to manage the flock without Zelda."

"It might be a good idea to keep your flock in the barn right now, Bill," Harry said. "With giant mosquitoes flying around, you don't want to take any chances." Harry rose and walked over to the window and looked out on the small town main street. "Isn't that funny? It looks like that Carl Dennis from Channel 10 out there with a camera man. He seems to be talking to everyone in town."

"I'm going to show him this bug," Bill said. "I'll be sure to bring it right back so you can take it to the university later." He grabbed the jar and both men headed out into the cool morning air.

A small crowd of people had gathered around the reporter and were taking turns speaking about the earthquake the previous night. Bill's sister Eileen was talking now about how her dog had tried desperately to get out of the house after the quake. She had little damage but woke to find the inside of the front door badly scarred and marked with blood from the dog's feet. She had been on her way to the vet when she saw the action. She was holding Coco in her arms and was showing the dog's feet to the camera.

After she finished, Bill walked up to his sister and hugged her close. Harry came along and took the dog and headed back to his clinic. Bill and Eileen followed him, until Carl Dennis called out Bill's name. He turned to find the camera aimed at him and a microphone in his face. Bill hadn't seen Carl in person since college. They had been friends growing up in this town. Their friendship ended when Bonnie decided to marry Bill and broke Carl's heart.

"It's good to see you again, Carl," Bill said.

"This is my old friend, Bill Marshall," Carl said to the camera. "Tell us about the earthquake last night. Did you have any damage?"

"Some. Lots of glasses and dishes were broken and one shed collapsed. My son Frank lost half of his roof a couple miles from our ranch," he replied.

"What in the world is in that jar?" Carl asked when he noticed the glass jar in Bill's hand.

"It's some kind of mosquito, I think," Bill replied. "It landed on me last night, right after the earthquake. So I swatted it and stepped on it." He held up the jar so the camera man could get a close up. "I brought it here to show Doc Watson, who says he'll take it to some professors he knows at UCSD today."

"That's really disgusting," Carl winced. "I've never seen a mosquito that size. Get an extreme close-up on this thing," he said to the camera man. "Thanks for sharing with us, Bill." Carl turned to talk to other residents and Bill headed back to the vet clinic.

Bill's phone vibrated in his pocket. He pulled it out and saw Bonnie was calling. He figured she had seen him on television. "Hi, honey," he said.

"We've got trouble in the barn, Bill. Cindy and I keep hearing crazy braying coming from in there. It sounds like the sheep are going mad. You've got to come home now," Bonnie said. "Frank went to work and it's just us here now."

"I'm on my way. Bye," Bill said as he rushed to the vet's office. He ran in and set the jar on the vet's desk and headed out to his pickup. He jumped in and started the engine. He threw it into gear and it lurched up to speed and headed the five short miles to his ranch. Those five miles seemed to take forever as he was desperate to find out what was wrong. It was not like Bonnie to be afraid to work with the sheep. He had trained her how to shear and they worked as a team when heavy work needed to be done.

A voice on the radio said, "So far, the reports of damage from last night's earthquake are very limited. I think we dodged a bullet on this one. There has been little effect from what is now being called an 8.8 quake. We'll keep you updated as new information becomes available." Bill pulled onto the short road to the ranch buildings and slammed on the brakes as he approached the ranch. He flew out of the truck and raced to the barn. He could hear the braying and crying of the animals inside. There was no smell of fire, but he couldn't take any chances with his prize flock and flung the doors open. Dozens of sheep raced toward him and he dived sideways so he wouldn't be trampled by them. The sheep ran around the open yard and raced to get as far from the barn as possible. When the sheep had exited, he slammed the doors closed and latched them.

He ran back to the house and opened the door. Bonnie, Cindy, and Cybil were sitting on the couch in tears. Bonnie had a shotgun on her lap. Bill rushed to her and kissed her and hugged Cindy and Cybil. He took the rifle from Bonnie and said, "Call Frank now and tell him to get here as fast as he can. I need you to help me gather the sheep and put them in the fenced pasture. They seem to be calming down. While you two do that, I'm going to check on the barn."

Bill ran out the door again and headed back to the barn. He could see his sheep on the opposite side of the property near a small pond where they appeared to be calming down and drinking water. At least that part of the battle was over for now. He carefully opened the man-door and stepped in. It was very quiet and dark inside now, with a few rays of light shining between the slats on the walls. Nothing was moving and there was no sound. At the far end of the barn, he could see four sheep lying down on their sides. He approached them slowly. They did not move and he could not see their chests move as they breathed. He was certain they were dead. Perhaps they had been trampled by the other sheep when they panicked. Perhaps one of those giant mosquitoes had bitten them. Or maybe a coyote got in to escape the quake. As he reached the first two animals, he could see they were clearly dead, but couldn't find any marks from being trampled. He rolled the first one over and found two large puncture marks on its neck. He found the same thing on the second.

Something was very wrong here. He cocked his shotgun. The third sheep looked like a bag of bones, as though all the muscles and organs had been removed without cutting the skin. It had several bite marks all over its body. A movement caught his eye and he stepped back. The fourth sheep appeared to be moving away from him, as though something was dragging it. He stepped cautiously forward until he was within ten feet of the carcass. A small pair of black eyes was watching him from just above the dead animal. He couldn't see the rest of it though. A strange feeling came over Bill and he started to step backward. He looked from side to side and began to see more black eyes staring back. Quick movements caught his eye but he could not see what was happening. He had moved backward most of the way to the door when Frank flung the big doors open behind him.

With the sunlight flooding in, Bill could now see the large spiders all over the barn. They hissed at the light and moved toward the back of the barn. The bodies of the spiders were six inches in diameter and their legs were a foot long, making the animals almost three feet across. They were hairy and their fur was almost like a zebra with black and white stripes. One of the spiders made its move and ran toward Bill, who stumbled and fell backward. Frank ran forward and grabbed the shotgun, aimed it at the advancing bug and shot it point blank. Fragments of the spider flew through the barn. The rest of the spiders retreated into the relative darkness at the back of the building. Frank helped his father to his feet and they left the barn and latched the doors.

Chapter 3

Several trucks pulled onto Bill Marshall's property, including the one from Channel 10. Carl's truck parked next to a SWAT team vehicle. Several officers were donning body armor and preparing their weapons. Two more large trucks were over by the pond where the Marshalls were loading their sheep on board. Bill found a site several miles away where he could keep his sheep until his property was safe again. Doc Watson was with him and examined each of the remaining sheep for any injuries.

"Well, Bill, I've looked at them all," Harry said. "Two more have those bites, but otherwise seem to be okay. They were probably bitten just before you let them out of the barn. Several sheep have traces of the black and white hair you mentioned on their hooves. We'll probably find a few trampled spiders in there now."

"Thanks Harry," Bill said, relieved that most of his herd would be safe. "This is just unbelievable. Where could these things have come from?"

"I called Doctor Ernie Brewster at UCSD after I heard about the spiders," he replied. "He and a team of his people are coming here to collect samples. He has never heard of giant mosquitoes or zebra-striped giant spiders. Ernie told me he might expect something like that in the Amazon or on a desert island somewhere, but never in San Diego County."

"Are you talking about me?" a man in a white lab coat said as he approached them. "Harry, it's great to see you again." He turned to Bill and extended his hand. "You must be Bill Marshall. I'm Ernie Brewster from UCSD. Harry said you have some things to show me. It's got to be amazing to have a SWAT team here."

"Nice to meet you, Ernie," Bill said. He turned to find Frank. "Hey Frank, please go get that jar with the mosquito for the doctor here!" Bill faced the two doctors. "I'm glad you're both here. All of this is unbelievable to me. The SWAT team is here to check out the barn. They are waiting for some bomb disposal suits. When we told them about the spiders, they didn't want to risk anyone being bitten.

"I already talked to their commander when I arrived," Ernie said. "I'm going to wear one of those suits and go in with them. We've got to get at least one live spider. We have traps with us that we will fill with meat and position in the barn. Hopefully a few will go inside and get caught." Frank returned with the jar and handed it to Ernie. "Holy cow, what the heck is that thing?"

"We hoped you would know, doc," Frank said.

"Honestly, I've never heard of a mosquito this big. It is definitely a mosquito though. You can see the proboscis it uses to attack its victim," Ernie said. "Utterly amazing. Have you seen any more of these things?"

"Thankfully no," Bill answered. "But there were dozens of those spiders in the barn. You should have no problem getting some of them. How am I supposed to get rid of those things?"

"After we analyze the samples, we should be able to find a way to eliminate them," Ernie said. "Hopefully we can find their native habitat and return them there. I'd hate to just kill them. This is a miraculous event for science. Tell me about what happened with your sheep?"

"When I opened the barn, the animals rushed like crazy for the doors. I had to jump aside to avoid being trampled myself. I've never seen them that agitated," Bill replied. "When I went back inside, I found four dead sheep. Two had just been bitten and a spider was dragging another away. The last one looked like nothing but skin and bones. Like an empty sack where a sheep used to live. It had bite marks all over."

"Interesting," Ernie said. "Spiders use their venom to liquefy the bodies of their prey. Then they suck it out. It's odd to find them working together. Normally, spiders are solitary. They would never share their food with another."

"Excuse me, Bill," Bonnie said. "The drivers are ready to take the sheep out of here. They need you to sign off on their paperwork. Sorry for the interruption, gentlemen."

"No problem Mrs. Marshall," Ernie replied. "I think the SWAT team is ready for me now. Let me tell you one last thing. You and your family cannot stay here now. Those spiders hunt at night. If more of them are out there, they might try to feed on you. If there are too many of them, you wouldn't stand a chance."

"Don't worry, Ernie," Bill said. "We're leaving the area right after you guys go into the barn. My sister has room for us in town. But thanks for the warning." The Marshalls walked over to the trucks now loaded with their flock. Ernie and Harry headed back to toward the barn.

When Ernie arrived at the SWAT truck, he stepped up to Captain Lewis Washington who was reviewing the bomb suits that had been delivered. "It looks like we're ready, Captain," he said as he approached.

"Yes we are, and not a minute too soon," Lewis replied. "We've only got a couple hours of sunlight and we need to do something with these creatures before then."

"I recommend getting flood lights to surround the barn if we can't get control before then. These spiders seem to be afraid of bright light. If it gets dark, we can light up the area with the lamps and keep them inside until morning," Ernie replied.

"They are already on the way, Doc," the captain answered. "We have five bomb suits. You and one of your men will use two suits. Two of my strongest officers and I will use the others. We'll drag your traps inside the barn. The rest of my team will guard the perimeter. If any of those creatures attempt to escape, they have orders to shoot."

The five men donned the heavy suits. Other officers checked to make certain the closures were sealed and helped them move the traps near the doors to the barn. SWAT officers positioned themselves around the barn to cover every possible exit. Five stood near the main doors with the men in bomb suits. At exactly 4:00 p.m. the doors were pulled open.

A horrible hissing sound rose inside the dark barn. Things could be seen scurrying back from the doors. The five men each took the cable from a trap and began to walk forward, dragging the traps behind them. Captain Washington was in the middle and slightly ahead of the others. The two doctors were on either side of him. The SWAT officers were on the outside of the line as it advanced into the barn. As the traps moved past the entrance, two of them became entangled with the door frame.

Two officers stationed near the doors slung their rifles across their backs and headed to the traps. All the civilians were held twenty yards back from the doors. The first officer wriggled the trap free and it began moving forward again. The policeman took his rifle and began to move back. The second officer released the trap and pushed it into the barn. As he stepped back, a spider fell from the ceiling of the barn and landed on his chest. He immediately fell to the ground and other officers rushed to his aid. The man and spider rolled on the ground as the man frantically tried to dislodge the monster. Its legs were holding on tight. The officer could feel it trying to bite him through his vest and pushed it back with all his might. Another officer arrived and knocked the spider off with the butt of his rifle. He grabbed his comrade and began dragging him away. The spider rolled onto its feet and looked around for another target. Another officer close by pulled his revolver and shot the beast squarely between its eyes. Fragments of spider splattered on the barn doors.

Inside the barn, the five traps were now well inside, so the men started moving backward toward the doors. As they moved backward, they could see what seemed like hundreds of tiny black eyes watching them. The spiders seemed to sense the meat inside the traps and began to move forward. As the men approached the doors, dozens of spiders lunged forward. Most headed for the traps, but others came toward the men who tried to get out as quickly as they could in the heavy suits. Professor Brewster stumbled and fell as several spiders attached themselves to his suit. The SWAT officers knocked the bugs off and tried to drag him forward. Other spiders joined the fight and several jumped on to each of the men in bomb suits as they finally left the barn.

Captain Washington ripped the legs off a spider that attached itself to his head. He swung his arms and other spiders flew through the air. As each landed, one of his men shot them dead. The rest of the spiders rushed back into the barn. One spider was still outside the barn and had firmly attached itself to Ernie's helmet. Inside his suit, Ernie could see it desperately trying to bite through the heavy glass faceplate. Captain Washington grabbed the spider, pulled it loose, and held it over his head. He pulled his revolver and shot it through the head. The barn doors had been closed and locked. The crowd watching the scene was silent and in shock.

Lewis pulled off his helmet and sat on the ground next to Ernie. He helped pull off his helmet.

"Doc, you're lucky I got there when I did," he panted. "That bastard was almost through the glass."

"Thanks, Captain," Ernie huffed. "I've never been so afraid in my life. I could see it looking at me as it tried again and again to bite my face. These creatures are not from this planet. God knows how or why they are here now.

Bill Marshall had come over and stood near the two men. "How many did you see? Do you think we can get rid of them?"

"Right now, Mr. Marshall," Lewis began, "if it were up to me, I'd burn this barn to the ground. Those things are horrible monsters. I'd burn it now, but there may be more out there."

"Captain, do you have some robots that can extract those traps? It's too dangerous to go in there again," Ernie said.

"Now that we have an idea what we're up against, that's the only way we're going to attempt to get those traps," Lewis said.

"Captain, can I show you something?" one of the officers said.

"What is it, Wilson?" he replied. "I think we're a bit busy right now."

"Captain, after I helped get one of the traps inside, one of those spiders attacked me," Ron Wilson said. Thankfully, Joe knocked it off and Willie killed it. But look at my body armor vest."

Lewis looked in disbelief at the vest. Most of the fabric had been shredded and ripped off. Many of the armor plates inside were dented and broken. "Why are you still alive, Wilson?"

"Besides Willie's shooting, look at my badge. This was right underneath the broken armor plate," Ron replied.

"Holy shit, man!" was all Lewis Washington could say. The badge was scrapped until most of the lettering was gone. Two deep dents pushed almost through the metal.

Carl Dennis moved forward with his cameraman. "Captain Washington, I can tell you that all of San Diego is in shock after what we've just seen. Do you have a message for our audience?"

"Stay out of this area. If you live within a mile or two, get out now!" Carl said. "We are going to cordon off this area to keep everyone away. After we extract the traps, we will burn the barn to the ground."

"Bill Marshall, please tell my audience what you're thinking now," Carl said as he held the microphone to Bill.

"I can still hear them hissing inside," Bill said. "They sound very angry, probably because many are in the traps now. I think we all better get out of here as fast as we can."

Chapter 4

Bonnie, Eileen, and Cindy were talking in the kitchen and putting the last touches on dinner. Bill sat with his son Frank and his brother-in-law Justin Cramer in the living room, each sipping a cold beer. Eileen and Justin's teenage daughters Tiffany and Helen were watching television with little Cybil in the family room.

"Bill, I still cannot believe the video from your farm," Justin said. "Those spiders were huge and vicious. You are lucky to be alive!"

"I know. There are several people lucky to be alive tonight. I only hope they got their samples and can find out where those things came from," Bill replied. "I only lost four sheep, so if they can just get rid of those things, maybe life can go back to normal."

"Uncle Bill, they're showing your farm again on TV," Tiffany yelled. "It's that professor again." The three men hurried into the family room and stood behind the couch.

"So tell me, Professor, what's happening now?" Carl Dennis said. He looked tired after a long day on the beat.

"We asked for and received Marine support now," Ernie Brewster said. "They have five robots in the barn attempting to extract our traps. Three other robots are looking around to assess the overall situation. Hopefully, we will be able to examine these spiders and find out where they came from."

"There's a lot of light out here for eight o'clock; what's that about?" Carl asked.

"These spiders don't like bright light. We're flooding the area to keep them inside the barn. If they escape, they could wreak havoc all over the county in a day or two," Ernie replied. "If anyone out there sees anything like these creatures, stay far away. They are extremely dangerous. Several people have already been attacked, including me."

"The traps are being taken out now," Carl said as the camera panned to show the five boxes coming out of the barn, pulled by their robots. The hissing from the boxes and from inside the barn was very loud.

"Move all nonessential personnel back!" shouted Marine Colonel Art Roback as he brushed past Ernie and Carl. "We don't know what these creatures will do. I want a fifty-yard perimeter now!" Fifty marines moved forward and began pushing the crowd back.

"Colonel, Ten News, can you tell us what's happening, sir?" Carl asked.

"Son, you seem like a nice man," Art said as he faced the camera. "I don't want to see one of these spiders sucking your guts out tonight, so please move back thirty yards. After the situation is under control, I'll come back and talk to you." Two marines moved Carl and his camera man back. "Professor, get your truck up here so we can load these traps and then your team needs to leave the area."

The truck backed into the view and several men started loading the hissing boxes inside the truck. The marines formed a semicircle around them for protection. One of the boxes fell from the truck and rolled on the ground. The scientists turned and ran while the marines moved toward it. The hissing was deafening, but the box held. The marines lifted it up onto the truck. After the last box was loaded and lashed down, three marines climbed into the back and strapped boxes onto the crates. They then closed and latched the door.

Carl was next to Ernie Brewster when Colonel Roback walked up. "Professor, you are cleared to leave the area. We have attached high power incendiary devices to each of your traps. I'll send an APC with a squad of marines behind your vehicle. If there is any indication the traps have been compromised, we will radio your drivers. If we do so, they must stop immediately and exit the vehicle as fast as they can. We will then detonate our incendiaries. There is no way we will allow those creatures to escape. Do you understand, sir?"

"Yes, Colonel," Ernie said. "Let us hope that doesn't become necessary."

"There's no room for hope here. Let's all just get our jobs done," Art said.

"What's the plan now, Colonel?" Carl asked.

"Thank you for moving back, sir," Art began. "Our robots reported seeing more than one hundred of these spiders outside the traps. If anything were to happen to these lights, those things would be all over the area attacking anything or anyone breathing. My orders are to burn this barn to the ground and make certain all the spiders inside are dead. The show is now over. All civilians are strongly requested to leave these premises now. There is some chance a few of these spiders will escape. I cannot guarantee anyone's safety if that happens. Once we begin this part of the operation, several air assets will be deployed here. If we lose control on the ground, they are ordered to fire on this location and make certain that nothing escapes alive."

"Dinner's ready everyone," Bonnie said as she came up behind Bill and put her arms around him. "It's just a barn, sweetheart."

"I know we can always raise another barn. But I just don't understand how this happened. It's like we stepped through a door to another planet when the earthquake hit. I worry about what could happen next," he sighed. "Let's eat something."

Eileen made a pot roast and salad for dinner. Eileen learned to cook from her mother. She had that certain knack for seasoning, and everything she tried to make turned out great. Justin opened a bottle of California cabernet sauvignon to enjoy with dinner. Justin fancied himself a bit of a wine expert, and had built a wine cellar under the house. Bill enjoyed wine too, but preferred a bitter India Pale Ale. Tonight, however, all the adults drank wine.

Tiffany and Helen talked nonstop about school, and their parents were happily caught up in the discussion. College wasn't far away for either, and Justin and Eileen knew an empty nest was waiting for them, so they enjoyed each day together as a family. Bill was lost in thought about the farm. He could picture his beautiful barn burned to ashes with hundreds of cooked spiders littering the floor. He wondered if his insurance would cover an invasion by monster spiders. He felt relatively certain the rest of his property was okay. If the marines had bombed it, they would have heard the noise from only two miles away.

"Dad, are you okay?" Frank asked. "You look like you're hypnotized."

"I'm sorry everyone," Bill replied. "I guess my mind is on overload today. Sis, the food is really great, like always, but I'm just not that hungry. I started thinking about the sheep and those spiders and lost my appetite. I'm sorry. If it's okay, I'll grab a beer and watch TV for a bit." He rose and kissed Eileen and Bonnie on the cheek and went into the kitchen. He took a beer from the refrigerator, opened it, and returned to the family room.

The TV was off, and he had no desire to hear more about the farm now. He sat quietly looking out the window. His phone vibrated in his pocket. He took it out and answered it, "Hello?"

"Hi Bill, it's Ernie Brewster, how are you doing tonight?" the professor said.

"I'm okay, I guess," he replied. "How is it going with your spiders?"

"Hard to say. We got them back here safely and put them in an isolation cell with steel walls. We have a total of twenty live spiders. They went crazy for a while and attacked the walls and doors. Thankfully, they couldn't do any damage. We fed them and they calmed down a lot then. We were able to get some DNA from some of the spider fragments from the attack earlier. I have to tell you I've never seen DNA like that," Ernie said.

"How do you mean, Doc?" Bill asked.

"Bill, on Earth all creatures with DNA have many similarities. It's like we're all distant relatives from the same family. But the DNA in these spiders is completely different," Ernie continued. "It's like they are from another planet. And it was the same with that mosquito. It was completely different from any Earth DNA and also from the spiders."

"So, you're telling me they are not from Earth and not even from the same planet as each other," Bill repeated. "How did this happen? You might want to check again in case there was an error."

"We've already sent sample tissue to several other universities," Ernie said. "It will take some time to get results back, but I'm pretty sure our evidence is correct."

"Now we just have to find out how and why all of this is happening," Bill replied. "I don't think there are any tests for that."

"Let's just hope more strange things like this don't happen," Ernie said. "One big mosquito was odd but not terribly dangerous. A few hundred man-eating spiders is another story. I don't even want to speculate what might happen next."

"I wish I had an idea. All I know is this started after the earthquake," Bill said.

"I don't know any answers either, Bill. But I wanted you to know what we found since it is impacting your family the most. Try to get some sleep, and I'll let you know when I learn anything new. Good night, Bill," Ernie said.

"Good night, Ernie, and thanks for your help," Bill said and disconnected. "Where are those damn dogs?" he said to the empty room.

ℭhapter 5

Bill awoke with a start with his heart beating rapidly. He was still sitting in the overstuffed chair in Eileen's family room. He could see Frank sleeping on the couch. Cybil was sleeping in her sleeping bag by his feet. The clock on the mantle said it was two thirty in the morning. He realized he must have dozed off after talking to Professor Brewster. He stood carefully so as not to disturb Cybil and went to the bathroom. He returned after brushing his teeth and walked back to the chair. Some movement outside the window caught his eye.

He went to the window and looked out at the quiet street. A cloud of birds was flying around the closest street light. He thought about that and looked again. It was a cloud of the giant mosquitoes, he was sure of that. Now as he looked, it seemed like the street was moving. He squinted and could make out hundreds of giant spiders moving along the street away from the direction to his house. This could not be happening. He had to be dreaming. He went back to the bathroom and splashed water on his face. On the way back, he grabbed his shotgun and pistol just to be safe. As he approached the window, one of the spiders jumped onto the glass. He could see it looking in his eyes with its mandibles moving back and forth. He did not know what to do. If he shot it, hundreds more would rush in and kill them all. If it broke though the glass, they would all die anyway.

He leveled his rifle on the spider and debated whether to shoot. A large animal shot into view and

31

grabbed the spider in its mouth and chewed voraciously. At first Bill thought it was a large wolf, but when he looked more closely, it had no hair and leathery black skin. The eyes were blue and Bill thought it, too, was looking directly at him. Then the beast jumped away and into the street. It and several others like it were grabbing and eating the spiders as fast as they could. Bill's mind was racing in circles. There was no way he could fight off all of these creatures. Everyone in town would likely die that night no matter what he did next.

Bill thought about poor Cybil lying there sleeping so peacefully. What would happen to his granddaughter?

The window crashed open as one of the large beasts jumped through and knocked Bill to the ground. It stood on top of his chest, breathing down on him. Cybil screamed and Frank jumped to his feet. The animal glanced over at Cybil and licked its lips. Bill raised his pistol to the animal's head and pulled the trigger. Blood and gore splashed against the wall and on his face, and the animal fell over dead. Frank grabbed Cybil, and Bill tossed the shotgun to his free hand. "Get to the back of the house now!" he shouted as several spiders climbed through the window. Bill tried to move away from the window while training the gun on the advancing creatures. Bill shot the closest one, but another raced forward and bit him on the leg before he could shoot it. He kicked it off and shot it as it flew across the room. Several dozen spiders were in the room now, and Bill only had a few bullets left. The venom was affecting his mind now, and he found it difficult to focus on the advancing spiders. He knew his life was over and prayed for his family to be safe.

As he was about to black out, a very tall man burst through the door. He was wearing full body armor unlike anything Bill had seen. The man held out his left hand and shouted, "A-Nak-Fla!" A brilliant flash of green light filled the room and all the spiders froze in place. The man came to Bill and pulled a small device from his belt. He jabbed Bill in the thigh near the spider bite. "Don't worry, this will eliminate the venom. Please don't move. I'll be right back." The man raced back into the street. Bill could see him through the broken wall where the window had been. He held some kind of gun in his right hand that shot balls of light wherever he aimed it. He raised his left hand again and again shouting different phrases. Blinding lights of various colors illuminated the night sky. Bill was already feeling much better but thought he better do as he was told.

As quiet returned, Frank cracked open the door and saw the scene in the living room. "Are you okay, Dad?" Frank asked.

"I'm going to be okay. How's everyone else?" Bill asked.

"We're fine but scared out of our minds. What happened out here?" Frank said as he walked over and sat with his father. "You were bitten by that spider, weren't you?"

"Yes, but some guy came in and froze them all. Then he jabbed me in the leg and said it would eliminate the venom," Bill said.

"Some guy? What guy, Dad?" Frank asked.

"That would be me," said the man in the black armor who had returned. He pulled off his helmet and smiled at the two men. "Hello there, my name is Lance Allright. I think I got all of them."

"Thanks for saving my life, Lance, but who are you?" Bill asked.

"You can probably get up now. The anti-venom has had time to do its work," Lance said. "Besides, I need your help to make sure this doesn't happen again. I don't know if you'd really understand who I am, so I want one of you to come with me. Don't worry, you'll be completely safe."

"Lance, my name's Bill Marshall," he replied. "You saved my life, so the least I can do is see what you want me to see. But you're sure all these things are dead, aren't you?"

Lance laughed. He picked up one of the spiders and dropped it to the floor. It shattered as though it was made of glass. "Oh, I'm sure they're dead. Let's go before something else bad happens."

"I'm not sure I like this Dad," Frank said. "Maybe I should go too?"

"Sorry, Frank, but I need you to take care of our family now," Bill shook his head. "You have to remember that if Lance hadn't shown up, we'd all be dead already. I owe him this."

Bill felt remarkably well, all things considered. Five minutes ago, he was laying three-fourths dead on the floor with hundreds of ravenous creatures about to kill his whole family. Now he was running down the street with the man who saved the lives of every person in town. He felt like a young man again, full of excitement for what would happen next.

Thirty minutes later, the excitement had worn off. He and Lance had passed his farm and continued into the woods behind the house. He passed the burned shell of his barn and wondered if he would ever get his sheep back. Deep in the woods, they came upon a hole in the ground. Lance started to crawl down into the hole.

"What exactly is this, Lance?" Bill asked, out of breath.

"This hole was created by the earthquake," Lance said. "It opened this cave that had never been discovered before. Climb on down, Bill, we're almost there."

Bill climbed down and they found themselves in a dark cavern. Lance pulled another device from his belt and slapped it against the wall. Bright light filled the chamber. Primitive paintings covered the walls. Lance raced further down the cavern between tall stalagmites. Bill could hear water dripping and soon a small stream ran by their feet. Lance turned down another dark passage and slapped another lighting device to the wall. The large room was full of crystals. They grew from every wall, the ceiling, and the floor. Bill imagined this is how he would feel if he were inside a massive diamond. Lance stopped at the far end of the room in front of a crystal wall.

"What is this place, Lance?" Bill asked as he stood beside him. Lance had to be seven feet tall, as he stood a head and one-half over Bill.

"It's just a crystal cave, Bill," Lance said. "This wall is what I brought you to see." The wall was one giant crystal, except for the large crack in the center. The wall was one hundred feet tall and two hundred feet wide.

"Wow!" Bill exclaimed. "That's a big crystal, Lance. But it's broken there in the middle."

"This isn't just a crystal, it's a single diamond," Lance said. "This is the Heartstone. Come over here and look at the crack in the middle."

They walked to reach the crack which was ten feet wide and two and one-half feet tall. Bill blinked when he thought he could see a field of green grass on the other side of the stone. Most of the view was fuzzy due to imperfections in the stone. Through the open crack, the scene was as vivid as looking out an open window. Past the field of grass, he saw a small stone building and a great stand of tall trees in the distance. "That's some illusion, Lance," Bill said. "How does the Heartstone do that?"

"That's no illusion, Bill," Lance smiled. "That is my home planet. Come on, you have to climb through with me." Lance put his hand on Bill's shoulder.

"That's another planet?" Bill scoffed. "I thought you just wanted to show me how to stop those monsters from coming back, not go to another world!"

"Bill, I asked you to trust me. I'll bring you back in no time. But stepping through this is part of the job. The Heartstone cracked during the earthquake. That's why there was little damage from the strong earthquake. Most of the force was absorbed by the Heartstone. Now that it's broken, it has opened a way into your world from many other planets and galaxies. I stopped more damage by locking my portal key on your world. I can't leave it that way forever. Eventually, another world will attach to your portal and more terrible things can come through," Lance explained.

"Lance, I gave you my word, so I will go. What do I do now?" Bill asked.

"Just climb through the Heartstone, Bill," Lance said. "When you get to the other side, you'll be in that grassy field. When I see you there, I will follow. Now hurry, please."

Bill climbed into the crack and began to move forward. The Heartstone was at least a hundred feet thick, and much of the broken crystal was very sharp. He could feel the crystal cutting through the knees of his pants and his hands. When he had almost reached the other side, his stomach flipped. He felt very woozy and dizzy. He could still hear Lance yelling at him.

Finally, he reached the end of the Heartstone and fell out onto the green grass.

Chapter 6

Lance climbed out of the Heartstone and stood in the field of grass next to Bill, who was panting for breath and lying flat on the ground. Bill's head was spinning and he felt as though he had a terrible hangover. Lance took Bill's arm and pulled him to his feet. Bill wavered back and forth, but eventually he felt a bit better. "I feel terrible, Lance. What happened to me?" he asked.

"Stepping through a portal can be very nauseating at first. You'll feel better soon. Come on and follow me to the house, and I'll get you some coffee. That always helps me," Lance said as he turned and started walking up the hill.

Bill looked back where he had fallen from the Heartstone. There was a large circular metal structure next to him. A series of flashing red lights were affixed to the outer edge. The Heartstone seemed to be right in front of him with its jagged edges. It filled the opening and seemed right next to him. The view seemed to flicker slightly as though it was a projection and not the true stone. "What is this thing?" he asked.

"That's my portal key, Bill, now hurry up!" Lance shouted from halfway up the hill. "I have a couple new friends who want to see you!" Bill hurried to catch up with Lance. He reached his side just as Lance approached the door to the small stone house. "Bill, welcome to my home," he said as he opened the door and stepped in. As Bill followed him inside, Zelda and Chachis yipped and rushed to see him.

"Where did you find these dogs, Lance?" he said as he petted Zelda and picked up Chachis, who eagerly licked his face. "They ran away when the earthquake hit. I was sure those spiders got them."

"Lucky for you, the dogs found me," Lance laughed. "For entertainment, I like to let the portal key attach randomly to other portals. It's like a slide show of galactic realities. There is a safety system to keep anything dangerous from coming though my portal key. I happened to be looking at your Heartstone when I saw it crack open. I knew that was a very bad thing, but before I could lock on, the image switched to another portal. Not knowing what else to do, I came here and had a little dinner. After an hour or so, I heard a scratching sound at my door and opened it. Zelda had Chachis in her mouth. Chachis had been stung by one of those large mosquitoes. Fortunately, I had some universal antidote and Chachis recovered quickly."

"That's amazing! My little granddaughter will be so happy to have her dog back," Bill smiled. "And Zelda can help me with my ranch again. I don't know how to thank you, Lance."

"It was my pleasure, Bill. We don't have animals like these here. I have really enjoyed their company," Lance said. "Perhaps when this is over, I can get a dog from your world and bring it back here with me? Running the portal key is lonely work." Lance poured fresh coffee into two large mugs and sat at the small table. Bill sat opposite him, with both dogs as his feet.

"So what do we do to stop the monsters invading my world, Lance?" Bill asked. "I came here and you promised to tell me if I did."

"The only way I know is to install a portal key on your end," Lance said.

"You mean like that circular thing at the bottom of the hill?" Bill asked. "Do we just put it at the opening in the Heartstone?"

"It's not that simple, Bill, and I'm not really sure we can do it," Lance began as he sipped the hot coffee. "Let me tell you about Heartstones first. Maybe that will make it clear. Every habitable planet has a least one portal. The portals link all of creation together, kind of like a safety valve for the universe. They are a natural phenomenon, like thunder and lightning. They formed when each planet accumulated from the primordial clouds of dust. From what I have been told, each portal is blocked by a Heartstone. We believe these stones allow the portals to link all of creation without allowing things to physically move."

"But your portal doesn't have a Heartstone, Lance," Bill said.

"I'm glad you noticed that," Lance replied. "Actually, it did once. As sentient societies evolve, they will eventually wonder how they can ever find other civilizations given the unimaginable distances in space. They will build space ships and try to explore, but find it impossible to survive for hundreds of years in cramped space ships. We did all of that on this planet several thousand years ago. Eventually, we gave up and focused on our lives here. A major earthquake in this area opened a hidden cavern long ago. Scientists eventually found a crystal room with a single giant diamond at one end. It was our Heartstone. They watched the scenes of other planets and galaxies through the crystal and finally realized what they were looking at. In the exact center of the Heartstone was a portal through space."

"So, did they move the Heartstone up here then?" Bill asked.

"No, the Heartstone cannot be moved. It is the natural vessel of the portal. Our scientists knew they could not break the Heartstone without allowing every other galaxy and planet unfettered access to our world. A thousand years ago, they developed the portal key device like the one at the bottom of my hill. Only then did they begin to break the Heartstone. A large army was stationed here during that time in case some hordes rushed through our portal. Thankfully that never happened. When the last of the Heartstone was removed, there was only a shimmering circle of light, about fifteen feet in diameter. They moved the portal key in place and the portal snapped into the center," Lance finished as he rose to get another cup of coffee.

"So, the earthquake broke the Heartstone on Earth and allowed those mosquitoes and spiders to flood my ranch?" Bill asked. "How did you stop it?"

"When we find a new world we want to explore, we lock its coordinates into the portal key. When your dogs showed up here, I knew they had to have come from the planet with the cracked Heartstone. I put on my battle armor and gathered my weapons. Then I parked myself in front of the portal key and waited until I saw that cracked stone again. I waited all night and half of the next day, just watching the portal key. When I saw the broken crystal, I saved the coordinates and locked my portal to the one on Earth. That's when I found you," Lance remembered.

"So, Earth is safe now," Bill said. "That's good news!"

"Not entirely, Bill," Lance said. "I can't leave my portal locked to yours forever. Thousands of scientists and normal citizens use our portal key to travel to other worlds. We now have settlements on fifty other planets and the only way we can travel or trade is through this portal key. I've reported all of this to my bosses, and they are sympathetic to the needs of your planet. But if there is an emergency somewhere that requires me to unlock the portal, your planet will be subject to more invasions."

"So, what do we do now? Can we fix the Heartstone? Can we move a portal key to Earth to block attackers? You've got to give me some hope," Bill said.

"A Heartstone cannot be fixed. It is a force of nature, and blocks the open portal. If it breaks, that's it. The only way to block the portal is to remove the entire Heartstone and place a portal key in its place," Lance replied. "And there are plenty of problems with that too."

"What kind of problems, Lance?" Bill asked.

"The technology of the portal key is thousands of years beyond your planet, Bill. We believe only highly advanced planets should have that technology. Otherwise, savage societies can wage war by sending armies through the portals. Your race is still very primitive," Lance replied.

"So, we're doomed. Is that what you're saying?" Bill asked. "You told me you were going to help me, remember?"

"My people have great faith, Bill. It should be impossible for an earthquake to crack a Heartstone. Those stones were created by the planet to block the unblockable and to keep the universe safe. The cracking of the Earth Heartstone is a sign from God we cannot ignore," Lance replied. "We will install a portal key on Earth. However, we need your planet to make a leap of faith and knowledge too. They must leave their petty differences in the dust of time and be a compassionate society."

"Do you think that's possible?" Bill asked. "Watching the news everyday makes me believe it is too much to ask. I want to try, though."

"Trying is all any of us can do," Lance smiled. "It is getting late. I have a spare room with another bed, Bill. Let's get some sleep and see what tomorrow brings."

"Shouldn't I be going back? My family is probably worrying about me," Bill said.

"Trust me again, friend," Lance said. "Several elders will arrive tomorrow morning. You and I will travel through the portal key with them to your world. We will make certain your dogs get to their homes too. You must convince our elders your planet should be saved. You and I need to convince your leaders that the time for peace is now. I think a bit of sleep will do us both good."

Chapter 7

Colonel Art Roback walked slowly down the street through Valley Center with fifty marines in full battle gear. Strewn around them were hundreds of bodies of giant spiders and large wolf-like creatures. Giant mosquitoes lay in piles under street light poles. It was eerily quiet for a Saturday morning. Ahead on the right side, they could see a man sitting on his porch with a shotgun across his lap. The front window of the house was smashed, leaving a gaping hole, and the front door appeared to have been kicked open. As the soldiers approached, the man leaned his shotgun against the side of the house and stood up.

"Sir, are you okay?" the colonel shouted.

"Yes, sir," Frank Marshall replied. "It's been quiet here for several hours."

"What in the world happened here last night, son?" Art said as he crossed the small yard and climbed onto the porch. "You were at the sheep ranch yesterday, right?"

"Yes, Colonel," Frank replied. "I remember you too. That ranch belongs to my dad, Bill Marshall. My name's Frank."

"It looks like we didn't get all of those damn spiders with the fire," Art said. "Are these things dead? I see some of the creatures have been shot with something, but others look like they're frozen or something." He tapped one spider with his boot and it didn't move. "We can't be too careful with things like this."

Frank smiled, "Oh, they're dead all right." He picked up one of the spiders and dropped it onto the porch, where it shattered into thousands of fragments. "It was the strangest thing I've ever seen, Colonel."

"Tell us what happened, Frank," Art said as he sat on the porch. "Is your family okay? Was anyone hurt here?"

"My family's okay," he began. "I haven't tried knocking on any doors. I imagine folks are too scared to come out, in case more of these things return. Now that you guys are here, maybe they will. From here, it looks like only my aunt's house here was attacked."

"What do you remember, son?" Art asked again.

"Not much, Colonel. Actually, I was asleep on the couch there. My dad had been asleep on the armchair, and my daughter was sleeping in her sleeping bag in the middle of the floor. I heard a large crash and heard Cybil scream. I jumped up and saw that giant animal on top of my dad," he said, pointing to the dead wolf on the floor of the living room. "I thought the animal was going to kill us all, but my dad shot it dead with his pistol. Then a bunch of those spiders crawled in the open window and headed for us. My dad threw me his shotgun and told me to get Cybil to the back of the house with the others. I was certain my dad was going to die, and then those things would kill us and everyone else in town. I heard someone kick the front door in. I cracked the door open and saw a tall man in black body armor jab my dad in the thigh with something, and then he ran out into the street. I came back into the living room and saw my dad had been bitten by one of the spiders. He said the man had given him anti-venom. Then the man came back and said his name was Lance Allright and he needed one of us to go with him to make sure this kind of thing didn't happen again."

"Don't tell me your father was stupid enough to go?" Art asked.

"I guess he was. He said that if Lance hadn't been there, we would all have been dead, so he owed him that. I begged to go, but Dad said I needed to take care of the rest of the family until he got back," Frank said.

"You only saw the one man in body armor? There wasn't a platoon or any vehicles?" the marine asked.

"No, just Lance," Frank replied. "If I hadn't seen all the dead beasts out here with my own two eyes, I wouldn't have believed it. They left around three o'clock this morning. I've been sitting out here ever since. I don't know whether I'm waiting for my dad or more monsters. What branch of the service do you think Lance came from? He had weapons like I've never seen before."

"Tell me about them, Mr. Marshall," Art said.

"I couldn't tell a lot through the open crack in the door, but he had some kind of blaster in his right hand that shot balls of energy or something. He had something else in his left hand. He would hold his hand out and shout something. Then light would shoot out. That's how he froze the spiders," Frank replied.

"I have no idea, Frank," Art scratched his head. "I've been a marine for more than twenty years, and I've never seen anything like that. Of course, our government and some others always have secret things under development. I'll ask around and see what I can find out."

"Thanks, Colonel," Frank replied. "It still seems like a nightmare."

"I know. Those spiders in your father's barn were horrifying. I can't imagine hundreds of them running free through the streets. I'm amazed no one was hurt or killed." The colonel turned to a captain standing next to him. "Joe, call in a team to get rid of all of the dead animals. We need to get that Doctor Brewster from UCSD to look at them. Then send the men door to door to see if everyone is okay."

"Yes, sir," Captain Joe Smith replied as he left the porch and began giving out orders.

"Frank," Art said, "I could really use a cup of coffee now. And I'd like to talk to the rest of your family to see what else they might know. Do you think we can do that?"

"Sure, Colonel," Frank smiled. "Come on in. I know Aunt Eileen made some coffee a little while ago."

Bill Marshall awoke to mumbling sounds coming from outside the door. He felt great. The anti-venom must have other health benefits, he thought. The early morning sun was just peeking through the window as he rose, walked to the window, and opened the curtains. Two suns were rising above the horizon. One was small and bright white. The other was twice the size and somewhat yellow. He definitely wasn't on Earth anymore. He could see down the hill to the portal key. Ten men dressed like Lance stood around the device. As he watched, five of them stepped through the portal and were gone. The other five sat on the grass and watched the portal. He walked over to the door, cracked it open slightly and tried to listen to the conversation coming from the kitchen.

"Lance, we do appreciate what you have done," a woman's voice said. "But you know we cannot keep the lock on that Heartstone forever?"

"Of course I do, Elder Jane," Lance's voice replied. "But the broken stone on Earth is a sign that we must not ignore."

"Perhaps, Lance, but Heartstones do break from time to time," Jane said. "It is rare, but with an almost infinite number of planets and galaxies, it does happen a few times a year."

"I have to agree with Lance, Elder Jane," a man's voice broke in. "Did you see the break in the Earth Heartstone? It is not a typical break. Also, the sentinels on Earth came here to find Lance. That is another powerful sign."

"So it would seem. I haven't seen the image of the Earth Heartstone yet, Elder Paul," Jane replied. "What is strange about the break?"

"As you know, I have studied Heartstones for several hundred years. Each one is a single perfect crystal. In almost every case I've seen, when a Heartstone is broken by a natural phenomenon, it is a clean break, like a jeweler cutting a diamond. From one stone, you now have two," Elder Paul replied. "Lance, I sense your guest is listening to us."

"Bill Marshall, please join us," Elder Jane said. "We are talking about your world, so you are entitled to hear."

Bill opened the door and walked down the short hallway into the kitchen. Two men in red body armor stood by the door. Lance sat at his table with a man and woman who both appeared to be fifty or sixty years old. Chachis was sitting on the woman's lap, while Zelda sat at Lance's feet. As he approached, they rose and extended their hands.

"Bill, my name is Elder Jane Virtue. It is a pleasure to meet you. I must say your pet here is a lovely animal," she smiled. "And this is my colleague, Elder Paul Justice."

"Bill, it's good to meet you," Paul said. "You may not know it, but this is a monumental day. We haven't met with people from your planet in millions of years.

Not since the Exodus, right Elder Jane? It is a sign from God that your sentinels were able to find Sentinel Lance Allright! I am almost overwhelmed with joy!" Paul grabbed Bill and hugged him. "What a great day!"

"It's a pleasure to meet you both, but I have no idea what you are talking about," Bill replied. "You were talking about the crack in the Heartstone?" Bill sat down with the others, while Lance poured a cup of coffee for him. Lance placed several pastries on a tray and joined the group at the table.

"Yes, Bill, thanks for reminding me," Paul said. "Each Heartstone is a single crystal, and if an earthquake strikes with enough force, it should cleave into two pieces. Do you remember how many tremors hit during the earthquake, son?"

"There were three tremors that I remember. The quake struck in the early morning, and I may have missed one or two small ones before it woke me up," Bill remembered.

Elder Paul rose and paced slowly around the table. "Okay, if there were three tremors powerful enough to break a Heartstone, there should be no more than eight breaks. If there were five, that would mean thirty-two pieces. Look at this." Elder Paul held up a very thin tablet. On it they could see the portal key and the Earth Heartstone on the other side. The crack had doubled in size since Bill crawled through the night before. There were thousands of cracks and hundreds of small stones covering the floor of the break. "This Heartstone has been shattered like a block of glass hit by a giant hammer."

"The opening is much larger this morning than when Lance and I crawled through," Bill said. "It's like the whole stone is crumbling away on its own."

Elder Jane held her head in her hands. "Elder Paul, this is much worse than I could have imagined. Now what do we do?"

"Someone tell me what's happening?" Bill demanded.

"Bill, there are an almost infinite number of planets connected to each other through their portals. Almost all of them are blocked by Heartstones, which we believe is God's way of keeping the life on each planet safe while providing a safety valve for space and time," Paul replied. He rose and refilled his coffee and sat again. He took a pastry and bit into it, and washed it down with the hot coffee. "When societies become advanced enough, they discover their Heartstones. If they continue to advance, they may develop portal keys, like the one down the hill. That portal used to be inside a Heartstone deep in a cavern like yours. Once we had the technology, the hill and cave were removed. Then the stone was broken and the portal key put in its place. Now we have the ability to block our planet or travel wherever we wish."

"Yes, I know. Lance told me much of this last night. But what is so bad?" Bill asked.

"Not every society with advanced technology is peaceful, Bill," Paul continued. "We firmly believe that only peaceful societies can develop portal keys. However that doesn't mean they will always be peaceful. Some change and become brutal invaders who use this technology to conquer other worlds."

"But they are very rare, Elder Paul," Jane interrupted. "Bill must know they are very rare indeed."

"That is a fact. However, if there are a million peaceful societies in this universe, there can still be a few hundred bad ones too," Paul said.

"But those animals that attacked us on Earth were not intelligent," Bill said. "They were wild animals looking for food."

"Our portal key is locked on your world," Paul continued. "We have asked our people on other planets to look for other Heartstones broken like yours. We have found several that were broken about the same time as the Earth stone. We are sending sentinels like Lance into those worlds and hope to find the creatures that invaded your world on them. We believe some savage society with portal keys has deliberately broken the stones in order to prepare for an invasion of Earth. They used those vile creatures from the other planets to test the strength of your defenses. Frankly, your defenses failed terribly."

"I told Bill last night if we don't put a portal key on Earth, eventually we need to move ours. That will leave Earth open for the next stages of the invasion," Lance said. "We can't let that happen, Elders. They would be destroyed."

"We understand and will try our best," Elder Jane replied. "We have already sent five sentinels to Earth to guard the broken Heartstone. We have five more here that we can send if needed. Eventually, we need to reopen this portal key. Hopefully, those sentinels can control the Heartstone if we need to move our portal for a short period."

"What exactly is a sentinel?" Bill asked. "I've heard you call Lance one, and I think you said something earlier about my sentinels finding Lance."

"Bill, Lance and the others down the hill in black armor have the rank of Sentinel on our planets. They are trained in many military and scientific pursuits. Their mission is to protect our portal keys," Elder Jane said. "We believe each planet has its own natural sentinels to protect the Heartstone. Lance told us about the cave paintings near the Heartstone. Those are a clear sign ancient people knew they were guarding something important. The paintings were a warning to others. Lance told us your dogs came through the Heartstone to this place. You cannot imagine how impossible that is. The portal in a Heartstone randomly aligns with all of the other portals in the universe. What are the odds those dogs would end up here? We also know another society was locking your portal on the planets where those mosquitoes, spiders, and wolves came from. Logic would dictate that your dogs would end up on one of those planets. But they did not. They waited for this specific portal and came through. They were waiting for this place, because they knew Lance would help and protect them, and you. If they hadn't come through, Lance may never have come to your world and destroyed the invaders. These dogs are what we call natural sentinels."

"That's amazing, but pretty hard to believe," Bill said. "They're just dogs."

"Bill, you told me the dogs ran away right when the earthquake hit," Lance said. "Why would they do that?"

"We believe they sensed the break in the Heartstone and rushed to stop any attack," Paul said. "Of course, they didn't have the weapons to fight everything that came through. There were probably many other creatures that tried to get to that spot. There were all sentinels."

"Is the cavern on your property, Bill?" Elder Jane asked.

"I'm not sure, but it probably is. When we ran there last night, it was dark but quite close to my house," Bill answered.

"Then you are probably a sentinel too, Bill," Jane replied. "You had animals on your ranch that attracted the spiders, right? That gave your people time to stop them there. Unfortunately, your people did not understand the threat and would have been overwhelmed if not for Lance. When the creatures returned, they could have gone anywhere. They did not. They came looking for you, Bill. Lance could not find any creatures other than on that one block five miles from the Heartstone. What are the odds of that, Bill?"

"What do we do now, Elders?" Bill asked.

"I think it's time we go to your planet, Bill," Paul said. "We'll take our personal guards and the other five sentinels. We need to talk to some of your elders about this danger. Only if we all work together can we stop all of this."

"Who do you think is behind this?" Bill asked.

"We have no idea yet," Jane replied. "We have other portal keys working on that now. But with millions of portals, we may not know until they attack Earth. It's also possible that Earth is a diversion, and they really want to attack us. There's no need to speculate on that now, Bill. Let's go to Earth so your family can know you are safe. Then we'll see what happens next."

Bill felt his body being pulled into the portal. His arms seemed to stretch to the breaking point as he reached through. His head twisted and contorted as did each part of his body as it moved through. He knew he had to be almost through, but could not see or hear anything. As his last foot crossed the portal, he found himself lying in the crack in the Heartstone. Two strong hands grabbed his and pulled him through. Something had been placed on the floor of the crack to keep the broken surface from cutting through skin and clothing. At the end of the stone, the sentinel pulled him free and stood him on his feet.

"Thank you," Bill gasped, still recovering from his second trip through a portal. "I'm Bill Marshall."

"You are welcome, Bill," the tall man in black armor said. "I'm Sentinel Arthur Makepeace." Arthur pulled Bill aside as Lance followed him through the crystal. Significant changes had been made to the cave since the night before. Permanent lights were in place and a new floor had been installed. At the far end of the crystal chamber, the two elders were arguing with a huge man in red body armor. Lance put his arm on Bill's shoulder and led him in that direction.

"Ah, the local sentinel," the man in the red armor said. "Bill Marshall, I am General Alvin Archer. How do you do, sir?"

"I'm well, General," Bill said. "Your men have done a lot to improve this cave in a few hours, sir."

"I can't take credit for that, Bill," Alvin said. "The sentinels have done all the work. I was told the military in this area is now involved, and I thought another military man could help in this matter."

"Alvin, we believe the Elders are in the best position to negotiate here," Elder Jane said.

"Nonsense, Elder Jane," Alvin scoffed. "I am prepared to have a hundred men here with enough weapons to keep anything else from coming through this stone. You need my help, with all due respect."

"He is correct, Jane," Elder Paul said. "We have been getting requests to use the portal for several hours now. We don't have much time. We need a line of defense here now."

"Great!" Alvin exclaimed. "My men are already on the way with the needed equipment. Everything has been measured to fit through the hole in the Heartstone."

"Sentinel Makepeace," Elder Jane began, "stay here with five others until the military arrives. Do not allow anyone to move the portal key until they do so."

"Yes, Elder," Arthur said. "I've asked for ten more sentinels to stay on the other side in case of any other issues."

"Okay, Lance, you lead the way," Elder Jane said. The floor of the cave had been leveled and light filled each room. In the brightly lit chamber, Bill was better able to view the ancient wall paintings. There were definitely warnings showing terrifying beasts emerging from the crystal chamber. The small hole Bill had slipped through the previous night had been enlarged and a metal stairway led up to the surface. The two body guards ascended first, followed by the sentinels, and finally the general, elders, and Bill. Another sentinel was stationed outside the opening, on the lookout for any creatures attempting to return to their own worlds.

It was a short walk out of the woods and toward Bill's home. "So, Bill, is the cavern on your property?" Elder Jane asked.

"Yes, Elder Jane, it is," Bill replied. "My family has owned this land for generations."

"It makes perfect sense to me," Elder Paul said. "The family name is Marshall, which is also a lawman's name, like a sentinel. It's funny how that works."

As they came around the side of the house, they could see a number of SWAT officers and marines searching the ashes and rubble of the barn. Colonel Art Roback saw the group approach and came to meet them. "It's early for Halloween, Bill," Art said. "I don't believe I know your friends."

"Colonel Roback, this is General Archer and Elders Virtue and Justice," Bill said. "Lance here is the one who killed all the creatures in town and took me with him."

"Right," Art scoffed. "But seriously, what asylum did you all come from?"

A massive explosion came from the woods. A large fireball rose into the sky followed by black smoke. Bill turned to see the two guards blocking all access to the elders. The general and sentinels had turned and rushed back into the woods. Colonel Roback called the marines who followed them.

"Take this, Bill" one of the guards said as he handed a blaster to Bill. "You must guard your Heartstone now. We will stay here and protect the elders."

Thoroughly confused, Bill turned and followed the marines back into the woods. The sounds of shouts and weapon fire filled his ears. As he approached the entrance to the cave, two sentinels were holding off a very tall soldier in green armor brandishing two blasters. Arthur raised his left hand toward the soldier. Before he could utter a word, the soldier backhanded him and he fell to the ground. The other sentinel had his blaster raised and began to back off. A pack of the wolf-like creatures poured out of the cave entrance. One jumped on Arthur and the two wrestled on the ground. The rest surrounded the other sentinel who had backed ten yards from the entrance. The green soldier stood in position and seemed to be laughing. Trying to fight off panic, Bill raised the blaster and shot the green soldier, hitting him square in the chest. He flew backward from the impact and down into the cave. The wolves looked disoriented without their leader. They saw Bill standing twenty yards in front of them and growled deeply. Then they charged.

The marines opened fire on the wolves and most were quickly dispatched. Only one was still coming and Bill was too frightened to move. The other sentinel raised his hand and shouted, "Undo Altor!" A flash of blue light shot from the device in his left hand and hit the wolf, which winced and fell to the ground at Bill's feet. Arthur Makepeace had killed the wolf that attacked him and he rushed to Bill's defense.

"Bill, are you okay?" Arthur panted. His body armor was badly damaged and his chest was deeply scarred. Several fang marks had dented his helmet, but it held. "That was a hell of a shot. Thanks. You wait here." He ran down into the cave. It was deadly quiet as the marine contingent approached. The two elders and their guards were also coming in his direction.

"What is the name of God is going on here, Mr. Marshall?" Art shouted. "And what kind of crazy weapon are you holding there?"

"I'm not sure myself, Colonel," Bill said as he let the blaster drop to the ground. "Those wolves are like the one that broke through my window last night. Excuse me, sir, but I have to go check on my friend in the cave." Bill picked up the blaster and ran down into the cave.

"Don't worry, Colonel," Elder Jane said. "We can explain everything. Let us wait here until we find out what's happening down in the cavern."

"I'll go there myself, madam," Art said. "I don't need anyone to tell me."

"Colonel, please bear with us a few minutes," Elder Jane continued. "This is a very serious situation and we do not wish to risk any more lives. It was foolish for Sentient Bill Marshall to reenter the cave as well. Let our team do their work. We need you and your men to guard the cave entrance now in case more enemies emerge. Once we regain control over the interior, we will show you as well."

The cave was dark and full of smoke. Most of the lights had been damaged and the few remaining ones flickered. Bill could see the green soldier lying on his back. The center of his body armor was blown off and a large hole went through his body. His helmet had been removed. The face was not human. The skin appeared to be scaly and green. The large eyes were bright yellow with up and down slits for pupils. Bill heard labored breathing and crawled forward. Sitting against the wall was General Alvin Archer. Great gashes were ripped through his armor and blood seeped from the slits. An open wound on his head dripped more blood down his face. His fractured helmet sat next to him. "General, are you all right?" Bill whispered. The general looked blearily at him. He smiled and put his arm on Bill's shoulder.

"War is hell, son," Alvin said. "I think we stopped them this time. Arthur said you shot that fellow over there. Thanks for that. He and his wolves did this to me." Sentinel Makepeace came out of the smoke and kneeled beside them. "How's the battle, Sentinel?"

"We've stopped the encroachment sir. We lost two sentinels and have two more wounded. I don't know how we lost connection through the portal," Arthur said.

"Where's Lance?" Bill asked.

"He's okay Bill," Arthur replied. "He was hit several times by blasts through the Heartstone, but wasn't hurt badly. The two sentinels who didn't make it were coming through the Heartstone when the connection was lost. Lance said the connection slipped and a number of blaster shots came through the open portal, killing the two. The pack of wolves and five soldiers then came through. The bodies of the sentinels slowed them down enough for us to dispatch all but one. Thank you for saving me, Sentinel Marshall. I owe you my life."

Lance Allright entered the room and slapped two lighting disks onto the walls. His black armor was badly scorched as though a torch had been held to several spots. His helmet was also cracked. He pulled off his helmet and kneeled near the others. "General, we have restored the connection, sir. Arthur and I will take you through the portal now. We have an emergency flyer waiting to take you to the hospital." He turned to Bill. "I heard you got the last combatant, Bill. Congratulations Sentinel."

"What about my troops?" Alvin asked. "Are they here yet?"

"They are now unloading their material by the portal key, sir. They do not want to cross until you get back safely. Bill, come with us to the crystal room," Lance replied. Lance and Arthur picked the general up and carried him into the other room. Bill grabbed the general's helmet and followed them.

The remaining sentinels had their blasters leveled at the portal in case the connection was lost again. The bodies of the fallen had been moved to the side of the room. Arthur crawled backwards into the opening in the Heartstone. He pulled on the shoulders of the general and began backing into the opening. Lance turned to Bill and said, "Bill, take this." He handed him the device on his left hand and a small book. "This explains how the illuminator works. I've asked for an armor suit to be sent through along with the soldiers. That is for you now, Sentinel Marshall. After you visit your family, I need you to come back to my house. Arthur and I will instruct you on how to be a sentinel."

"Lance, I don't think I'm sentinel material. It was a lucky shot that killed that green soldier," Bill said.

"It doesn't work that way, Bill," Lance smiled. "The Heartstone has chosen you as its sentinel. I think you are beginning to know that. We will all be here. More than one hundred of our soldiers are coming through in the next few minutes to protect the portal. But we need a true sentinel for this planet. That can only be you, Bill. It is your destiny. You must now go out there and talk to the Colonel and any other leaders you can find and tell them about this. Bring them to our worlds to make them believe. I'll come back in a couple of days. Take care, Sentinel." Lance crawled into the Heartstone and grabbed the general's feet.

"You take care too, Sentinel!" Bill shouted as the three crossed the portal and arrived on the grass field near Lance's cottage. Bill could see paramedics take the general and load him into some sort of flying device which lifted off and dashed out of sight. He could see Lance and Arthur look back and wave at him. He waved back as the first soldiers crossed into the Heartstone.

Chapter 10

Bill Marshall walked down the street toward his sister's home. Sentinel Lionel Forthright, Zelda, and Chachis walked with him. All the carnage from the previous night had been cleaned up and a number of marines patrolled the streets. Frank Marshall was sitting on the porch with the shotgun still on his lap when he spotted his father. He set down the gun and rushed to meet him. Father and son hugged tightly. "Dad, I'm so glad you're safe!"

"It's good to see you safe too, son," Bill said. "How is everyone else?"

"Everyone's fine but worried about you, Dad. You found Chachis and Zelda too!" Frank laughed as he grabbed his dog and let her lick his face. "Cybil will be so happy to see her again. Where did you find them?"

"You wouldn't believe me if I told you, son," Bill smiled. "I want you to meet Sentinel Lionel Forthright. Lionel, this is my son Frank."

"It's nice to meet you, sir," Frank said shaking the sentinel's hand.

"Greetings Sentinel Frank Marshall," Lionel said.

"Huh?" Frank replied.

"Don't worry about that just yet either Frank. Let's go inside," Bill said. There was a warm reunion when they entered the house. Bonnie had been almost out of her mind with worry after Bill had disappeared the night before. Frank had told them about the giant wolves and spiders and how Bill had left with the tall stranger. The whole family had hidden in the back of the house, unable to sleep all night long. Frank sat outside the broken window with the shotgun, not knowing what would happen next.

Eileen invited everyone to sit in the living room while she made coffee and warmed some pastries. The younger children were sent to the family room to watch television and play with the recovered dogs. "So, what do you do, Lionel?" Eileen asked the question on everyone's minds.

He smiled broadly and said, "I am a sentinel, Eileen. It is my duty to guard portal keys."

"Okay, I'll bite," Justin said. "What's a portal key?"

"This is going to blow your minds," Bill replied. "Every planet in the universe has at least one portal. They act as safety valves for space and time. There is one a hundred yards behind the house."

"Yes, that is correct," Lionel continued. "In their natural state, the portal is locked deep inside a massive crystal, which we call a Heartstone. We believe that is so because God wishes to keep some normalcy in His Universe. Without the Heartstone, all manner of creatures could pass from their worlds to any other. Unfortunately, the Heartstone here was damaged during the recent earthquake. That is why those strange creatures came here and attacked your sheep and Sentinel Marshall here." Cybil walked into the room carrying Chachis in her arms. "Hello there," Lionel said.

"Cybil sweetie, you need to go back with your cousins and watch TV," Eileen said.

"Good morning, Sentinel," Cybil said. "How are things in Ballantine these days?"

"Cybil, that's enough," Cindy said as she rose to escort her out of the room.

"Please, let her stay. This is amazing," Lionel said.

"What are you talking about, Lionel?" Bill asked.

"Ballantine is my home town, Bill," he replied. "It seems clear to me that your granddaughter has a strong connection to the Heartstone. It is reaching out to her mind." He turned to Cybil and said, "Things are well in Ballantine. Thank you for asking. Please continue, Sentinel Cybil. What do you know about the last two days?"

"It's a bit fuzzy, but I remember Chachis telling me there was a problem with the stone, and that Zelda had already gone to investigate. Chachis left to find her and help. As the crack got bigger, the vorrath flew through. I bet that one Grandpa whacked didn't see it coming." She giggled. "When the opening was bigger, those ugly zongo ran through. I knew they were attacking Grandpa's sheep, but I didn't know what to do, so I hid. Finally, the hole was big enough for the ulluba. They came to get Grandpa, but Sentinel Lance came to the rescue," Cybil said. Then she crawled onto the sofa with her parents.

"How does she know that?" Bill asked. "Is she making it up and just being right?"

"You have all lived near the Heartstone most of your lives," Lionel replied. "The stone chose your family to be its sentinels. You all probably have similar abilities, but Cybil is a small child. She is guileless. When the stone touches her, she embraces it. Bill, do you have any pieces of the Heartstone with you?"

Bill pulled two small stones out of his pocket and set them on the table. "I just wanted to show Bonnie. I wasn't going to keep them."

"That's okay, Bill," Lionel laughed. "You are the sentinel and it is your stone. As far as I'm concerned, it is your property. Give the pieces to Cybil and Frank and let's see what they discover."

Cybil took the stone and turned it over and over in her small hand. She held it up to her eye and looked through it. She shuddered and threw the stone across the room. "Ballanan," she said and started to cry.

Cindy grabbed her daughter and held her. "What did that thing do to her?" she shouted.

"No, she's right," Frank said. "It is the Ballanan tribe from Orto Nong. They broke the stone. They broke all the stones and sent those creatures here to test our defenses. Then they sent their soldiers." Frank turned to his father and put his hand on his knee. "Dad, you killed one of their leaders. Next time, they will come for you." Frank let the crystal fall from his hand to the floor. "How did I know that?"

"You are a natural sentinel of the Heartstone, Frank. All of you are to some degree. The stone chose you and now you must help protect this planet from invaders," Lionel said. "We are sending troops and equipment to guard your portal until your people can handle it themselves. We will keep you safe."

Cybil rubbed her eyes, looked up and said, "Sentinel, the retort has arrived and is operational."

"Thank God for that," Lionel said.

"Lionel, what's a retort?" Bill asked.

"The retort is a defensive tool that keeps aggressors from passing through the portal. On my world, that technology is built into the portal key. Until we can install a portal key here, the retort should keep anyone or thing trying to attack from passing through," Lionel replied. "But since the Ballanan were able to break the crystal, I'm not one hundred percent certain." He turned to Cindy. "Cindy, I need to ask Cybil one more question. I want to give her both stones first. The Heartstone will not injure your daughter. She is one with it and it loves her. I promise. Please, may I continue?"

"One question and that's it," Cindy demanded.

Lionel picked up the stone at Frank's feet and walked to where Cybil had thrown the other. Then he returned to Cybil who was holding out her hands and gave her the stones. "Thank you, Sentinel."

"You're welcome, Sentinel," Lionel smiled. "Cybil, please don't be afraid. I don't want you to look into the stones. Can you tell me if the Ballanan are black mages?"

Cybil smiled and giggled. "Black mages, hardly. Black mages did take over Orto Nong many generations ago. The people were treated terribly and most of them died. But what the black mages did not know is there was a second Heartstone on the planet. That stone was more powerful than their magic. It created diseases that preyed on the black mages, killing most of them. Finally, the second Heartstone cleaved itself into millions of blades. The Ballanan found the blades and made swords from them. They attacked the black mages who could not defend themselves against a Heartstone weapon. Eventually, they retreated through their portal and left Orto Nong forever."

Lionel looked confused. "But Sentinel, all of our weapons are built with Heartstone elements and yet we had difficulty fighting the Ballanan. How could that be?"

"One question, Lionel. That's it," Cindy interrupted.

"It's okay, Mommy," Cybil said. "I'm not afraid. Normally, Heartstone weapons do have limits,

Sentinel. However, in this case, the second stone sacrificed itself to save the people on its world. That act made those blades invincible."

"So I guess our world is helpless," Bill sighed.

"Don't be silly, Grandpa," Cybil laughed. "Those weapons are invincible only if used to defend Orto Nong. No Heartstone would give power to invade another planet. All Heartstones were created to protect planets, not attack them. You two are funny." Cybil yawned. "Well, I think I'm going to watch some TV now." She jumped from the couch and gave the two stones to Bill. Then she walked out of the room.

"What do we do now, Lionel?" Bill asked.

"Sentinels Allright and Makepeace will return in two days," he began. "They will train you and Frank to be sentinels. I will guard your home today and tonight. Then another will take my place tomorrow morning. The army is moving troops to the cavern and more sentinels will likely arrive. Hopefully, the retort will give us time to prepare for the next attack. The fact the Ballanan could destroy this stone is very troubling. They have power unlike anything we have ever seen. Hopefully, the elders will develop a plan."

"Lionel, something just flashed through my mind," Bill said. "I think there is another Heartstone on Earth." He passed the two stones to Frank.

"Bill, a sentinel wouldn't think, he would know," Lionel replied.

"There is another stone," Frank said. "And I know where it is."

"This could change everything, Sentinels," Lionel smiled.

"One last question, Lionel," Bill said. "What are black mages?"

"It's almost too terrifying to mention, Bill," Lionel replied. "Civilizations continue to advance after developing portal keys. Most become centers of science, trade, and exploration. Some others decide they have the power to control the universe. The black mages are on a mission to dominate the universe by twisting the power of the Heartstones to their will. We have never had contact with any of them, but others have and told us how terrible they can be. If black mages had broken the Heartstone, none of us would be alive to talk about it now."

Chapter 11

The night was too quiet. Bill Marshall was accustomed to the sounds of crickets chirping outside his farm house. The occasional hoot of a passing owl would normally remind him that nature is hard at work even in the middle of the night. Even when he was asleep, his ears were focused on the sounds of the local coyotes. He had lost more than one lamb to the intruders who were brazen enough to make their way into the barn. Tonight though, there was no sound outside. He could only hear Bonnie breathing deeply as she slept next to him.

Bill rolled over and looked at his alarm clock, which read 3:30 a.m. He climbed out of bed and walked over to the small window overlooking the front of the house. In the harsh light of the security lamps he could see ten Ballanan soldiers marching toward the house. The dark green of their battle armor looked almost black. Their faces were stern and angry through the faceplates on their helmets. Bill rushed downstairs and grabbed his shotgun and pistol and waited. He could hear their footsteps coming up the few steps and onto the porch. He stuck the pistol into his belt, leveled the shotgun at the door and crouched behind the sofa. He wondered what they were waiting for and what had happened to the sentinels in the crystal cavern.

Two soldiers knocked open the front door. Two others jumped through the front windows. Before he could shoot, a soldier slapped the shotgun out of his hand and knocked him to the ground. Another

77

grabbed the pistol out of his waistband and threw it across the floor. One of the soldiers kneeled next to Bill and removed his helmet. His scaly green skin was streaked with sweat. He pressed his blaster against Bill's head and laughed. "So, Sentinel, this is how it ends for you!"

Bill woke up with a start. His heart was pounding and he was drenched in sweat. He was still in Eileen's living room, sitting in the same chair as the night of the attack. Frank was sleeping on the sofa and little Cybil was snug in her sleeping bag at his feet. He looked at his watch, which read 4:00 a.m. Bill stood and walked to the door, not certain if he should open it or not after the horrible nightmare. Finally, he opened it slightly, and Lionel Forthright, who had been standing on the porch, turned to see who it was. "Bill, are you well? Pardon me for saying so, but you look terrible," Lionel said.

"I had a bad dream. I dreamt I was sleeping in my ranch house and ten of those Ballanan soldiers came to kill me," he replied. "Is everything okay in the cave?"

"I report every five minutes," Lionel said. "Three minutes ago everything was fine. You should try to get some more sleep."

"No chance of that now, Lionel," Bill laughed. "I'm going to make some coffee. Would you like a cup?" Lionel nodded and Bill walked to the kitchen. He found Bonnie sitting at the dinette table in the dark, sipping a cup of coffee. Bill went to her and kissed her on the forehead. "What's wrong, sweetheart?" he asked as he pulled another cup from the cupboard and filled it.

"Bill, what is happening to our lives?" Bonnie asked. "A few days ago, we ran a small ranch raising sheep for milk and wool. Now, you're some kind of soldier protecting an opening in space to keep monsters from killing us all. That's not normal, Bill."

"I don't understand how this could happen any more than you," Bill sighed. "I loved that other life. It's all I ever wanted to do. I just had a nightmare where those green soldiers broke into our house and were about to blow my head off. I think I'm in way over my head as a sentinel."

Lionel was standing at the door to the kitchen with another Sentinel. "I'm sorry to intrude, but Sentinel August Reason has arrived to take my place."

The new sentinel removed her helmet, allowing her long red hair to flow out. She was quite beautiful and smiled broadly. "It's an honor to meet and protect you and your family."

Bonnie and Bill shook hands with the new sentinel, who put on her helmet and left to guard the house. Bill poured a cup of coffee for Lionel and invited him to join them. He set his helmet on the counter and sat with them, sipping the hot coffee. "I didn't mean to overhear your conversation, but it is totally understandable to be hesitant and afraid at this point," Lionel said. "On the planets of my civilization, the Heartstones have been broken for many generations. However, the stones still pick the sentinels."

"How can that be if the stones are gone?" Bonnie asked.

"All the pieces of the stones are kept," Lionel responded. "They just do not block the portal anymore. The portal key does that job now. When the first portal key was placed, it took an enormous amount of energy to make it function. After many generations, it was found the Heartstone fragments generate almost unlimited power. That was when we created the blasters and illuminators we sentinels carry. Finally, a group of elders came up with the idea of building a foundation block for the portal key with fragments of the Heartstone. That's why the portal key that Bill went through has no visible source of power. The stones at its base generate it all."

"But how do the stones still pick sentinels?" Bill asked.

"Around our planet, we have special monuments where pieces of the Heartstone are kept on display. Anyone can visit them at any time. Sentinels guard each facility around the clock," Lionel began. "The stone is mounted into a circular frame standing on a marble column. When a person looks through the stone, they may see many things. Most see the room on the other side of the stone, as though it were a pane of glass. If a person is hoping to understand the purpose of their life when they look, they will see the answer. I saw myself standing on the other side of the stone, wearing this uniform. As a young child, my grandmother, Elder Jane Virtue, saw herself as an elder."

Bill pulled the two stone fragments from his pocket and laid them on the table. "So, if I want to know my future, all I have to do is look through one of these rocks?"

"It might work, Bill. On my planet, we all have faith the Heartstone has that power. If you believe in the power of the stone and have faith that it knows your purpose in life, I believe you will see it through the stone," Lionel replied. "If you have doubts or if you are deeply concerned about something else, it probably won't work. You told me about your dream and it's obvious how worried you are about your family. I'm not sure it would work now."

Bill pushed a stone toward Bonnie. He picked up the other and looked at it, turning it over in his hand. It was about the size of a grape with a very slight pink tint. It sparkled in the light of the small room. He thought about everything that had happened in the last few days. He remembered crawling through the Heartstone and arriving near Sentinel Allright's house. He remembered the horrible spiders and wolves that had nearly killed everyone he cared for. He looked up to see Bonnie looking into the other stone. She set it down and pushed it back to Bill. "What did you see, Bonnie?" Bill asked.

A few tears starting down her cheeks and she smiled. "I'm not sure. Everyone was there and we were all happy. We were in a large hall full of people in a huge building that seemed to be made of marble. You were sitting a few feet away from me in one of those black armor suits. Two men were putting some kind of robes on me, like what a judge wears. Only these robes were not black. The robe was glistening white with a slightly pink edge. Lionel, what do you think that means?"

"It sounds like you will become an elder on this planet, Bonnie," Lionel replied. "That is a very good sign. I am very happy for you."

"What does an elder do?" she asked. "I'm not sure I like the sound of it. It makes me sound old."

Lionel laughed. "Not at all, Bonnie," he said. "The elders form the leadership for our society. They are selected by the people and the stones. They work together to provide justice, fairness, and equality among the people. They also work with the elders on our other planets to negotiate trade and other agreements. Finally, they work with other cultures on mutual defense and scientific progress."

"Wow!" Bill said. "I'm very proud of you, sweetheart!" He placed the stone near his left eye and looked through. The stone dropped out of his hand and splashed into his coffee. "I guess I am a sentinel."

"What else did you see, Bill," Lionel urged. "Every detail is important."

"I was wearing the black armor like you, Lionel," Bill stammered. "I was standing next to Bonnie in her robes, but we weren't at a celebration. It was very dark and cold. I could see my breath as I spoke, but couldn't hear what I was saying. We were standing in front of a long bench with twenty or more elders staring down at us. But the elders weren't human. They were Ballanan."

"Oh my God, Bill," Bonnie cried. "That's awful. Lionel, does this mean they are going to capture us?"

"I honestly don't know, Bonnie," he replied. "My instincts tell me no. I don't think the Ballanan would take any of us to meet their elders. If anything, I think they would just kill any captives. Let's try not to read too much into this. I told you current circumstances could cause you to see something that is not true. My grandmother will be coming here in a few days and we can ask her. Her connection to the stones is amazing. Try to relax and get some rest. I'm going to the cave now and return to my planet. I should be back in two or three days. There are now more than one hundred soldiers and fifty sentinels near the cave. I feel confident everyone will be safe from now on. Bill, do you still have the illuminator Lance gave you?"

Bill stood and walked over to the cupboard. He pulled open a small drawer and withdrew the device. He returned to the table and handed it to Lionel. "Does Lance need this back now?" he asked.

"No, but I need to adjust it for you," Lionel said. He pulled a small tool from his belt and worked on the small device until it popped open. Lionel removed the small blue stone from it and carefully put the stone into a small box on his belt. "This stone is from Far Sun, the planet Lance and I come from. You could use that stone, but one from your own world will work much better for you." He reached into another compartment on his belt and pulled out a number of small stones with the same pink tint as those Bill took from the cave. "I just need to find one that fits. Ah, this is it." The stone fit the opening perfectly. Lionel used the tool to close the illuminator and handed it back to Bill. "Okay, Bill, let's go out back and I can train you on this for a while before I go." As he stood, he turned to Bonnie, and said, "Bonnie, please find a safe place to keep all of these stones. Everyone in your family should keep one on their person at all times, except when bathing, of course. Bill will keep the illuminator on his hand at all times, so he is fine. The stones will warn you if something bad might happen. They will also try to guard you. That is the key to being a sentinel. You guard the stone and the stone will guard you. I can't tell you how important that is. Okay, Bill, let's go."

Chapter 12

The sentinel tactical vehicle rolled up the calm street toward Justin and Eileen Cramer's home. The vehicle exterior was shiny black metal and the large windows were dark gray blast proof glass. Some sort of weapon was mounted on the roof, but the hatch for the gunner was closed. The six studded tires punched small holes through the asphalt roadway. The locals had returned to some semblance of normalcy after the horrible night three days ago. The neighbor across the street from the Cramers Dan Wilbur was mowing his yard as the vehicle approached and parked against the curb of the Cramer house. Dan stopped and shut off his mower. He stared at the vehicle and wondered if it was Army or Marine.

The driver door opened and Sentinel Arthur Makepeace climbed out and into the bright sunny morning in San Diego County. He noticed the man standing over his mower and waved. "Good morning, sir," Lionel said.

"Morning, soldier," Dan replied. "I've never seen a truck like that. What branch of service are you in?"

Arthur walked over to the man and extended his hand. "My name is Arthur Makepeace, and I am a sentinel. How do you do?"

Dan looked up at the tall man in the black armor and replied, "My name is Dan Wilbur, Sentinel. My neighbor Justin told me about you guys and how you saved us from those wild bugs and wolves that ran through here a couple days ago. Thank you for that, young man."

Lance Allright had exited on the opposite side of the truck and was watching the two men across the street. "You are welcome, Mr. Wilbur, but that would have been my friend over there," Arthur replied as he pointed to the other sentinel. "He was the one who came to your rescue. Please be assured many of us are here now to stop further incursions."

"Good. I do have a problem that needs fixing, Sentinel," Dan said as he looked up and down the street. "That night, one of those wolves broke into my basement. I have an old dog kennel down there that we don't use anymore. Damned if that beast didn't get stuck in that cage."

"You're telling me you have an ulluba in your basement right now?" Arthur gasped. He waved frantically at Lance who rushed across the street.

"Yes, I do," Dan replied. "It was pretty mad for a day or so. I tried to tell the marines, but they just laughed at me. Yesterday, I threw some meat into the cage and the thing settled right down. My wife tells me we are in mortal danger, but the thing just sits there eating and sleeping now."

Arthur turned to Lance. "This is Mr. Wilbur, Lance. He claims to have a live ulluba captured in his basement."

"You guys can just call me Dan," the neighbor said.

"This is very intriguing, Dan," Lance began. "And now it calmed down and is just sitting around in your cage?"

"Come take a look for yourselves," Dan urged. "My wife Val says either it goes or I do. Can you two take care of it for me?"

"Give us a few minutes, Dan," Lance replied. "I need to get Sentinel Bill Marshall over here too. Something very strange is going on around here." The two sentinels ran back to their vehicle, where Lance withdrew his helmet and a large bag. They rang the Cramer's door bell and entered the house.

"I'll just keep mowing while I wait," Dan shouted.

"It's good to see you both again," Bill Marshall smiled as he shook the two men's hands. "What do we do now?"

"We have a change of plans, Bill," Lance said. "Your neighbor Dan Wilbur claims to have a live ulluba in his basement."

"You are kidding, right?" Bill laughed. "A real ulluba should have killed everyone and destroyed the house looking for me, wouldn't it?"

"It should have done that, Bill, but your neighbor says it's just sitting in a cage and resting," Arthur replied. "We brought sentinel armor for you, Frank, and Cybil." He withdrew a set of armor and handed it to Bill. "You need to go and put this on now so we can all go see for ourselves."

"You brought armor for my granddaughter? Are you both crazy? She's not going to be a sentinel. She's just a little girl," Bill argued.

"Calm down, Bill," Lance replied. "Cybil is not going to go fighting anything. But you know how strong her connection is to the Heartstone. She needs armor for protection. Please put on the suit now. We can talk more about the overall situation after we figure out what to do with the ulluba."

Bill took the armor and went to a bedroom for privacy. A few minutes later, Bonnie and Eileen came through the front door after having dropped the children at school. Both were startled to see the tall sentinels in their living room again. "What are you two doing here?" Eileen asked.

"We have returned as we promised to work with Bill and Frank," Lionel said.

Bill Marshall walked down the short hallway and joined the others. The black armor suit reached from his neck to his ankles. He wore heavy gloves that looked to be part leather and part metal. A wide belt held several pouches and a single clip on his right hip. "How do I look?" he said, grinning from ear to ear.

"Like my guardian angel," Bonnie said.

"Like a crazy man," Eileen laughed.

"You look almost like a sentinel, Bill Marshall," Lance said. He reached into his bag and removed a pair of heavy boots and presented them to Bill, who pulled them onto his stocking feet. Lance reached in again and withdrew a blaster. He checked the setting to make sure it was on stun only. "No sentinel is complete without a gun, Bill." Lance walked over to Bill and clipped the blaster on the belt. "Do you have your illuminator?"

Bill extended his left arm and opened the palm, showing the device in place. Lance took a small coupling on the illuminator and attached it to the glove. "Now you have all the power of the suit to support the illuminator." He pulled a helmet from his bag and handed it to Bill. "Let's go."

"Wait a minute," Bonnie said. "Where are you three headed?"

Bill answered, "Eileen, your crazy neighbor claims to have one of those wolf things in his basement. We're going to check it out."

"Sentinels, I'm not sure my husband is ready for battle just yet," Bonnie said. "Can't you two handle this?"

"Yes, we could," Lance said, "But there is something strange about this ulluba. Your neighbor claims it is calm and living in a kennel in his basement. That's just not normal. This is Bill's planet to protect, and we may need his help to understand what's going on."

"Should I get those pieces of Heartstone to help?" Bill asked. "Now I only have the little one in the illuminator."

"That's not true anymore, Bill," Lance smiled. "Your suit, helmet, boots, and blaster all contain pieces of your stone. From now on, you must always have the stones with you." He turned to Bonnie who appeared on the verge of tears, and put his hand on her shoulder. "Bonnie, please don't worry. Arthur and I will keep Bill safe. This should only take a few minutes. Why don't you two make us some breakfast? We can all eat together when we come back."

Dan Wilbur was sitting on the top step of his porch as the three sentinels left the Cramer house and headed across the street. He was sipping a glass of fresh lemonade Val had prepared for him. It was going to be very hot today. As they crossed his freshly mown lawn, he stood up to greet them. "Hey Bill, what are you doing in the fancy outfit?"

"I'm just along for the ride, Dan," he smiled. "How's Val and the kids?"

Before he could answer, Lance interrupted, "I think we should don our helmets now. We have no idea what to expect inside. Mr. Wilbur, please lead us to your basement, but let us go in first for your own safety."

They entered the front door of the Wilbur house. Val was sitting on an easy chair watching television. "It's about time, Dan," she scowled. "Get that damned animal out of my house." They walked through the dining room to the kitchen. On the far wall of the kitchen was a single door that led downstairs.

Dan went to the door and stopped. "Well, this is the door to the basement. What do you want me to do now?" he said.

"Stay here with Arthur, Dan," Lance said. "Bill and I will go downstairs and check things out." He turned to Arthur and said, "You know what to do if the ulluba tries to come upstairs." Arthur nodded and the other two stepped through the door. He closed the door after them.

"Now we just wait, Dan," Arthur said as he drew his blaster and pointed it at the closed door. "We should probably be a few feet away from the door in case the ulluba crashes through."

Lance was two steps ahead of Bill. A naked light bulb swung on a long cord over their heads as they continued downward. "Bill, can you see the red image on your heads-up display?" Lance asked.

"No, all I see is a green image shaped like a wolf," Bill replied.

Lance stopped on the step. "That's even stranger. The stones in your suit do not detect any danger. That's why your image is green. My stones feel differently, I guess." They continued downward. After three more steps, Lance could see the edge of the cage. Two steps later, he could see the full empty cage. "Bill, the ulluba escaped from the kennel. Draw your blaster and be ready to shoot."

Bill held his blaster aimed downward to avoid shooting Lance by mistake. As the sentinel approached the bottom of the stairs, the ulluba began to snarl and growl. Lance aimed his blaster at the beast, which had moved to a leather couch and was watching him closely. Bill hurried to get to the bottom of the stairs to help his friend. The ulluba was standing on the couch and appeared to be ready to strike. It bared its fangs and its eyes were narrow and foreboding.

Lance was ready to fire when Bill reached the bottom of the stairway. The ulluba noticed Bill and stared at him. After a moment of uncertainty, the ulluba stopped growling and began to wag its tail. It rolled over onto its back and began to whimper as though it wanted someone to rub its belly.

Instinctively, Bill walked toward the ulluba. Lance tried to grab him by the shoulder, but it was too late. Bill sat on the couch next to the massive animal and began to rub its belly and pet it. "That's a good girl," Bill cooed. The ulluba began to lick his faceplate and gloves.

Lance noticed the image in his display had changed to green as well and removed his helmet. "Well, if that isn't the craziest thing I've ever seen," he laughed. The ulluba crawled off the couch and crossed to Lance and began to rub itself on his legs. He reached down and petted its back, making its tail wag even more.

The sentinels put the ulluba in their vehicle in case it had a change in attitude. The three then returned to the Cramer house and joined Eileen and Bonnie, who were sitting at the dinette table. Arthur took a dish of water and some raw meat back to the ulluba, which wagged its tail frantically at the sight of the meal. Then he returned to the group.

Eileen had made a hearty breakfast of bacon, eggs, toast, and hash browns for the sentinels. The five sat together enjoying the meal and each other's company. "Lance," Eileen said, "I never thought to ask if people from your planet eat food like this. I hope it's okay."

Lance laughed, "Eileen, everything is great. Thank you for asking though. While much of the wildlife on our planet is very different, our body's need for carbohydrates, fat and protein are no different from yours. Sentinels like Arthur and I travel to many different planets and are accustomed to different foods. Thank you again for inviting us to eat with your family."

"What are we going to do with the ulluba?" Bill asked. "I'm not sure I'm ready for a six-foot hairless dog with razor sharp fangs." He sipped his coffee.

"All of this is very unusual, Bill," Lionel replied. "The ulluba that came through the stone a few nights ago were vicious killers. Dan even said the one we captured was wild and crazy for some time before it settled down."

"Not to mention Bill's helmet never sensed danger as he went downstairs," Lance interrupted. "None of this makes sense."

"Oh my God," Bonnie said. She had turned as white as a ghost. The others turned to see what was behind them. Cybil was leading the ulluba into the kitchen. She stroked the top of its head and its tail wagged happily. "Cybil, come over here and try not to scare the animal."

"Lance, why did you have Buffy locked in your car?" Cybil said, still standing next to the ulluba.

"You gave the ulluba a name, honey?" Bill said.

"No, Buffy was always her name," Cybil smiled.

Lance stood and walked over to Cybil and lifted her in the air. He turned and carried her back to Bonnie and set her in her grandmother's lap. He went back to the animal and knelt beside it, rubbing its ears. "So, you're Buffy, huh?" he asked. Lance turned to Cybil and said, "Cybil, can you hear Buffy speaking to you?"

"Not really," Cybil said, looking confused. "It was Chachis and Zelda who told me that was her name."

"But how could the dogs tell you that? And how would they know?" Bonnie asked.

Cybil looked around the table. "I don't really know, but ever since I got this piece of stone, it's like they're talking into my head. Zelda said Chachis had been stung by one of those vorrath and was dying. But Zelda didn't know what to do, so she took Chachis and hid in a corner of the crystal cave. When the zongo crawled through the stone, a few saw Zelda and tried to attack, but she bared her teeth and growled and most backed off. The ulluba came next and they attacked the zongo who were trying to get Zelda. Buffy was the last ulluba to come through the stone and saw Chachis was wounded. She stayed with them until she saw Lance's planet through the stone and told Zelda to take Chachis through the stone quickly before the image changed."

"Wow!" Bill replied. "Thanks, Cybil. I sure wish they would talk to me too."

"I'm sure they are trying to, Grandpa," Cybil smiled. "Maybe you're just not listening."

The doorbell rang and Eileen rose to answer it. In a minute, she returned with Elder Jane Virtue and her bodyguard. Lance and Arthur rose and offered their chairs. After everyone was introduced, the elder hugged her grandson, Arthur, and asked him to stand watch outside with her bodyguard. Then she and Lance sat and joined the group. "Would you like some breakfast?" Bonnie asked. "We have plenty."

"No thank you, Bonnie," Elder Jane said. "But the coffee does smell good. I could use a cup of that, please." She turned her attention to the sentinels while Bonnie rose to retrieve a cup from the cupboard. "I am stunned to see an ulluba here in the room with us. What is the meaning of this, Lance?"

"This creature seems to be domesticated, Elder," he replied. "According to Cybil, it is responsible for getting the other dogs through the portal to our world. Frankly, I am at a loss to explain it. We were hoping you might have an idea." While he spoke, the ulluba rose and rubbed itself against the elder's legs and sat next to her on the floor.

"Yes, this is intriguing," she said. "We know nothing of the world this animal comes from, but the coincidence does give me a thought." She bent over and patted Buffy on the head. "I know you reported the attackers in green armor were Ballanan, and definitely not black mages, but this all seems like mind control to me. Do we know when the ulluba became docile like this?"

"Our neighbor across the street, Dan Wilbur, claims it was wild for a day or so after getting trapped in his kennel," Bill replied. "It calmed down suddenly when he fed it."

"Yes, I think I am seeing a timeline in my mind now," she said. "I believe the Ballanan leader that Sentinel Bill killed was controlling the minds of the ulluba during this attack. When that soldier was killed, the control was lost."

"But after I shot the Ballanan, the ulluba attacked me," Bill argued. "Why didn't they calm down too?"

"Well, I can't be certain, but that Ballanan was the only leader they had," she replied. "In the shock of the killing, they turned on you for fear you might shoot them next."

"So, all the ulluba are the pets of the Ballanan," Bonnie said. "They're like junkyard dogs. They are peaceful and happy when their owners are around, but become vicious when left alone at night to guard the property."

"Something like that, except they are not from Orto Nong," Elder Jane began. "The Ballanan broke the Heartstones on the planets where the vorrath and zongo came from first. I doubt much mind control was necessary as both species are naturally vicious predators. When they broke the stone on the ulluba's home world, the animals likely came as sentinels to protect the stone. Then the Ballanan used mind control to make them come to this world and attack."

"It's an interesting theory, Elder," Bill replied. "But how can we know if you're right?"

Jane Virtue sighed heavily and said, "Unfortunately, the only way to be sure is to travel to the ulluba's home planet and see what we find."

"But won't the ulluba guarding the broken stone attack us when we pass through the portal?" Bill asked.

"Perhaps, Bill," she smiled, "but they seem to have strong intuition. This creature is acting like my pet, so it must feel I am no danger to it. Of course, there may be Ballanan warriors there recruiting more of them to attack." She put her hand on Lance's shoulder. "Lance, I think you and Bill should take this ulluba and check it out."

Chapter 14

The Marshall ranch was a hive of activity. Earth movers clawed away at the ground to reach the crystal cave. The Marine Corps cleared a five-mile radius around the cave for security. A team of scientists worked feverishly to remove the cave paintings and other artifacts before they were lost forever. Others worked to extract the rest of the crystal chamber. Bill Marshall felt alien in the sentinel gear. Lionel, Lance, and Buffy walked along with him. Sentinel August Reason was standing with three other sentinels at the opening to the cave. She followed Bill and his team down into the cavern.

"Elder Paul Justice ordered me to accompany you to the planet of the ulluba," she said. "We have had ten other portal keys looking for that location, and we've narrowed it down to four possibilities. That means we'll have to keep trying until we find the correct one."

"Hopefully Buffy will be able to spot her home planet," Bill smiled.

August rubbed the ulluba's ears. "Buffy, that's a cute name for a frightening beast like this. I hope you're right. I certainly don't want to arrive on the vorrath or zongo planets."

Ten soldiers in red armor kept guard in the painting room. The paintings were almost all gone, and those warnings would never been seen near the portal again. Workers carried trays loaded with pieces of the

Heartstone toward the surface. Everyone stopped what they were doing when the ulluba walked past them.

"Oh, I almost forgot," August said as she reached into a pouch on her belt. "I made this collar for the ulluba. It has pieces of your Heartstone on it, Bill." She knelt next to the animal and fastened the collar around her neck. "Now that's a pretty ulluba," she giggled.

"Wow!" Bill gasped. "I think I can see through Buffy's eyes now. It must be the stones. Lance, take Buffy into the crystal cave while I wait here with my eyes closed."

Through his closed eyes, Bill could see that the opening in the Heartstone was large enough for three men to walk through abreast. Three sentinels guarded the portal. The open funnel of the retort was aimed directly at the center of the portal. Through the stone, he could see other worlds passing one by one. The scene changed every ten seconds, and each world was more fantastic than he could have imagined. A vast jungle appeared through the stone. Suddenly, a flock of dozens of vorrath raced toward the portal. The retort glowed to life and the vorrath were trapped on their side. After a few seconds, the view changed to a dark cave with an intact Heartstone. "Come here, Buffy," Bill thought to himself. It seemed as though he was looking up at himself, so he opened his eyes to find Buffy standing right next to him.

"Good girl," he said, patting her head. He and the ulluba walked into the crystal cave to find exactly what he saw in his mind. "I guess we eliminated one possibility."

"How did you know that, Bill?" Lance asked.

"I can see through Buffy's eyes now that she's wearing the stones," Bill replied. "I don't understand it, but it was incredible."

"I guess I'll have to order armor for her, too, now!" Lance laughed. He knelt next to Buffy and turned her head to look at him. "Okay, Buffy, you need to take us to your home. Bark when you see it through the portal and we'll use the retort to lock the connection." The ulluba wagged her tail and licked Lance's face.

August walked up to Sentinel Brian Master, the retort operator. "Brian, please select the next of the chosen planets and lock on." A dark cave was visible through the portal. The Heartstone was crumbling, just like the one on Earth. Brian shone a light through the portal and the room lit up. It seemed too quiet and completely lifeless. After a moment, the entire cave seemed to come to life as millions of zongo surged forward toward the open portal. The retort held them back until Brian was able to disengage the planet.

"I'll make sure to lock out that portal too, August," Brian said. "I guess we know where the spiders came from now." Another cave appeared through the portal. There was plenty of natural light as an opening was only a hundred feet or so from the portal. The Heartstone was crumbling there as well, except the opening was only eight feet in diameter.

Thunderous sound could be heard and a cascade of falling water masked the opening to the cave. Buffy barked and wagged her tail. Then she ran through the portal and hopped and jumped in the cave on the other planet.

"That's our cue," Lance said. "Helmets on and blasters to stun everyone." He put his hand on Bill's shoulder. "Bill, you come right behind me and don't be afraid. This is all part of our mission to save Earth. Lionel and August will be behind you. Keep your blaster in your hand, just in case." Lance smiled warmly as he donned his helmet and drew his blaster. Then he turned and ran through the opening. He crouched low on the other side and waved Bill through.

Bill knew he was an idiot for doing so, but he pulled on his helmet and drew his blaster. He thought about Bonnie and the rest of his family waiting at home. He smiled to himself and ran into the Heartstone. While the Earth stone had flooring installed, the other was covered with loose bits of crystal. Bill felt instantly nauseated by the jump and sliding uncontrollably forward. Lance grabbed him tightly before he could fall to the ground.

"Good job, Sentinel," Lance said. "Believe me, it gets easier. Do that a few thousand times and it's no big deal." Lionel and August strolled through more leisurely and both were laughing.

"Bill, you're such a card," August said. "Lance is a big show-off. Next time, unless you're in danger, just walk through." She hugged him. "Where's Buffy?"

"She's standing at the entrance to the cave waiting for us," Lionel said. "What are your orders, Lance?"

"August, you stay at the cave opening with Bill," Lance began. "Lionel and I will check the rest of the cave for a while to make certain it is secure. We'll be back in ten minutes. Let's go Lionel." The two sentinels examined a number of tunnels that led off the crystal chamber. Bill and August walked to the mouth of the cave to join Buffy.

The opening was approximately eight feet wide and ten feet tall. A massive waterfall fell twenty feet away from the sheer rock face. The water crashed several hundred feet below into a large lake. There were no ledges or other features around the opening. Clearly, Buffy had not entered the cave here. "Bill, when we want to talk to our team, we say the word "com" and then pause a second. Then anything we say can be heard by all of us," August said. "Com. There is no way to leave through the cave mouth. It's a sheer drop of five hundred and eighteen feet. There are no ledges to use either. Out."

"Copy that. We've checked a few of the other tunnels, but all were dead ends. Lionel and I are in the last one now and it must be the way out. Take the tunnel on the far left side of the stone and you should find us. Out," Lance replied.

"Copy that, Lance. Bill and I are on our way. Com out," August said. "You see, Bill, it's very easy. Come on now, we have to catch up. Buffy, come on." They left the crystal room and headed into the narrow tunnel. The floor was well worn and smooth, a clear sign of foot traffic. After several bends, they found themselves in a large chamber with the other sentinels. Rows of stone benches radiated outward from the tunnel they came through. There were stands for oil lights throughout the room. "This looks like some kind of church," August said. "We are definitely going in the right direction."

There was a single opening on the far side of the room, and the group hurried toward it. That opening was a twenty-foot tunnel that opened onto the surface of the planet. A giant set of stone steps led down to the surface two hundred feet below. A large, ancient city stretched out before them. Rough hills and jungle surrounded the buildings. Thin trails of smoke rose from hundreds of small stone houses. A large stone temple was directly opposite the cave and several dozen priests could be seen emerging from it. Dozens of ulluba were sitting quietly on the stone steps. They sensed something and turned to see the sentinels at the opening. The ulluba began to growl and bark. Several raced up the steps to confront the Beings that were in the temple. As they approached the top of the steps, Buffy stepped forward and barked loudly. The rest of the ulluba stopped and whimpered. It seemed clear Buffy was their leader.

Dozens of soldiers raced through the open square toward the temple stairs. They wielded bronze spears and brightly colored shields. The ulluba turned to the soldiers and began to growl. Most of the soldiers stopped advancing and were stunned the guardians were not attacking the strangers. One soldier raised his spear in the air and threw it towards the sentinels.

The spear was aimed directly at Lionel, who reached out with his left hand and grabbed it out of the air. He dropped the weapon and stood silently. The warriors did not know what to do and began to argue among themselves. Two priests joined them and quieted them down. Their faces were bright red from anger and paint.

Lance opened a small bag on his belt and withdrew four pieces of Heartstone and offered them to the others. "These are pieces from the stone on this planet. Put one in your communicators," he said. He opened a small panel on the chest plate of Bill's armor and snapped the stone in place.

Bill was shocked. "Wow! That's amazing. I can understand what they're saying," he said. "But how can they understand us?"

"Lionel and August, be prepared to get Bill out of here," Lance replied. "Bill, wait here with the others. Buffy and I are going to say hello to our hosts." He motioned to Buffy who began to follow him down the steps.

"I don't think that's a good idea, Lance," Bill shouted after him.

"It's the only way, Bill," Lance replied. "You knew the job of a sentinel wouldn't be easy." The group of warriors and priests were stunned to see the single soldier and ulluba walking toward them. Lance had clipped his blaster onto his belt. The soldiers pointed their spears menacingly at Lance, but began to back off as the pack of ulluba followed behind him. The two priests held their ground and scowled.

"You filth have defiled our temple and corrupted our sentinels," one of the priests said. "How dare you come back here to steal more of our sentinels? You think the four of you can fight all of our soldiers? We are not afraid of you."

Lance held out his right hand to reveal a small piece of Heartstone from his own planet. The priest looked confused and looked around at the others. After a moment of hesitation, he reached forward slowly and took the offering in his hand. "My name is Sentinel Lance Allright. My friends and I have come to your world to understand why some ulluba came to our planet and attacked us."

"How do you speak our language?" the priest replied. "What kind of black mage magic is that?"

"You can understand me because you hold a piece of the Heartstone from my home planet," Lance explained. "We borrowed four small pieces of your stone so we could understand you as well."

"I have no idea what you are talking about," the priest said. He turned to the other priest and said, "You understand him too, Malua, right?"

"No, Chief Priest, I cannot," Malua replied. "How is it possible for you?"

The Chief Priest gave the stone to the other and said, "You talk to him then."

"Priest Malua, I was just telling your Chief Priest that my name is Lance Allright," he said. "It is the stone in your hand that has joined our minds so we can communicate. Please believe that we have come in peace."

Malua let the stone drop from his hand and stood motionless as if in a trance. The Chief Priest picked up the stone again. "You must pardon Malua, he is a fool. Why should any of us listen to you? I can order my men to kill you where you stand, Lance. Give me one good reason not to."

"There has been a coordinated attack on Heartstones on several planets, including yours. At least one Ballanan soldier came through your stone and used mind control to force ulluba through the stone to attack another peaceful planet," Lance remarked. "We don't know why they did it, but we know they can now attack any planet with their armies. The first soldier only took a few ulluba. The next ones may invade your world. Your weak weapons will be useless against them. They are not black mages, but still could kill you and everyone here with no remorse."

"It was only a couple days ago when the lizard men came through the stone," the priest recalled. "There were hundreds of worshippers in the temple when they came through. They were slaughtered without mercy. I only survived as I was buried in a mound of dead bodies. They did not look much different from you. How can we be sure you are not more lizard men here to kill more?"

"I can give you two reasons to believe me," Lance said. "You know firsthand the power of the Ballanan warriors. Do you think any of you would still be alive if I was one of them?"

"That is a good point," the priest replied. "Perhaps you have more insidious plans for me. What's your second point?"

Lance pulled off his helmet, revealing his human features. "You can now see I am not a Ballanan warrior," he said. "You must understand that your people are in grave danger. We will help you if you allow us to do so. We have equipment that may stop the Ballanan from entering your world. But you will have to allow us to occupy the crystal cave." He turned to the other sentinels at the top of the steps and shouted, "Bill, please go back to the crystal cave and ask Brian to bring fragments of the Far Sun stone. We need to get more of these people to understand us."

Bill waved and started back through the temple and into the tunnel. When he arrived in the crystal cave, he walked over to stand in front of the break. The opening had increased to ten feet in diameter already, and more pieces of stone rained down onto the floor of the cave. He could see the retort on Earth through the stone and waved at the sentinels there. When he got Brian's attention, he made the request for the stones. Then he turned back to return to the entrance when an odd feeling overcame Bill and he spun around to see three Ballanan warriors rushing through the stone. Before he could react, the leader hit him across the chest with his arm causing him to fly backwards and crash into the wall of the cave. He felt himself losing consciousness and fought to hold on.

He looked up and realized he was alone in the cave. His chest plate was dented and several puncture marks almost reached through to his skin. Looking through the stone, he could see a dark cave which he presumed was the Ballanan planet. There were no signs of life, but he did see a machine pointed at the Heartstone. He struggled to his feet and drew his blaster, adjusting it to high. He aimed carefully at the machine and fired. The plasma ball shot through the opening and stuck the machine which blew into pieces. Instantly, the image changed and the crystal cave on Earth reappeared. He called to the sentinels and three rushed through to join him. They headed back down the tunnel toward the temple, where they could hear the sounds of blasters firing just ahead.

The Ballanan warriors were hiding behind the benches firing at the sentinels guarding the exit from the cave. Bill could see Lionel lying flat on his face next to Buffy who had also been shot. Lance and August peeked around the entrance of the cave and fired at the two Ballanan who were still in the fight. Brian Master whispered, "Com. On my command, do the San-Fa command with your illuminators." He could see Lance nodding his approval as he ducked behind the wall just as a plasma blast flashed by his head. "Let's go team!" He and the other two sentinels stood in the opening facing the Ballanan who had not yet noticed them. Bill took his place by their side and raised his left hand. "San-Fa," the sentinels shouted.

Green light shot from the illuminators, forming a wall between them and the Ballanan, who heard the commotion and turned to face them. They enemy fired their blasters at the sentinels, but the plasma was absorbed into the green wall which strengthened and continued toward them. Bill could see August and Lance doing the same, and a second green wall approached the Ballanan from the opposite direction. The Ballanan stood back to back and continued to fire at the green walls which grew stronger with each plasma blast they absorbed. After a minute, the two walls met and the enemy was trapped inside. A few seconds later, the two Ballanan collapsed and fell to the ground dead.

Brian clapped Bill on the shoulder and handed him the bag of stones. "Great job, Sentinel! I've got to get back to the retort before we lose the connection again. We'll take Lionel and the ulluba with us." The group rushed to the fallen warriors and carried them back toward the crystal cave, where the Earth cavern could still be seen on the other side. Five soldiers in red armor were watching for danger. Brian and his team carried Lionel back through the portal where he could be cared for.

Lance picked up Buffy gingerly. She winced in pain. "Bill, don't worry, Lionel and Buffy will both be okay. You and August stay here while I carry the ulluba back. Keep your blasters aimed at the portal just in case," he said. He turned and walked through the portal. Bill could see two soldiers take the animal carefully and carry it out of the crystal room. Lance and Brian stood together talking for several minutes.

Then he returned through the portal and joined them again. "What happened in here, Bill?"

"I asked Brian for the crystals and was coming back when a deep feeling of dread overcame me," Bill replied. "I turned around and saw the Ballanan soldiers coming through the portal. Before I could react, the first one struck me and knocked me across the room where I hit the wall hard." He pointed to the cuts in his armor. "He almost broke my armor, but thank God it held. When I could move, I noticed the soldiers had left. I looked through the portal and saw some kind of machine pointed at me. I shot it with my blaster and it exploded. Instantly, I could see Brian and the others on Earth. That's when they came through."

"Lance, it sounds like the Ballanan have a portal lock device," August said. "We're very lucky it wasn't guarded better or many more could have come through."

"You're right August," he replied. "I wonder why they came here anyway. These people are very primitive. The ulluba were good weapons, but now that we're involved, those animals aren't a real threat to Earth."

"Do you think they were looking for me, Lance?" Bill asked. "Remember what Frank said when he held the Heartstone."

"The next time they'll be looking for you," Lance repeated. "I suppose that is possible, but why would they come here? How would they know you weren't on

Earth? Let's not worry about that right now. We need to go see how the locals are doing." He turned to August and said, "You need to get another sentinel over here to help you guard this end. And tell the elders we need a retort and permanent crew to manage this portal. Try to hurry since we don't know how long we can keep the connection. Hopefully, Bill destroying their portal lock will give us time."

"Yes, Lance," August said. She walked through the stone and began talking to the team there.

"Come on, Bill," Lance said. "We need to talk to the locals and see if they have been hurt." The two left the crystal cave and headed back to the temple.

Chapter 15

When Bill and Lance returned to the temple, the bodies of the fallen Ballanan were gone. The warriors had carried them out of the temple to display the enemy to the locals who formed a large circle around the bodies. Bill and Lance hurried down the stone steps toward the group after removing their helmets so they were not confused with the Ballanan. Lance moved through the crowd toward the bodies while Bill offered small chips of Heartstone to the people so he and Lance could communicate with them. As Bill approached Lance, he could see he was arguing with the Chief Priest.

"Joco, what are you doing with these bodies?" Lance shouted.

"It is our custom to view the bodies of our vanquished foes before we burn them," the Chief Priest said. "However, it wasn't long ago when we would have eaten their flesh to gain from their strength."

"Bill, come over here and help me out," Lance said. "We need to check their armor for pieces of their own Heartstone. That's the only way we'll be able to communicate with them when we arrive on their world."

"I hope you're kidding, Lance," Bill laughed. "You want us to go to their world so they can kill us more easily? That doesn't make any sense at all."

Lance was scouring one of the bodies for hidden compartments in the armor. After a few moments, he found several pieces of a dark blue Heartstone imbedded in the suit. "See? Here, Bill, the compartments are right here. I've found five pieces already." He stood up and faced Bill. "We need to know why the Ballanan are attacking these planets. They are not black mages, but their planet used to be ruled by them. Until we learn their motivation, there is little chance we can make them stop. Killing their soldiers will only enrage them all the more."

August rejoined the two others in the circle of natives. "Lance, five sentinels are guarding the cave now. A second retort should be available in a few hours. The big risk is breaking the connection to Earth long enough to connect to Far Sun where it is being prepared. Hopefully, those sentinels can stop another incursion."

"August, Lance wants to travel to Orto Nong to find out why the Ballanan are attacking us. Isn't that crazy?" Bill asked.

She put her hand on his shoulder and said, "Crazy yes, but also critical. We can't install retorts on every planet to stop these guys. We need to make them want to stop."

Lance had returned to examining the other bodies and had accumulated a large stash of Heartstone fragments. Finally satisfied, he stood and offered stone fragments to Bill, August, and Chief Priest Joco. "Keep these stones. When the Ballanan come back, we should be able to understand them."

"When they come back?" Joco asked. "So, it's just a matter of time? What can my people do if your forces cannot stop them?"

A huge explosion rocked the city. A ball of fire and black smoke shot out the temple entrance. Debris showered down on the circle of villagers. Dozens of Ballanan warriors emerged from the tunnel and headed down the steps while firing their blasters at the crowd.

"Run!" Lance shouted over the screams of the crowd. The crowd broke up and ran down the narrow stone streets away from the temple grounds. Hundreds of villagers flooded out of their homes and joined the others trying to flee the city and escape into the surrounding jungle. Blaster fire flew over their heads and into the crowd. Wounded villagers fell down only to be trampled by others desperate to escape. Fragments of stone flew into the air where blaster shots struck the surrounding buildings.

After two blocks, Lance grabbed Bill and August by the arms and pulled them into a narrow alley. The floor of the alley was littered with debris from surrounding buildings. They kept their backs against the wall as they watched the crowd race by. After a few seconds, the alley became very quiet. Shortly thereafter, they could hear several Ballanan warriors approaching. "Naka, this is the most fun I've had in ages," one voice said.

"Ibu, this is not a shooting gallery. These creatures are harboring black mages. The elders have confirmed that," Naka replied.

"I know, Naka, but can't I enjoy my work?" Ibu asked.

"Shut up the both of you," a third voice said, very close to the sentinels now. "We would have finished our assignment already if not for those other soldiers. Just be quiet and keep following the crowd."

Lance raised his left arm and jumped out of the alley to face the three advancing soldiers. Before they could react, he shouted "Chak-tak!" and a pink light shot from his illuminator. He motioned for the others to join him. The three soldiers seemed to be frozen in place.

"Lance, is that what you did to the zongo on my planet?" Bill asked.

"Of course not, Bill," Lance smiled. "These three are temporarily paralyzed in place. It should last ten or twenty minutes if we're lucky." He pulled fragments of the Far Sun Heartstone and placed them on the Ballanan warriors. "My name is Lance Allright, and I am a sentinel from Far Sun. Your forces have attacked this planet as well as others without provocation. I heard you say that the locals are harboring black mages, but I cannot believe that is true. My people are also enemies of the black mages, but we can't help you if you keep attacking innocents. When you return to Orto Nong, tell your superiors we will help you battle any black mages, but will fight against you if you continue to attack peaceful populations." He returned to August and Bill. "Okay, that's all we can do here. The portal is obviously compromised, so we need to hide out until more troops can take the temple back.

Perhaps we'll find out something in the jungle. Let's get out of here before they come after us." The three hurried down the street to the edge of the deserted city and out into the countryside.

The first couple miles of land were cultivated to provide food for the large city. A few stone roadways led toward other cities. Lance chose a narrow dirt road that crawled by a few farmsteads and then ended at the jungle's edge. They sat on a mound of dirt that marked the end of the road. Several miles away, a cloud of smoke rose over the abandoned city. August used the maximum zoom on her visor to look for approaching troops, but none could be found. "My guess is they are scouring the city for people and perhaps a black mage or two," she said.

"Looking for gold and other valuables to steal while more soldiers arrive," Lance replied. "The city was fairly small. Now they have an entire planet to search. I just hope those three take my message back."

"Lance, what if the Ballanan are right about black mages?" Bill asked. "Doesn't that mean there are black mages on Earth too?"

"I've thought about that too, Bill," Lance replied. "But it seems unlikely. The ancient texts tell us black mages make others believe whatever they want them to. The mages may still be on Orto Nong too, having convinced the Ballanan to look elsewhere."

"And five sentinels have died defending this planet," August said. "I still can't believe I left them just minutes before the attack. I should have died there too."

"Nonsense, August," Bill said. "God has some other fate in store for the three of us."

"That's right, Bill," Lance said. "And I think it's time we started to find out what that is. Let's get out of here before they come looking for us." They stood and began to walk down a narrow dirt path that led into the dense jungle.

Chapter 16

Night fell quickly in the jungle. Two hours after entering the jungle, it was pitch black. The three set their helmets to night vision and continued down the path in the eerie green light. Bright floating blobs of light marked fire bugs floating about looking for food. Other animals could be seen as hot spots scurrying around in the jungle around them. August was in the lead and motioned back to the others to kneel down. The brightly lit image of a campfire and several people was ten yards ahead. They listened intently and tried to stay absolutely quiet.

"Joco, please stay calm," said Malua. "It is only a flesh wound and I am preparing a poultice to help with the healing."

"Malua, you fool, I am dying," Joco said. "Those evil lizard men have killed your Chief Priest, and you fiddle around with herbs and berries. Pray for me and pray for all of your lives."

August whispered, "Com. I am reading only villagers and no Ballanan in the area at all, Lance."

Lance replied, "Okay, let's go in. Com out." He removed his helmet and spoke out loud, "Joco, it's Lance. We are coming to your camp. Please don't be surprised." The three sentinels moved out of the darkness into the firelight. August stepped forward to check the Chief Priest's wounds. Lance and Bill sat by the fire. "You are all very lucky to be alive."

"Alive for now, Lance," Joco winced in pain. "I was hit by one of the Ballanan and feel my life force fading quickly."

August removed a small vial from her belt and injected its contents into the priest's wound. "I think you'll be okay in the morning, Joco. It was just a blaster burn, but I'm glad we found you."

"All of God's blessings on you, sentinel," Malua said. "You have saved our priest's life and our lives are now forfeit to you."

"Oh, shut up, Malua," Joco said, already feeling much better. "All of us are living on borrowed time now that our sacred temple has fallen. I'm surprised you three are still alive. Why did you bring those lizard men back here to our planet?"

"We didn't have anything to do with that, Joco," Lance said. "We did learn something today though. Those warriors believe black mages are living on this planet. That's who they came looking for."

"That's preposterous!" the Chief Priest laughed. "Black mages on Goola, that's pretty funny. Look at me! Do I look all powerful to any of you?"

"We don't understand it either, Joco," Bill replied. "If what the Ballanan believe is true, then there are black mages on my home world too. Since the temple and portal are now in their hands, we have few options."

"Joco, there must be something about this planet that makes them believe black mages might live here," Lance said. "Are their any rumors or myths about strange places or events that we might check out?"

"There are no black mages on this planet!" Joco shouted. "I would know if there were." At that moment, a large python slithered into the camp and approached the Chief Priest. He tried to move away, but the beast slowly started to crawl over his legs. The other villagers began to move away and shouted prayers at the sky. Lance stood and picked up the twenty-foot snake and tossed it into the underbrush. He then withdrew a small black box with a glass dome on top and set it next to the fire. He pressed down on the dome and a blue dome of light emanated from the device and grew until it formed a twenty-foot shield around the campsite.

Malua fell to his knees and clutched his hands together in front of Lance. "Mighty Lance, you are our savior. You have defeated the Bagli with your bare hands. Chief Priest, you must tell Lance about the hidden lands. You owe him your life!"

"The hidden lands? That sounds interesting," August said.

"Oh all right!" Joco acquiesced. "But the consequences will be on your head, Malua."

"What and where are the hidden lands, Joco?" Lance asked.

"Our most sacred text, the Book of Nan, tells the story of Nan-bo-Nan, a visitor from the Underworld who came to Goola long ago to escape the evil there. Nan-bo-Nan was a god who chose this planet as her home and promised to protect us from evil for all time. In exchange for this protection, she asked us to pray to her and to stay far from her home, which is deep in the hidden lands. But it is strictly forbidden to enter those lands. Those who enter are immediately killed and their souls are sent to the Underworld for eternal torture."

"Well, since she has broken her promise, I think it's time we visit this Nan-bo-Nan," Lance said. "Where is this place?"

"Far from here, Lance. It would take months to reach the hidden lands. I'm certain the lizard men would find us long before we reach it," Joco said. "And if we do arrive, we will be killed immediately."

"I understand your fear, Joco," Lance replied. "You must remember that Nan-bo-Nan has already broken her promise. The Ballanan have invaded your planet and killed many of your people. I need you to lead us to the hidden lands. If you do not wish to go further, that is fine. My team will carry on until we find this Nan-bo-Nan. Either way, you are going to take us there. There is no discussion on that point."

"Fine," Joco relented. "We will not survive many days here in the jungle without your assistance. The hidden lands are far from this pestilence, so it will be safer for us too. But do not expect us to follow you further than the edge of the hidden lands."

"That's a good deal. We accept," Lance said. "How far do you think it is?"

"No one knows. We have never attempted to travel there. Now that we have no homes or temple, we have less incentive to stay put. Our ancient text says the hidden lands are barren and rocky with massive mountains all around, so it must be very far from here," Joco said. "We should all get some rest now. It will be easier to travel when the sun is up."

"Just so you know, the perimeter shield device I set up works both ways," Lance smiled. "It will keep all the creatures of the jungle away tonight, but it will also keep you from running away. Good night, everyone."

Bill Marshall slept very well in the jungle. The controlled atmosphere within his suit kept him cool and comfortable in the steamy jungle. He awoke to find one of the villagers throwing greens and tubers into a pot of boiling water. When he looked at the pot, the system in his helmet told him the soup was two hundred and thirty four degrees and all the ingredients were edible. The priests were arguing about everything, including the direction to the hidden lands. Twenty yards away, he could see Lance sitting up in the branches of a tree. He rose and walked over to him. "Good morning, Lance!"

"Good morning, Bill," he replied. "I'm just checking the surroundings for any Ballanan warriors. It doesn't look like they are following us yet. I am getting some odd signals from the city though. They are clearly still in control and bringing more equipment through as quickly as they can."

"That can't be good," Bill replied. "Where's August? I haven't seen her yet."

"I sent her to get some fresh water to the north of here," he said. "Why don't you go give her a hand?"

"Will do," Bill replied as he turned to head north. He walked back through the camp where the villagers were eating the stew. Malua offered a cup to Bill but he waved him off and continued back into the jungle. "Com. August, where are you? Lance sent me to help." No response. He kept moving north. After five minutes, he could hear falling water. After climbing over a small ridge, he came upon a small lake being fed by a waterfall. His helmet read that the water was pure. He continued forward to the edge of the lake until he noticed August standing under the waterfall bathing. "Oops! Sorry about that," he said as he turned around.

"Good morning, Bill," August shouted over the water. "You should come in; the water is fresh and cold. It feels wonderful."

"That's okay, maybe later," he replied. "Lance asked me to come and help you gather water. What should I do?"

"What do you want to do, Bill?" she whispered from right behind him. He turned to see her standing inches away from him, nude. Drops of water fell from her hair and rolled down her breasts and belly as she smiled at him. She pulled off his helmet and dropped it onto the ground. Then she grabbed his head with both hands and pulled him to her, kissing him on the lips. "You know, Bill, you are very cute. What do you think of me?"

"August, you know I'm married," he stammered.

"That's not what I asked, Sentinel. Now answer the question," she demanded.

"August, you are a very beautiful and sensuous woman," he replied. "And I can't believe this is happening to me."

She laughed. "Bill, you are adorable. There are some containers over there. Just fill them up. You can help me carry them back to the camp." She kissed him on the cheek and went to dry off and put on her uniform.

As he filled the last container, she joined him, taking two of the containers. "Thanks for the help, Bill." She leaned close so her mouth was next to his ear and said, "And just so you know, anytime you want to join me in a lake or anywhere else, just let me know. There is just something about a natural sentinel that is irresistible to me."

Bill was blushing bright red as the two walked back to the camp. When they arrived, they found Lance enjoying a bowl of the stew. "You two need to try this, it's really good," Lance said. "I don't know when I had anything so fresh and delicious."

"I know exactly what you mean, Lance," Bill said. August laughed out loud.

Chapter 18

The group traveled two more days and was still mired in the jungle. None of the villagers had ever left their city and had no idea where high mountain country could be found. With no knowledge of the geography of the planet, the sentinels were helpless too. Lance kept them on a northward course assuming that cooler weather would eventually lead to different terrain, however, that could be many weeks away. Thankfully, food was abundant and the villagers made delicious food from the unusual plant and animal life. Water was also plentiful and August used every trick in her book to make certain that Bill would find her naked somewhere every day.

On the fourth day, the terrain became hilly, although the jungle remained thick and foreboding. Lance would race to the top of each new hill hoping to find mountains on the horizon, but today there were only more hills. In the afternoon, rain drenched the group and they sought shelter anywhere they could find it. As the sun began to head toward the horizon, the sky cleared and the temperatures shot up again. The heat was unbearable for the villagers who did not have sentinel suits to protect them, so the group was forced to stop. August had gone to the nearest hilltop to check for Ballanan readings. Her voice spoke in Bill and Lance's helmets, "We've got company coming. I'm on my way there."

Moments later, she ran to the group sitting in a clearing. "Everyone out into the jungle, now!" she shouted. Bill and Lance pulled the villagers to their feet and led them back into the cover. A thin metallic sound approached from a great distance. She stood between Lance and Bill and spoke quietly, "We've got a flying craft of some kind headed this way. I don't think they saw me, but there's no way to tell. We've got to stay hidden until they go away. They probably have infrared sensors, but hopefully the heat of the jungle will block that."

A small craft flew over the clearing and hovered. With his helmet, Lance could see two pilots and one gunner in the back of the ship. It hovered for a few minutes and began to circle the area. "This could take a long time," Lance said.

"What choice do we have?" Bill asked.

"Tactic 87 Lance?" August said.

"You know, that's just crazy enough to work. I saw a lake fifty yards to the east. Give me five minutes and then execute," Lance said. He ran off into the bush.

"What's Tactic 87, August?" Bill asked.

"You're part of it, Bill. You'll find out soon enough," August said. She pulled off her helmet and faced the villagers. "Joco, you and your team stay here. Don't move or they'll find you and kill you. We're going to distract them. Okay, Bill, it's up to you and me now." She grabbed his hand and pulled him eastward. "Leave your helmet here, Bill. You won't need it."

The sky craft was directly overhead as they dashed through the undergrowth. Bill thought he could hear August singing, but realized that must be the sound of the craft. They entered a large open space with a broad lake. August pointed upward so Bill could see Lance positioned high in a tree. "Okay, Billy boy, no time for arguing. Take off your clothes and do it quick before the craft gets here," she said as she pulled open her suit and dropped it to the ground.

"But August, I don't understand," Bill argued.

She reached forward and pulled open his suit. "I told you not to argue, now strip!" When she was nude, she raced out into the lake up to her knees. "Get over here Bill! They are almost here."

Bill decided he had been thinking too much. He took off his underwear and ran out into the water with August, who immediately threw her arms around his neck. "Now, that's not so bad, is it?" she asked as she pressed her body against him. "Now kiss me like your life depends on it, because it does." They kissed and she pushed her belly against his and pulled him down into the water. Suddenly, she was on top of him, grinding her hips and smiling down at him. "You see the ship, honey?" she asked.

"It's right above us," he sighed. "It looks like they're coming down to get a better look."

"They always do," she laughed as she arched her back to give the crew a really good look. "Good old Tactic 87. It never fails with males." She leaned forward and kissed him on the mouth.

Bill could feel himself entering her and looked away and thought of the vorrath and zongo in a desperate attempt to distract himself. As he looked up, he saw Lance launch himself from the tree into the cockpit of the craft. He shot the gunner whose dead body fell not ten feet from them in the water. August had already jumped up and raced back to her uniform and blaster. The two pilots were fighting hand to hand with Lance. Bill stumbled to his feet and headed back to the shore. As he approached, August fired her blaster and the pilot's head exploded. Lance then threw the other pilot out and he plummeted to the water below. When he tried to stand, August shot him dead.

Lance had gained control of the craft and signaled down to the others who waved at him. He pointed toward the clearing and flew away. August dropped her blaster and threw her arms around Bill's neck. "Damn that Lance," she whispered in his ear. "Ten seconds later and I would have been much happier." She kissed his mouth. "Bill, you are great at Tactic 87, but please don't tell me if you perform it with anyone else."

Bill smiled at her and kissed her cheek. "I promise, August. I promise." The two dressed quickly and searched the warriors for Heartstone fragments. Then they returned to the clearing where Lance had enlisted two villagers to clear the blood and gore from the craft.

"Thanks Bill. I didn't know if you could pull that off or not," Lance said. "But August can be very convincing. I thought you were getting into it a bit too."

He turned to face the craft. "But now we have transportation out of this damn jungle. On my way back here, I took it up to ten thousand and could see mountains a few hundred miles from here. It looks like it's fully gassed up, so we're ready to go whenever we get our gear on board."

"The sooner the better, Lance," August said. "Those guys are not going to report on schedule and then someone's going to come looking for them. We don't want to be around when that happens."

Joco approached the group and said, "You expect us to travel in the sky? That is not possible. Only birds, gods, and demons can fly."

"Joco, don't be unreasonable," August replied. "You would have been dead already if not for us. This is your one chance to survive. We're all going together. You made a commitment to help us find the hidden lands, and you are going to fulfill that. Got it?" she shouted as she thumped him on the chest with her index finger.

Malua joined the group. "Everything is loaded on the craft. We are at your disposal, Sentinels."

"Everyone on board," Lance said. "Joco and I will sit up front so he can look for landmarks. Bill and August will keep an eye on the rest of you. Since you've never been in the air before, there is a significant chance you might get sick. I want all the villagers sitting on the outside. If you're going to vomit do it outside, or you'll be doing the cleanup again.

After clamoring on board and buckling themselves down, the craft lifted off and rose to just over the tree tops. Then it shot northward at full speed.

Chapter 19

Bill Marshall woke suddenly. He was sitting in the back of the flyer. August was sleeping with her head on his shoulder. The villagers were staring at the land zipping by below them. He tried to remember how he felt the first time he flew in an aircraft, but it was too long ago. Looking down on the planet must be an amazing experience for these ancient people. The jungle had given way to rolling, grassy hills. Large herds of animals could be seen grazing below. The flyer had risen to two or three thousand feet above the ground. Looking forward, ranges of snowcapped mountains dominated the horizon. Every few minutes, the ship flew by a small village surrounded by a rough fence to keep predatory animals at bay. He could see the townspeople looking up in amazement at the machine flying through the sky like a bird.

"I'm glad you woke up, Bill," Lance said. "You and August have been sleeping for a couple of hours. How do you feel?"

"I feel great, Lance. It looks like you have found the hidden lands," he replied.

"Maybe, I don't know. Joco only has his memory of the ancient texts to guide him. I'm hoping there will be some sign demarking the forbidden territories. Otherwise, we could fly around this planet a thousand times and not find anything," Lance said.

"Chang-A! Chang-A!" Joco shouted.

"What are you talking about, Joco?" Lance asked.

"Can you see the city ahead of us? That is Chang-A, the temple city that marks the entrance to the hidden lands," Joco said. "We must not let them see us flying or they will consider us demons. All of this is written in the sacred texts. Please listen to me."

"Very well, Joco," Lance replied. "I'll set us down in that small wooded area over there. Then we can camouflage the ship and proceed on foot. Bill, you should wake up August so she can help." Lance turned the ship away from the rapidly approaching city and headed toward a small forest in a shallow, broad valley a couple miles to the east.

Bill took August's hand and squeezed it. "August, we're getting ready to land," he said.

She opened her large green eyes and looked at Bill. She smiled and pressed her face against his arm. "Thanks for the shoulder, Bill. I must have been exhausted. Tactic 87 can do that to a person."

"I know," Bill smiled. "I just woke up myself. There is a big city a couple miles from here that Joco says marks the beginning of the hidden lands. We're setting down not far from there."

The flyer slowed and hovered over the woods while Lance looked for a suitable spot to touch down. A small clearing in the center of the woods fit the bill completely. A small creek cut through the middle of the opening. Lance set the ship down on the western bank of the creek and powered down. Joco and Malua immediately jumped out and fell to their knees to thank God for their survival. The sentinels climbed out with the villagers and began to gather branches to help conceal the ship. While it wouldn't be possible to completely hide it, they hoped the strangeness of the metal ship would be enough to keep any locals away. When they had done their best, Lance asked Joco and Malua to sit with him and the other sentinels to discuss their next steps.

"This is a difficult situation, Lance," Joco said. "I doubt the lizard men have come this far yet, so the people of Chang-A have no idea what's going on. Perhaps you should avoid the city altogether and just take the flyer and go."

"Well, we don't know how far we need to travel in the hidden lands to find Nan-bo-Nan. We will need provisions for the trip," Lance argued. "Perhaps the people of Chang-A are not as timid as you are and may accompany us."

"Oh, no, no, no!" Malua cried. "Chang-A was built to honor Nan-bo-Nan. The priests there would never allow such a thing."

"Malua is correct, Lance," Joco said. "Each year, every city is required to send one priest here to study with the Grand Master. All the priests who have come here are adamant that the hidden lands remain just that.

"So you and Malua have been here before," August replied.

"No. Our city is too sacred for a priest to ever leave," Joco said. "The Grand Master knows our stone temple is the seat of power for the entire planet. Each year, a priest from Chang-A comes to our city to help run the temple."

"Why didn't you tell us this before?" August asked. "We could have used someone knowledgeable about the hidden lands."

"We could not. As I told Lance, when the lizard men first came to our city, they slaughtered everyone in the temple. I only survived as I was buried in other bodies. Priest Eboa was killed that day. He had just arrived from Chang-A two months earlier. We sent a messenger to tell the Grand Master, but he probably is still traveling this way on foot," Joco replied.

"Well, we need to learn more about Nan-bo-Nan and the hidden lands before we attempt to travel there," Lance concluded. "Given that, we might as well go to Chang-A and see what happens next. Let's pack up and head to the city. August, please secure the flyer with most of our supplies so we can travel light."

"Yes, Lance," she replied. "I've already done that. "I recommend the priests and villagers surround us so the city dwellers are not too suspicious."

"Excellent idea," Lance said. "Let's get going."

The weather in this area was much cooler than the jungle. A few scattered clouds blew about above them as they walked through the sparse trees. Thankfully, there were fewer bugs here. To show any locals that they were also human, the sentinels had their helmets clipped to their belts. At the edge of the woods, a narrow dirt path led forward toward the crest of the next hill. As they climbed over the summit, the tall stone walls of Chang-A appeared on the next hilltop. Their path intersected a large cobblestone road that led to the city gates. A few people were walking in both directions on the road, but stopped suddenly when they noticed the strange group approaching them. The sentinels were much taller than the locals. Even Bill was almost a head taller than the Chief Priest and the others. August was several inches taller than Bill, and Lance was the tallest of them all. What a shock it must have been to those ancient people to see the modern body armor and differing complexions of the sentinels.

As they stepped onto the cobblestone path, many of the pilgrims recognized the Chief Priest's robes and bowed deeply. He gestured with his hand to reassure and bless them. August stepped awkwardly on a broken stone and stumbled. Bill grabbed her waist and held her steady. She smiled at him and kissed his cheek. Bill blushed again. As they approached, the city gates opened and dozens of people flooded out to look at the strangers. Among them were several soldiers holding bronze-tipped spears and wearing elaborate brass and enameled breastplates. While the townsfolk continued forward, the soldiers formed a line across the road and held their spears menacingly.

"Lance, please give me some stone fragments so the soldiers will understand you," Joco said. Lance opened a small bag and withdrew a few pieces, handing them to the Chief Priest. He moved ahead of the group and approached the soldiers, who bowed perfunctorily. He offered them stone fragments as a gift from his temple, which they accepted gratefully. Then he waved Lance forward. "Lance, you may now speak to these men. This one is Captain Iko Bali. He is their commander and a spokesman for the Grand Master."

"Greetings, Captain," Lance said. "I am Sentinel Lance Allright, and my friends and I have come here to warn you about an invasion that has forced your temple city in the jungle to be abandoned."

"Yes, Iko, what the sentinel says is true," Joco said. "I have seen the lizard men with my own eyes. Hundreds of villagers have been slaughtered, including the priest the Grand Master sent to us."

"Lizard men?" Iko laughed. "I don't believe you, Priest."

"When they come here and kill you all, it will be too late to believe me. I am Chief Priest of Non, the jungle temple city. I demand my right to meet with the Grand Master," Joco ordered. "These sentinels saved me and my entourage. They have come to find out what the lizard men are doing here and to stop them from killing us all."

"Well, I still don't believe you, but you do have the right to meet the Grand Master," Iko replied. "I don't think I can allow your sentinels to enter the city."

"What are you afraid of, Captain?" August said as she approached the group. "There are three of us and you probably have thousands of soldiers. And I am just a weak woman. You have no need to fear us."

Iko took a step backward. "I am not afraid of you, woman, but your hair of fire is frightening my men."

"I'm sorry about that Iko," she smiled. "But red hair is common where I live." She kneeled down next to him. "Please go ahead and touch it. It's just hair." Iko looked at his men who had stepped back instinctively when he did. They looked terrified. Slowly, he moved his hand forward, afraid the hair might cause him to burst into flames. Finally, he touched it. He ran his hand all over her head and then asked his troops to do the same. They all touched her hair and began to laugh and smile. "See, nothing to be afraid of. If you want confirmation, just ask Bill over here."

"Okay, I suppose you just are taller and look different," Iko replied. "If the Chief Priest commands your presence, then I will comply. Please come in. Our city is your city."

The soldiers turned and began to walk back to the gate. The crowd of people began to sing and dance around the group. Looking up, Bill could see dozens more people lining the top of the city walls waving at them. After they passed through the gate, the massive wooden gates were closed behind them.

<h1 style="text-align:center">Chapter 20</h1>

General Alvin Archer had recovered from his wounds and was directing the operation to install a portal key on Earth. Only a thin ring of Heartstone remained of the original massive crystal. Sections of the new portal key had been moving through the portal for days now. The largest block of the original stone was already buried beneath the portal, ready to power the key for all time. Elder Paul Justice stood next to the general and watched the progress of the work crew.

"When will the final pieces of the portal key arrive, Alvin?" Paul asked.

"The keystone will be arriving at the Far Sun portal key in a few hours. Once that is brought here, we can begin assembly of the device," the general replied. "As you know, this is now the most critical time, so I've ordered a thousand more soldiers to come here and guard the portal. In those hours between the removal of the last pieces of stone and the initiation of the portal key, we will have much less control over what passes through. Imagine ten thousand Ballanan warriors surging through at that moment. We must be prepared."

"That is a horrifying thought, Alvin," the elder said. "Have any of our portals been able to connect to the ulluba planet yet? I am very concerned about our sentinels, especially Bill Marshall."

143

"I feel the same way, Paul," the general sighed. "But no, it seems the Ballanan have locked Orto Nong with that portal. I think we must expect the worst on that planet. Our eight sentinels could not hold back an entire army. If there is a bright side, we have recovered some Heartstone fragments from the Ballanan we have killed. Perhaps we will be able to use those to communicate with them. It just doesn't make sense that they attack helpless planets like this. All the societies of Orto Nong have never been known to be warmongering."

"Yes, but that planet was ruled by black mages for a long time," Paul said as he put his hand on the general's shoulder. "Perhaps their DNA has infected the Ballanan, or there may still be black mages on Orto Nong and the Ballanan do not know they are being controlled. I agree that we need to capture some of their officers alive, if possible, to find out why they are coming here and to the ulluba planet."

A line of soldiers stood on the other side of the portal. They approached the portal awaiting the command to pass through. Sentinel Arthur Makepeace was manning the retort and signaled them to move forward. Suddenly, the image of Far Sun was lost and the dark cave of the zongo planet appeared. It seemed very quiet for a second, and then a wave of zongo rushed toward the portal. The retort glowed to life and held them back. Two seconds later, Far Sun appeared again.

"What in God's name just happened, Sentinel?" the general screamed.

"I don't know sir. We lost connection for five seconds, but all the systems on the retort seem normal," Arthur answered.

A sentinel on Far Sun walked through the portal and approached them. "General, I am Sentinel Dennis Lawman. The Far Sun portal key had a power surge of unknown origin. Our portal went completely blank. Thankfully, no one was in transition at the time or they might have been lost outside of space-time. All systems now report normal."

"Sentinel, this is very troubling," Elder Paul said. "Other than losing connection, was there any other unusual issue?"

"Not on our side, Elder," Dennis replied.

"Elder, I did notice something here," Arthur said. "Just as the retort surged to block the zongo, a thin trail of black smoke slipped from the other side, but it dissipated almost immediately."

"So there was a fire or something in the cave," Alvin said. "That doesn't seem like a big deal."

"Hmm. I don't know, Alvin," Paul replied. "That kind of minute occurrence can mean many things. If there really was a fire in the zongo cave, why didn't we see the flames? It could have been a carrier signal for something. We need to analyze the readings from the retort and portal key to see if anything else was amiss. I need to leave now, though. I am expected to meet Elder Jane Virtue at the United Nations in New York tomorrow. We have an appointment the following day to meet with various heads of state and then make a speech to the General Assembly."

"So finally, the Earth people are wising up to the serious nature of all of this," Alvin smiled. "That's very good."

"We'll see," Paul replied. "I would have expected more action on their part in such an important matter. Dennis, please return to Far Sun and start moving the troops here. Arthur, prepare to receive them. And I want both of you to get the data from your systems to the Elder Council so we can review it as quickly as possible. Alvin, good luck here. If you need anything from the Council, just let any of us know." He shook their hands and walked away with his personal guard.

"You heard the Elder, men," the general said. "And don't let any more incidents happen. My troops deserve a safe trip here." Dennis stepped back through the portal and signaled the portal key was ready. One by one, the soldiers stepped through the portal and onto Earth.

The retort had recorded another unusual occurrence, but that tiny anomaly was as yet unknown. A single ant had crawled through the portal just before the retort came to life to stop the onslaught of zongo. It was tiny, at just a centimeter long, and it crawled through the Heartstone toward the open meadow that used to be the crystal cave. Rather than walking along the flooring that had been installed, it chose to crawl over the broken bits of stone along the edge of the flooring. That choice was very precipitous as the line of soldiers began to cross the portal and marched through the stone to join their companions. The stone fragments were many times larger than the insect, which had to spend time to crawl up and over each one. The sun was setting when the tiny ant finally finished walking through the Heartstone and climbed down onto the freshly planted grass filling the open meadow that used to be the floor of the cave. As it became increasingly dark, floodlights were turned on to illuminate the area near the portal. Heavy blaster emplacements were manned by the new soldiers, who pointed their deadly weapons at the portal. A large crew worked to assemble the portal key which was to be installed the following day. The ant kept moving forward, now following the gradual incline of the land toward the Marshall ranch.

It was early the next morning before the lonely ant managed to reach the edge of the forest. It had crawled around the tents of sleeping soldiers and across several new roads constructed to move supplies to and from the portal. It was approaching noon when the ant found itself deep in the woods. As it crawled over leaf litter on the ground, it found itself surrounded by several spiders. Their mandibles were flexing in anticipation of the fresh meal. The ant did not try to move. It was completely surrounded. The thin trail of black smoke that had crossed the portal with the ant now reformed over the ant. The spiders moved back slightly at the odd sight. As they watched, the black smoke moved down toward the ant. It stood on its hind legs and breathed in the black smoke. A sense of dread filled the spiders and they moved back again. The ant began to twitch and swell. Its exoskeleton cracked and its organs poured out and continued to grow. It winced and twisted as it grew.

The spiders hastened their retreat as the ant grew thousands of times larger. The five-foot-tall blob of ant entrails twisted and churned. After another moment, it began to solidify. A moment later, it had morphed into a human figure. The shattered exoskeleton transformed into sentinel armor. The mandibles melted into a mouth, and the face contorted until Sentinel Lionel Forthright stood in the woods. He smiled broadly and breathed in the warm air. He looked down at the spiders that were frozen in fear. Laughing out loud, he stepped forward and crushed them under his foot. He quickly scanned the area and finding himself alone, he walked away calmly.

Chapter 21

Elder Jane Virtue sat at the breakfast table with Bonnie Marshall and Eileen and Justin Cramer. The elder's personal guard stood calmly by the back door. Justin rose to pour coffee for the group, and handed cups to each of his guests. "Okay Elder," he started. "We are here and are listening. What happened to my brother-in-law?"

Jane sipped the hot coffee and looked at the family gathered around her. "Honestly, we don't know at this time. Ballanan warriors locked their portal onto the Heartstone on the ulluba planet. We have not been able to break their connection. Without a link to the portal, we must anticipate the worst. Sentinel Allright is one of our best men, but there may be hundreds or thousands of Ballanan on the planet by now."

Tears poured down Bonnie's cheeks and she held her head in her hands. Eileen reached out to hug her sister-in-law. "Bonnie, have faith. Bill is a strong man and will do whatever he can to come back to you."

"Why did this have to happen?" Bonnie cried. "We didn't ask for that damn portal to be on our ranch. Now I've lost my husband."

"I understand, Bonnie, but I think Eileen has a great point," Jane replied. "Remember what happened the night the wild beasts surged through the portal and attacked this house. Bill was on the verge of death when Lance suddenly appeared on the scene. All of

149

this happens for a reason. We just have to let time pass and lead us to the future God has destined for us."

Someone knocked on the door. The guard opened the door and let the sentinel into the room. As he pulled off his helmet, he said "Elder Virtue, I am Sentinel Lionel Forthright. I've been sent by Senior Elder Marku Ablam to accompany you on your visit to the United Nations."

Jane stood and shook the sentinel's hand. "Lionel, it is wonderful to see you back at your post. I was advised about your injuries on the ulluba planet. I am very pleased that you are back on duty."

"Thank you, Elder," Lionel replied. "Fortunately, the blast that struck me was a glancing blow or I may not have survived."

"Thank God for that," she said. "It is a bit unusual for a sentinel to be assigned as a bodyguard. I would have thought a personal guard would have been more appropriate."

"I'm sorry, Elder, I was just following orders," Lionel replied. "If you would like to confirm my orders with Elder Marku, I can certainly return to the portal until this is cleared up."

"That would be best, I think," she smiled. "These are difficult and confusing times. With the recent Ballanan attacks, I need to reconfirm everything. You don't mind, then?"

"Of course not, Elder," Lionel smiled back. "I am only a sentinel. It is not my role to make such decisions. I will return to the portal and help Sentinel Makepeace. Just let me know if you will need me or not."

"Thank you for your understanding, Sentinel," Jane said.

"Lionel, perhaps I can go with you," Bonnie said. "I haven't seen the ranch in a long time and Bill wanted me to gather our personal effects."

"Certainly, Mrs. Marshall, it would be my pleasure," the sentinel answered. "We can also get some others to help relocate any heavier items for you."

"Do you want me to go with you, Bonnie?" Justin said. "That ranch has a lot of bad memories for all of us."

"Don't be silly, Justin," she replied. "How could I be any safer than with a sentinel? Besides, there are hundreds of soldiers there. I'll be safer there than here."

"That is true," Lionel said. "I'll bring her back as quickly as possible."

"Very well," Elder Jane said. "I need to get to the airport to travel to New York now. We'll leave with you two. My transport should be arriving any minute. Thank you all for your hospitality."

Eileen shook Jane's hand saying, "You'll let us know if you find anything new, right?"

"Of course, I will," Jane replied. "Either an Elder or Sentinel will let you know anything as soon as we learn about it. Sentinel Forthright, would you like us to shuttle you and Bonnie to her ranch?"

"I would hate to delay your departure, Elder," Lionel said. "It is a short walk to the secure zone. What do you think, Mrs. Marshall?"

"I could use the fresh air and the walk, Elder," Bonnie said as she warmly shook Jane's hand. "Your work at the United Nations is critical to what happens next. But thank you very much for the offer." Everyone walked through the home and out the front door. After exchanging pleasantries, the Elder and her guard turned right and headed up the street. Lionel and Bonnie went the opposite direction toward the Marshall ranch. Justin and Eileen stood on the porch watching them walk down the street.

"Justin, what do you think about all of this?" his wife asked. "I'm so overwhelmed that I don't know what to feel anymore."

"I was certain we would all die that night when the monsters came to our neighborhood," he replied. "Since we're still here, I take that as a positive sign. Isn't that your cell phone I hear ringing?"

"I'm always forgetting that thing," she said as she went inside to get it. Justin stood there looking at his once tranquil neighborhood, now forever changed by the break in the Heartstone.

Eileen rushed out the door with the phone to her ear. "Bonnie! Bonnie!" she shouted. "It's Cindy calling about Cybil. There's a problem at the school."

Bonnie and Lionel had stopped and turned around. "What is it?" Bonnie shouted back.

"Apparently, Cybil broke down crying a few minutes ago and has been talking about black magic or something like that," Eileen replied. "Cindy's on her way to pick her up right now. She wants you to stay here until she gets here."

Elder Jane and her guard heard the shouting and had turned to come back to the Cramer home. Her guard had drawn his blaster and held it ready to fire. "Bonnie, come back here now!" she shouted.

Bonnie looked at the commotion and then at Lionel, who smiled at her warmly. "Don't worry, Bonnie, I'll protect you," he said. She smiled back at him. As the others watched, he gently put his hand on her shoulder and they both dissolved into a thin trail of black smoke, which almost immediately evaporated into thin air. The others rushed to the spot where they had been standing only seconds before.

"What the hell just happened here?" Justin screamed. "Where is my sister-in-law?"

"Silas, contact General Archer and find out about Sentinel Forthright," Jane said to her guard.

She sat heavily on the grass and held her head in her hands. "Oh my God, this is worse than I could have imagined."

Eileen and Justin stood over her. "Elder, what happened here?" she asked.

"Elder," Silas said, "according to Sentinel Makepeace, Lionel Forthright is still in a hospital recovering from his wounds."

"As I should have suspected," Jane cried. "Contact the Elder Council and arrange an emergency meeting. Elder Justice and I will continue on to New York. The meeting with the UN must not be delayed."

"Elder, my sister-in-law just vanished with one of your sentinels," Justin said. "What is going on? Where is she?"

Jane looked up at them with tears flowing down her cheeks. "I am so sorry. We should have been more on guard for this, but we had no idea. That was not one of our sentinels. It was a black mage."

"And what is a black mage?" Justin asked.

"They are a race of sorcerers with unimaginable powers," she replied. "We had never had contact with them before today. Many other planets have been conquered and ravaged by them over millions of years. Whenever we find a broken Heartstone on a planet with a less-advanced civilization, it is a clear indication of black mage infestation."

"Infestation? That makes them sound like a virus," Eileen said.

"More like parasites, actually," Jane replied. "We have no information on where they came from or where they are today, but when they take over a planet, they take everything they can and leave it barren and desolate. They provide no benefit to their adopted worlds. They only take. But as I said, their powers are unbelievable." She turned to her guard and asked, "Silas, your helmet didn't tell you that anything was unusual about the false sentinel?"

"No Elder," he replied. "My sensors even identified the Being's DNA as that of Lionel Forthright. He read completely normal."

"So now I've lost my brother-in-law and his wife," Justin said with tears in his eyes. "Eileen, I think I'm ready to pack up and get out of this town. We can take Frank, Cindy, and Cybil with us. We'll move as far from here as humanly possible."

"Please try to be calm," Jane said. "The mage took Bonnie for a reason. If he wanted her or any of us dead, we would be dead now. If he took her, it's because he wants her alive. We have to be patient."

"Be patient. You want us to be patient while our whole family vanishes," Justin smirked. "The real Lionel told us that Cybil has a uniquely strong connection to our Heartstone. What do we tell her parents when a mage comes for her?"

"Perhaps it would be best if you and your family went to Far Sun for a period of time," Jane replied. "Our security is much stronger there. You could stay far from our portal key to keep any enemies from finding you. We were planning to have Frank and Bill both take advanced sentinel training. Now is probably a good time. Perhaps one or both of you might do so as well."

"If it's safer than here, I agree," Justin said. "But can you protect us from black mages on your planet?"

"I don't know. What we do know is that Ballanan warriors and at least one black mage have been on this planet. We have never had any contact with either on Far Sun. Also we have a network of portal keys where we can better control the planetary portals," the elder replied. "It may not be perfect, but it has to be better than this."

"She's right, Justin," Eileen said. "We need to focus on protecting Bill and Bonnie's family now. They grew up on that ranch and probably have the strongest connection to the stone. Elder, we accept your offer."

"Wait a minute," Justin interrupted. "You grew up on that ranch too, honey."

"You will all be safer on Far Sun," Jane replied. "Silas, contact General Archer and have him send a transport and troops to escort these people to the portal and to Far Sun. I'll advise Elder Ablam while we travel to New York. He will make all the arrangements for everyone.

As she spoke, a transport vehicle came up the street and parked next to them. Twenty soldiers in blood-red body armor climbed out and began to form a perimeter around the Cramer house.

"It looks like you are in good hands now," the elder said. "I need to get going to New York. I will ask Sentinel Makepeace and General Archer to update me on everything until you are safely at the academy on Far Sun." She leaned forward and kissed both Eileen and Justin on the cheek. "Again, I am very sorry, but I could never imagine finding a black mage on this planet. My faith still tells me all of this will work out. We just have to find the lesson we are here to learn. I will visit you on Far Sun next week. Goodbye." Elder Jane and her guard walked back up the street. As they turned the corner on the next block, an SUV pulled up and Cindy and Cybil Marshall climbed out. Both were crying heavily. Eileen and Justin rushed to comfort them.

Chapter 22

Bill Marshall sat on a wooden stool in the tavern with a glass of whisky in his hand. Joco and Malua had been summoned to meet with the Grand Master. Lance had gone to acquire the necessary goods for their journey into the hidden lands. August had stayed in her room in the hotel and Bill was glad for that. Her aggression was wearing him down. Tactic 87 had almost broken his wedding vow. Half of his mind wished Lance had taken a couple minutes longer, while the other half wished he had never met August. The whisky was quite good for an ancient society. The nearby mountains supplied plenty of ice and the coldness of the drink was very refreshing. The bar was large and a crowd of locals filled the place. People were laughing and enjoying each other's company. Bill was content to be left alone.

Not being in the mood for only one drink, he put a piece of the Earth Heartstone on the bar. He convinced the barman to touch the stone when talking to him so they could communicate. He motioned him to come over now. The man touched the stone and Bill said, "I'll have another, please."

"Of course, sir," the man replied and turned to grab the bottle. He placed a couple more pieces of ice in his glass and began to fill it. Bill was lost in thought about home and did not notice at first that the bar had become dead quiet. When he did notice, he saw the bartender was overflowing his glass and whisky was pouring over the counter. He saw the man's attention was focused behind him and turned to see what was happening.

August had entered the tavern and was slowly approaching the bar. Every person in the bar was staring at her. Her red hair was full and flowing over her shoulders. Her green eyes sparkled in the candlelight. She wore what seemed to be a harem costume with a bikini top and bottom, with sheer strips of material flowing down like a long dress. The top barely covered half of her breasts and the bottom was cut well below her waist. She smiled broadly when she saw Bill watching her as well. She sat on the stool next to him and looked at the bartender and then down at the bar.

The barman noticed the river of whisky and quickly grabbed a rag to clean the mess. He was blushing red when he came to ask her for her drink order. She wore a pendant with a piece of the Far Sun Heartstone. She took the barman's hand and pressed it against her pendant and chest. "I'll have what he's having," she said, pointing to Bill's glass. As he stumbled to fill her order, she turned her attention to Bill. "I guess you approve of my outfit?" she asked.

"August, I keep telling you I'm married," he said.

"That's not what I asked you, Sentinel," she frowned as she put her hand on his knee.

He gently removed her hand and said, "August, you know you are one of the most beautiful women I've ever met. That outfit is stunning, but I'm still a married man," he said firmly.

That's better," she smiled. "You told me I'm pretty and my outfit is nice. Thank you, Bill." The crowd began to talk and laugh again. The barman put the glass of whisky in front of her and she lifted it to a toast. "Here's to the success of our mission, Bill," she said.

"I'll drink to that!" Bill replied as he touched his glass to hers. "Cheers!"

"I talked to Lance a few minutes ago," she began. "He has arranged for all the supplies we need. So far, no one here wants to go with us to the hidden lands. But I can't say I'm surprised. Nan-bo-Nan is a virtual deity on this planet."

"I know, but I don't blame Lance for trying," Bill replied as he sipped his drink. "If we do find anyone, we have to convince them to travel in the flyer, which is another issue. August, do you think there is a physical Being named Nan-bo-Nan or a religious symbol? Frankly, I'm not sure we'll find anything."

"That is a possibility, Bill," she replied. "But now that you've been through a few portals and have seen other worlds and peoples, you must have figured out the universe is a pretty magical and mysterious place. Many such legends have a basis in fact."

"But if the Heartstone here was just recently broken, how would Nan-bo-Nan have reached this planet?" Bill asked.

"That's another good question, Bill," she replied. "You've heard about black mages, haven't you?"

"Yes, a bit. When my granddaughter touched a piece of Heartstone, she said that black mages had ruled Orto Nong for a long time, until the Ballanan were able to send them back where they came from," he said.

"Wow! That's amazing. Your granddaughter is a seer?" August asked.

"She's only seven years old, but what is a seer?" he asked back.

August drained her glass and asked the bartender to refill it. Her cheeks were blushing with the heat of the strong drink. She turned Bill to face her and put both of her hands on his knees and smiled. "Each person has a different experience with a Heartstone. Many feel nothing. Others see their destiny. Some see outright falsehoods. But a very few see the past and the future of the planet the stone came from. A tiny fraction of people see the reality of the entire universe. We call those last two categories seers. Seers comprise less than one-tenth of one percent of a population. It's even rarer to find a seer who is also a natural Sentinel. You should be very proud."

"I'm not so sure about that," Bill replied. "The Heartstone has completely changed my life, and I'm not certain it's for the better. My ranch was destroyed and here I am, God knows how far from my wife and family, trying to stop an invasion that could kill everyone on Earth. I don't think I was cut out for this kind of work."

August was laughing. "Oh Bill, you're so funny. That's a very parochial view of what's going on in the universe. Let's say you lived fifty miles from the Heartstone and some other person was the natural Sentinel. That wouldn't stop the Ballanan from attacking Earth, and your family would be in similar danger. That other person would now be sitting here with my hands on his knees talking about the same thing. But that's not how it works at all. This is your destiny, Bill Marshall. Everything that has ever happened since the beginning of the universe was leading to this precise moment in time. It was your destiny to come here and fight along side Lance and me. And believe it or not, it was your destiny to perform Tactic 87 with me."

Bill laughed too. "I don't know if I can believe that, August. Since you know all of this, you must be a seer too."

She leaned forward and took his head in her hands, pulling his head toward her. She kissed him softly on the cheek and whispered, "Bill, you won't believe everything I know, but you will find out soon. I promise you that." She turned his head and kissed him on the lips. He pulled back quickly.

"August, I told you that I'm happily married," he said again.

"I know, and I'm sorry but I can't help myself," she said looking down. "Please don't hate me, Bill. Soon enough you'll understand all of this. Honestly, I don't want my obsession to affect our mission."

Bill lifted her head and looked into her eyes. "August, just relax. I could never hate you. You have to know that I'm flattered by your attention. There is part of me that would like nothing better than to make love to you, but I made a vow to another and I have to live up to that."

"I know," she said. "But everything I said about seers and the universe is true. It is your destiny to be here and to go to the hidden lands to find Nan-bo-Nan with Lance and me." As she spoke, Lance entered the tavern and walked up to them.

"August, that's not very professional attire for a Sentinel," he said. "Although I must say you look incredible."

"I'm sorry, Lance. I'll go change if you like," she replied.

"Good, because we've been summoned to see the Grand Master in one hour," he said. "Joco said his visit went very well. Let's go discuss strategy, team." The three left the tavern and returned to their hotel.

<h1 style="text-align:center">Chapter 23</h1>

The old man pushed his walking frame ahead of him down the crowded Manhattan sidewalk. He wore a long black coat that was visibly worn from many years of harsh winters. A tattered black hat sat on his balding head and a grimy scarf blew in the cold breeze. He was stooped over and his gnarled knuckles held onto the frame for dear life as the throng of people moved around him. His eyeglasses were smudged with fingerprints and one of the lenses was cracked. A line of police motorcycles moved by on the street barely ten feet from where he walked. He turned to watch them go by. In the middle of the line was a single black limousine. He could see the faces of Elders Jane Virtue and Paul Justice sitting in the back deep in conversation as it rushed by. He smiled and chuckled, then turned his attention back to his slow walk down the street.

Eventually he arrived at his destination and walked into the lobby of the high-rise building. A man in a suit stood behind the long marble counter. He said, "Good morning, sir. How may I help you?"

The old man removed his glasses and hat and set them on the counter. "Tell Mr. Umdala that Mr. Keedu is here, sonny."

"Of course, Mr. Keedu," the man replied. "Please wait while I contact his suite. You are welcome to sit if you like."

"Thank you, but I'll stand," the old man replied.

The man stepped over to his phone and dialed the appropriate number. After a moment, he returned. "Mr. Keedu, someone from Mr. Umdala's staff is on her way here to escort you."

"Thanks again, sonny," Mr. Keedu said.

After a couple minutes, an elevator car opened and a short, stocky woman in a business suit rushed out and over to the old man. "Mr. Keedu, it is an honor to serve you, sir. My name is Sopu Inki and I am Mr. Umdala's personal assistant. Please let me help you, sir." The woman and old man returned to the elevator and the door closed. The man behind the counter sat and opened his paper.

Inside the elevator car, Sopu looked at Mr. Keedu and thought, "Sir, there are recording devices throughout the public areas of the building."

Keedu nodded his head and thought, "Thank you for the warning. I suspected as much." When the elevator door opened again, they stepped into a large marble foyer. Two armed guards watched the room. When they saw Mr. Keedu, they bowed deeply. The head guard pressed a button and a steel door retracted into the wall, revealing the opening to Mr. Umdala's home. Keedu and the assistant walked inside and the steel door slid closed after them. The two guards looked at each other with looks of relief.

Once inside, Mr. Keedu pushed away the walking frame and stood up straight. His body contorted, twisted and stretched as though his head and feet were locked between battling vice-grips. A thin stream of black smoke surrounded him and his eyes glowed red. His face became almost molten and the features moved about. After a couple of minutes, the new Being was almost seven feet tall with large black eyes and greenish-brown skin. His ears were replaced with simple ear holes. His human clothes had changed into a suit of black body armor. White hair had grown out of his head and now reached down to the middle of his back, separated into two by a line of boney plates covering his spine. His fingers had grown almost twice as long with sharp black nails on each of the four fingers.

A man in a dark blue business suit entered the room and said, "Keedu, it is very unorthodox for you to come here."

"I know, Umdala, but it couldn't be helped," he replied. "Why are you morphed like that?"

"I have several meetings in the city today, Keedu. But I generally stay this way all the time to lessen the chance of any humans seeing me in my natural state," Umdala answered. "Sopu, my friend and I are going into my study. Make certain we are not interrupted for any reason." She bowed to both as they stepped into another room and closed the door.

Inside the study, Umdala poured two drinks and offered one to Keedu and pointed to two overstuffed chairs in the center of the room. As they sat, Umdala asked, "Why are you here, old friend? We made an oath to stay separated."

"Our separation has been a failure, Umdala," Keedu replied. "The Ballanan of Orto Nong have started a crusade to kill us all."

"Yes, I have felt them on this planet as well," Umdala said. "Fortunately, the sentinels of Far Sun are already here and are unwittingly protecting me. I am lucky this planet is fairly advanced. What has happened on your planet?"

"I am also quite lucky for different reasons," Keedu answered. "There are no sentient species on my planet, but the voracity of the zongo guarding the portal has discouraged them from attacking in force so far. But I fear it is only a matter of time before we are found and attacked. We must reorganize the Order again, Umdala."

"I don't know if that is possible, old friend," he said. "I have had no communication with other mages in hundreds of years. I have not felt any others until you stepped through the portal yesterday."

"None of us has the power to stop the Ballanan alone, Umdala," Keedu said. "We need at least ten mages to form a strong circle. Even that might not be enough. After all, the Order of mages on Orto Nong ultimately failed. I don't know if there are enough mages left to defend ourselves, but if we stay separated, we will most certainly die."

"You have forgotten our history, Keedu," Umdala laughed. "It was not the Ballanan who defeated them. It was the plagues and second Heartstone that turned the battle. Those mages were stupid. They sought to dominate and ravage their planet rather than blending in quietly as we do today. I exist here today with incredible wealth and, yet, no one knows my true name. Hundreds of thousands of humans work for my companies every day and know me to be the man sitting here next to you, not a black mage. Unless the Ballanan can overcome the sentinels and militaries of this world, I don't know how they can win."

"The Ballanan are obsessed. They would rather all die in combat than allow one mage to survive," Keedu said. "And although the sentinels are protecting you now, if they learn a black mage is living here, they will join the Ballanan to get you."

"I suppose there is some risk of that, Keedu," he replied. "But none of us have ever had interactions with Far Sun. Those sentinels have no reason to come after me."

"Then perhaps I have given them a reason to do so, Umdala," Keedu replied. He took off a chain around his neck and held it out. A small glass vial filled with black liquid was suspended from it. He pulled the stopper from the vial and poured out the liquid which turned to smoke as it left the vial. The smoke swirled about into a cloud that slowly coalesced and condensed until Bonnie Marshall stood before them. She appeared to be frozen in a trance.

"What did you do, Keedu?" Umdala sighed. "Please tell me this is a bad joke. If you have brought the humans and sentinels down on my head, I swear I will kill you now with my bare hands."

"Relax, Umdala. She is unharmed and we can return her to her home in an instant if needed. This female is a natural sentinel for this planet. When I sensed her powers, I knew we needed her. She can be the Keystone for our Circle. You know as well as I do that we need one to connect to other mages," Keedu replied.

"I can sense her connection to the stone as well," Umdala said. "But there is something else . . ."

"Ah, you can feel that too?" Keedu asked. "As soon as I entered the Heartstone on this planet, I felt it. Her connection to her mate is very strong. I can almost sense him now on Goola with other sentinels. And there are thousands of Ballanan looking for him and for a black mage there."

"Goola? There is no black mage on that world, Keedu," Umdala scoffed.

"Of course you are right, but the Ballanan are absolutely convinced there is," Keedu said with a broad smile crossing his face. "Now why do you think that is true, old friend? What could be on the planet that has the Ballanan certain one of our brothers is there? There is only one possibility, isn't there?"

"There is an ice wizard on Goola. Is that what you're saying?" Umdala asked.

"What else could it be?" Keedu laughed. "Nothing. There is no other possibility. Finally, after all these years, you and I have the opportunity to face our ultimate nemesis and regain our dignity."

"Keedu, you are an idiot," Umdala laughed. "That was so long ago, thousands of generations before we were born. Frankly, I don't know if those legends are true. And so what if it is true. Our home planet was destroyed by a nova long ago. Both the mages and wizards had to leave, so none of us have a home planet anymore. I never heard of any mage claiming to have found one of the ice wizards. They don't bother us and we don't bother them. Why not let the dead rest in peace?"

"You're honestly telling me you have no interest in finding this ice wizard," Keedu said. "I can't believe my ears. Look at me, Umdala. Look how we have devolved over the millennia. We used to look much like the humans, but our struggles to survive have forced our anatomy to change. If I were to walk out of this building in my natural state, the people would panic and trample each other to death to escape me. That is the damage the ice wizards did to us. At least that should get you mad."

"I agree that I'm interested in meeting an ice wizard," Umdala replied. "However, I don't want to fight an ancient war to recover some false sense of pride or a dead planet. But I owe you much old friend. I can agree to help connect to more mages and form a circle. We will need a minimum of eleven though, since I will likely step aside once that is done."

"I still think you are a coward and a fool, Umdala. However, I appreciate your help. Perhaps the others will convince one of us to agree with the other. In any event, I think it has been too long since we mages have worked together. At least here you can interact with other sentient Beings. On my planet, I've got spiders and that's about it," Keedu said. He sighed and drained his glass.

"Keedu, it might be some time before we can contact the other mages, and I have many visitors in this house," Umdala said as he pointed at Bonnie Marshall. "I'd appreciate it if you'd keep the human hidden and morph yourself to a more acceptable form."

"Of course, I understand," he replied. Keedu pursed his lips and blew a breath of air toward Bonnie, who instantly turned back into the cloud of black smoke, which swirled like a small tornado until it found the open mouth of the vial, where it condensed back into a liquid. He put the stopper back in the bottle and hung it around his neck. When Umdala stopped watching the smoke, he noticed the other mage had become a young man wearing blue jeans and a polo shirt. "I trust this is more acceptable?" he asked.

Chapter 24

The Temple of Serenity filled the center square of the walled city of Chang-A. It was the dead of night when the three sentinels marched toward the front of the temple, where fifty steps led up to the main entrance. A line of priests in red robes waited for them at the top. Joco and Malua were with the priests and waved the sentinels to quicken the pace. The three jogged up the steps and joined the group where Joco grabbed Lance's arm and began pulling him inside. "Lance, we are almost late! The Grand Master doesn't wait for anyone," he urged.

"Joco, you just told me of the meeting a few moments ago," Lance replied. "August had to change and we got here as quickly as we could."

The main hallway was dominated by fifty-foot marble columns supporting the ceiling, which was adorned with frescos of the local countryside. Bill noticed a painting of the stone temple in the jungle. The picture showed beams of light issuing from the open mouth of the cave. The group turned to the left through a large opening and into the audience chamber of the Grand Master. The floor of the room was a checkerboard of dark brown and white marble. The walls were covered with thick, ornate tapestries showing more idyllic scenes of the planet. Fifty feet ahead of them was a raised platform leading to the golden throne of the Grand Master. He was an old man, perhaps five feet tall at the most, with long white hair and beard. He wore thick red robes over a simple tunic and coarse leather thongs on his feet. He peered

173

back at them through thick glass spectacles. Fortunately, he was smiling. When they were five feet from the raised platform, Joco motioned them to stop. The entire group bowed deeply. "Master, I have brought the visitors as you requested," Joco said.

"Thank you, Chief Priest," the man replied. "Welcome, guests, to the sacred city of Chang-A. My name is Golo Ung, and I have the privilege to be the current Grand Master of this temple." He stood and approached them. He craned his neck to look up at Lance who was at least two feet taller than he. He extended his hand and shook Lance's. "I am told that you are Lance, the leader of this group. I welcome you."

"Thank you, Grand Master for your hospitality," Lance smiled.

"Please call me Golo," the Grand Master replied. "Since you are not one of our faithful, there is no need for formality." He patted him on the arm and stepped over to August. "My, you are a lovely woman. I believe we have met before."

"No sir," August said with a blush on her cheeks. "I don't think that is possible, but it is an honor to meet you."

"Perhaps you are right, my dear, but there is something very warm and familiar about you," he said as he kissed her hand. He looked at her again and thought about saying more but then moved along.

"Thank you," she replied, blushing bright red.

Golo stepped over to Bill, saying, "Ah, the seer. Welcome my friend. It is always good to meet those with strong connections to the spirit."

"It is an honor to meet you, Golo. My name is Bill," he said. "But I'm not certain that I am a seer."

Golo took Bill's hand in his and closed his eyes for a moment. When he opened them, he smiled. "Yes, there is not doubt that your connection to the spirit world is powerful." He turned to the Chief Priest and said, "Wouldn't you agree, Joco?"

"Of course, Grand Master," Joco replied.

Golo laughed. "No one ever disagrees with me here. I find that a bit unnerving, don't you Bill?"

"Sir, I am a married man, so I am quite used to having someone disagree with me," Bill replied.

The Grand Master laughed again. "Please, let us go to my private study," he said to the sentinels. "I've already spoken with the Chief Priest about your desire to venture into the hidden lands. I doubt he knows enough of your intentions to make a valid case. Perhaps the three of you can convince me." Golo led the sentinels through a small door at the rear of the audience chamber. Joco followed them meekly and closed the door behind him.

It was midnight in New York when Umdala and Keedu met in the inner sanctum of his penthouse. Twelve stone benches formed a ring about an elevated circular platform just large enough for Bonnie to stand upon. She was still frozen in place. The floor, ceiling, and walls were clad in highly-polished jet-black marble. Both mages were in their natural state and wore a small loincloth only. They sat on individual benches across from each other, facing Bonnie. Each was meditating, hardly breathing and moving their lips in a form of unspoken prayer or chant. Beads of sweat rolled down their faces and their eyes were clenched tightly as though forcing their minds to concentrate as much as possible. After several minutes, Keedu opened his eyes and screamed, "This isn't working, Umdala. What's wrong? Are we so old that we've forgotten something?"

Umdala picked up a small towel and mopped his face. "No Keedu, neither of us could ever forget the call to commune. It's something else. Look at the keystone. She looks totally peaceful and happy. That isn't right. If everything was good, she should be sweating and doubling over in pain. But somehow, the power is coming back at us. We both know that can mean only one thing."

"Do you think the ice wizard is helping her from so far away?" Keedu asked.

"Don't be stupid. Only a Cantu Bagwa on this planet can impact our call," Umdala said.

"Of course, I had forgotten," Keedu replied. "But why haven't we sensed him?"

"I can only imagine that this keystone is related to the Cantu Bagwa. Their spiritual connection is too direct for us to see it. You didn't sense anything when you were with this Being at her home?"

"No. Now that you mention it, there was a commotion that forced me to take the keystone by force," Keedu recalled. "Another female told this one her granddaughter was crying and screaming at school. This female was about to run away. At that moment, I took her with me before she escaped."

"That's a pretty important detail to omit, old friend," Umdala scoffed. "But I'm not surprised you didn't sense the Cantu Bagwa. If this seer and the Cantu Bagwa are related, then their subconscious minds were probably blocking for each other. You must return for the Cantu Bagwa."

"That would be suicidal and you know it," Keedu sneered. "Without a circle of mages, none of us have the power to defeat the Cantu Bagwa. But I am sensing something happening now. Touch my mind, Umdala and let us see what happens next."

Cybil Marshall was crying and fighting to get away from her father. Frank and Cindy had managed to pull together some luggage and were following Sentinel Arthur Makepeace down the slope toward the portal key, which had been installed hours earlier. "Daddy, I don't want to go to Far Sun. Grandma needs me here," she screamed.

"Honey, the sentinels say we can only be safe if we go to their planet," Frank replied. "There are black mages on Earth now and they will kill us if they can. We have to go now."

"I'm not afraid of any black mage," Cybil said. "I am the Cantu Bagwa and they are afraid of me!" She kept struggling to get away.

"What is she talking about, Frank?" Cindy asked. "She's been hollering and crying since I took her from school." She touched Arthur on the shoulder and asked, "Cybil is talking about a Cantu something or other. Do you know what that means?"

Arthur stopped in his tracks and turned to face the family. "No. I've never heard those words before. We will be meeting with Elder Justice at the academy. We can ask him."

"No, please Sentinel, listen to me!" Cybil screamed. "I am the Cantu Bagwa. I'm the only one who can save Earth from the black mages. You have to listen to me!"

Arthur stroked her hair softly. "I'm sorry, honey. I have my orders to get you folks to somewhere safe and that's where we're going." He turned and continued the march toward the portal key which was already locked on Far Sun. They could see Zelda and Chachis running around on the grassy hillside awaiting their family. It was a warm summer day in this part of Far Sun. Lance's small house was surrounded by wild flowers, and the sounds of birds singing could be heard.

As they approached, the sentinel manning the portal key controls told Arthur that everything was ready. Two other sentinels carried the luggage through the portal and began loading it on the flyer that was waiting to take them to the academy. Cindy turned and kissed Frank and then focused on Cybil, who was still struggling and crying. "Cybil, everything will be fine. We'll just walk through and be in the warm sun. You want to be with Zelda and Chachis, don't you?"

"Mommie, please listen to me," she cried. "Please don't take me away from here. Grandma and everyone else need me here. I'm the Cantu Bagwa. Please!"

Cindy kissed her forehead, turned and walked through the portal. She stumbled slightly as she passed the event horizon, but a sentinel on the other side took her hand to steady her. She turned and waved at Frank and Cybil.

"Daddy, please, this is important," Cybil cried. "Please don't do this."

Frank held her tight and said, "Honey, you aren't responsible for what happens in the universe. You are my little angel and I have to keep you safe. I love you." He walked through the portal and onto the grassy field. Cybil looked back through the portal, but knew all hope was lost now.

Keedu laughed until he was crying. "Umdala, I told you I felt something else. Let's start the chant again!" The two mages sat again and began to chant. Sweat poured from them and drops of blood slipped out of the corners of their eyes. Bonnie began to twitch and squirm. She screamed in pain and small cuts appeared all over her body and began to ooze blood. Her hair stood on end as if electrified. She clenched her hands so tightly that her nails cut the skin of her palms.

Outside in the night sky over New York, a vast black cloud began to spin over the city. It formed a cyclone which was centered over Umdala's building. The wind began to howl through the streets of Manhattan and made a deep moaning sound. That sound woke Elder Jane Virtue from a deep sleep in her hotel room. She could hear the window shaking in its frame. Startled, she rose and rushed to the curtains and threw them open. She could see driving rain and hail pelting the buildings and streets. Smaller ink-black funnel clouds dropped from the massive swirling vortex and raced up and down the streets. Trash blew around and the wind speed kept increasing. Dumpsters raced up and down and the few pedestrians clung to anything available to keep from being blown away. She felt a sharp pain in her forehead and put her hand to her head. A slow stream of blood dripped down into her eyes. "Oh my God," she gasped. "This is the end."

The storm ended as quickly as it had begun. The city was completely silent for a minute before the sounds of emergency vehicles began to blare. Bonnie had collapsed in a heap on the floor of the chamber. Umdala and Keedu wiped the sweat and blood from their faces and looked around. Ten other black mages were now seated in the room with them. All of them began to laugh and shout. Umdala opened bottles of whisky and passed them out to his new guests. Keedu hugged each of the new arrivals and thanked them for their help. After he greeted the last one, he walked over to Bonnie and waved his hand over her. Her body dissolved into black smoke and disappeared.

August had passed out on the floor of the private meeting room. Her body was ice cold and covered with sweat. Trickles of blood seeped from her ears and eyes. Bill shook her gently and tried to wake her. The Grand Master and Chief Priest were watching and chanting prayers. Lance pulled a vial from his belt and rushed to inject her. He stopped suddenly when he noticed that her red hair had changed to platinum blonde. "What is happening here?" he asked.

"I knew I had seen her before," Golo laughed. "I think she'll be fine in a moment."

"August, it's time for Tactic 87 again," Bill said to wake her up. Lance had kneeled next to Bill so he could inject the medicine in her thigh.

As Lance reached forward with the vial, her hand suddenly rose and blocked his. She opened her eyes and said, "That won't be necessary, Lance, I'm okay." The others were speechless. Her green eyes were now silver blue. Her body had also changed. Her formerly voluptuous figure was much leaner now. The sentinel uniform hung loosely on her.

"August, are you okay?" Bill asked. "I was so worried about you."

Golo laughed, "That is definitely not August, Bill."

He turned and frowned at the Grand Master. "What are you talking about? Of course it's August."

She sat up and looked at the others staring at her. "No Bill. Golo is right. But that's not important right now. Your planet is in terrible danger. A circle of black mages has formed. The Cantu Bagwa has been taken off the planet. We have to stop them before Earth becomes another Orto Nong."

"Sentinel, what is all this nonsense?" Lance barked. "What happened to you?"

She smiled at Lance. "I'm sorry, Lance, but all will be revealed in time. There is too much to do now to waste time talking." She took Bill's face in her hands and kissed his lips. "Bill, I'll do everything I can to help your family and planet." She turned to Lance and said, "I am sorry about this, and I will make sure August is returned to you." She put her arms around Bill's neck and the two disappeared in a cloud of fog. The temperature in the room dropped fifty degrees and the cloud quickly dissipated, leaving ice crystals on their clothes and the floor.

Golo laughed again and clapped Lance and Joco on the back. "I told you I had seen her before. Gentlemen, you have just met Nan-bo-Nan."

<h1 style="text-align:center">Chapter 25</h1>

Bill woke up in a large soft bed, covered with heavy blankets. He sat up and looked around. The room was extremely cold and he pulled the bed covers up to his neck. The interior was all white and had the appearance of being made from ice. A large window wall filled the opposite side of the room. Outside was a magnificent vista of mountains and deep valleys filled with glaciers. A few feather-like clouds dotted the bright blue sky. He looked around for his uniform but could not find it anywhere, and he was naked under the heavy blankets. He sat on the edge of the bed and tested the floor with a toe. It was definitely ice and he knew better than to step on it barefooted.

Nan-bo-Nan entered the room. She was still very beautiful, but now quite slim with shiny white hair flowing down to the middle of her back and those amazing silver-blue eyes. She was seven feet tall and wore a tight ice-blue bodysuit. She sat next to Bill. "Good morning. I guess the jump was too much for you, Bill. When we arrived here you had passed out, so I put you here. Don't worry; I don't sleep very often, so you were all alone. By the way, my name is Nan-bo-Nan, in case you hadn't figured that out yet. But you can call me Nan if you like."

"Where is my uniform, Nan?" he asked. "I have to get out of here and get back to Earth."

"Bill, I already told you I will help you," she smiled. "You need me. There are ten thousand Ballanan warriors marching this way. Another thousand are guarding the portal. You can't get home by fighting all of them. But I can do a lot."

"What happened to August?" he asked. "When did you take over her body and where is she now?"

She laughed, stood up and walked over to a wall cabinet. She pulled it open and withdrew an ice-blue uniform that looked like his sentinel outfit. "Here, Bill. I made some modifications to your clothes. It will now keep you warm here and is at least a hundred times stronger than before." She took the uniform and boots over to him. "I suggest you put them on under the covers. It's very cold here which is how I like it. There is a restroom through that door which is much warmer. You can take a shower if you like. After you're dressed, come through that other door and you will find me. I will take you to August and show you some other surprises." She bent over and kissed his forehead. Her lips were quite warm and her breath formed a little mist around his face. She turned to leave. When she reached the door, she turned back and said, "I didn't take over her body, silly. I would never force someone to do something. She is fine." She left the room and closed the door behind her.

Bill did take the shower and the hot water helped him feel alive again. He thought about how she said his planet was in terrible danger. He thought about Bonnie and the kids. He closed his eyes tightly to say a little prayer. In his mind, he saw Bonnie shaking in pain with hundreds of bleeding wounds all over her body. Her clothes were soaked in her own blood. He opened his eyes and shook his head to clear the image. He hurried to finish getting ready so he could ask Nan about the vision. The new uniform was extremely comfortable, as though it had been hand-tailored for him. He checked the different pockets to insure the pieces of Heartstone were still here. Alongside the pieces of Earth stone, he found at least ten other pieces of black and clear crystals. He tried on the helmet and the displays were completely different, although he instinctively knew what each one was for. Confused, he removed the helmet and clipped it onto his belt. Then he left the room to find Nan.

He walked down a short hallway and entered a massive open room. Forty feet ahead, he could see Nan and August Reason sitting together at a glass table drinking what appeared to be coffee. He rushed over to join them. August stood up and hugged him. "August, you're okay?"

"Yes, Bill," she smiled. "Nan told me what she did to you while pretending to be me. Sounds like fun," she laughed. "But just so you know, there is no such thing as Tactic 87. Let me get you a cup of coffee." She walked over to the counter and filled another cup.

"But Lance knew exactly what it was," Bill said. "How could that happen?"

"I placed the idea in his head, Bill," Nan laughed. "I told you I could never make someone do something they don't want to do. Lance wanted to stop the Ballanan and take their flyer. I just helped him do it my way." She took a sip of coffee and gave her cup to August to refill it. "I know you were distracted at the time, but didn't you see Lance jump from the tree?"

"Yes, it was amazing," he answered.

"Bill, honestly, I know you were excited, but Lance jumped from the tree one hundred feet to the flyer," she laughed. "How could he do that?"

"You helped him?" he asked.

"Exactly. Now I want to help you and your planet," Nan said. "When I felt the circle of mages form last night, it was more than my mind and body could bear. I could feel their hatred and vile intentions even from across the galaxy. I felt them reaching out to me as if daring me to stop them."

"Can you stop them, Nan?" August asked.

"I don't know. It's been so long since the last circle formed. After the loss of Orto Nong, the black mages became solitary, like the ice wizards. A single mage on a planet can live very well and control many things, but they cannot rule with impunity. We ice wizards are content to live quietly, but the Ballanan have drawn the mages together again," Nan said. "If the Ballanan found a single mage on a planet, they could kill him eventually; even though many of them would die as well. But a circle is another thing. I doubt all the Ballanan in the universe can compete with them. And without the Cantu Bagwa, there is little hope."

"What is a Cantu Bagwa?" Bill asked. "You mentioned that term last night."

"In the language of my home world, the Cantu Bagwa is the Singer of Praises, or Soul of the Planet," Nan replied. "A single Cantu Bagwa is always alive on every planet. They are the physical embodiment of the spirit of the planet. Everything on the planet obeys the Cantu Bagwa. I felt it when she was taken through the portal to Far Sun. At that moment, I also felt the rising strength of the black mages. If the Cantu Bagwa had stayed, the mages would not have been able to form the circle. With her gone, they can act freely and no one there can do anything about it."

"Why would someone take the Cantu Bagwa from Earth, Nan?" August asked.

"For protection, I imagine," she replied. "The Cantu Bagwa is not a super-human or supreme soldier. The Cantu Bagwa of Earth is a young girl. Neither the humans of Earth or of Far Sun know anything about this Being. To them, she is a little child in need of safety."

"My granddaughter is the Cantu Bagwa," Bill said. "I don't know how I know that, but she is. What do we do now, Nan?"

"Please believe me when I say that now we must wait here," Nan replied. "We need Lance to find us and the Ballanan army as well. We will require all of their help to save Earth now. The Ballanan want to fight black mages, so we will give them that chance."

"If the Ballanan are looking for mages, why are they here?" August asked.

"They are looking for me too," Nan replied. "I am not a mage, but the Ballanan cannot tell the difference. After all, the mages are my brothers."

"What?" Bill gasped.

"It's true, mostly," Nan replied. "The mages and wizards are the males and females of the only sentient species on my home planet. Over the millions of years, our species evolved away from male to female sexual procreation. While we are all still capable, our society began to procreate by self-cloning. Finally, our lifetimes became so extended that any procreation became unnecessary. Living separately, the two sexes changed. The men kept their aggressiveness, while the women became more and more peaceful. When we moved into the stars, we moved separately. Our home world was lost in a nova more than three billion Earth years ago. The men chose to conquer new planets and subjugate their populations. The women chose to become reclusive and live quiet lives helping the locals live in peace. It was the disaster on Orto Nong that helped the men to decide to live solitary lives. We have been doing so for a billion years."

"That seems very sad and lonely," August said.

"No. It's not so bad," she answered. "Bill heard the Grand Master last night saying he remembered me. I spent a lot of time with the people here. They have learned I am not a god, but just a person helping to protect them. But I don't want to take advantage of them either. That's why I was more than a little playful with Bill. I still crave physical intimacy, but must allow it to be the natural outpouring of love, not something coerced."

"A part of me wishes I could have been there for you, Nan," Bill said. "And now all the more so, with everything you are going to do to help us."

"Thank you Bill," Nan smiled and blushed. "I do have one other thing for you, but you must promise to remain calm."

"Okay, I promise," Bill said. He looked upward and said, "I am sensing Lance in the flyer. He is getting close to here."

"Very good, Bill," Nan replied. "You are a seer as Golo said. You'll be sensing the Ballanan soon. Why don't both of you come with me now." They rose and walked to another door on the far end of the room. She opened the door and a mist of fog poured out of the room. Nan took their hands and led them into the next room and closed the door behind them.

They stood in the cloud for a few seconds until it began to dissipate. They were in a small white room. In the center of the floor was long table holding a glass case. Bonnie Marshall was lying inside the case. Her skin was pale and seemed frozen. She had cuts all over her exposed skin, just as Bill had seen in the shower. "Get her out of there, Nan!" Bill shouted. "Is she okay?"

"Bill, you promised to be calm," Nan said. "Bonnie will be fine, but she is recovering now and we must not disturb her." She put her arm around Bill's shoulder and pulled him close to her. "This is what the black mages did to her. Her blood mixed with their own to open a portal through space. That portal allowed ten other mages to come to your planet." Frozen trails of tears were on Bill's cheeks and August hugged him. "When one of the mages attempted to lock her in his pendant, I intercepted her and brought her here. I doubt they have noticed she is missing yet. I used all of my strength to do that, which is why I fainted. She is very weak and needs several days to recover enough before we can safely wake her. That's a second reason we have to be patient and wait for the Ballanan warriors." She pulled Bill's face to her and kissed his lips. "Bill, I guarantee you that Bonnie will be fine if we just wait. Okay?"

Chapter 26

The alarm clock chirped in Jane Virtue's hotel room. She was having some difficulty opening her eyes, which seemed to be caked shut with sleep. She rubbed her eyelids and looked blearily around the small hotel room. Looking at her hands, she noticed dried blood in the congealed matter from her eyes. Her pillow case was also stained with blood. She stood tentatively and when she felt stable she walked over to the mirror. The whites of her eyes were deeply bloodshot. Jane was beginning to remember the storm overnight. She opened the curtain and looked around. The dark clouds still hung low in the sky, and rain poured down while lightning and thunder filled the city. The streets were littered with debris and crews were busily clearing them before the rush hour traffic began. A car would be coming for her in just over an hour, so she closed the curtain again and walked into the bathroom and turned on the light. She froze in terror. A message was written on the mirror in dried blood. She looked at her right index finger and realized that she had written it herself in her sleep. It said, "Your death is near, Elder."

Umdala entered the central chamber and noticed the other mages still sleeping on the floor and benches. He had taken human form again and was dressed in his best dark blue suit, ready for his busy day. He was due to meet at his attorney's office in an hour to discuss the terms of his company's latest acquisition. Later, he was due to have lunch at the United Nations, where several business leaders would meet with the visiting dignitaries from the Far Sun system. While the other businessmen were keen to expand their businesses to new planets, Umdala only wanted assurances the sentinels and military would continue to block the Ballanan from coming back to Earth. His life depended on those others protecting him. He felt that Keedu was a fool for convening the circle, but it was too late to think about that anymore.

"What kind of silly costume is that, Umdala?" one of the mages said as he woke.

"Baku, Umdala thinks he needs to fit in with the mortals here to protect himself from the Ballanan," Keedu said, rubbing his face and stumbling to his feet. The other mages began to stir and watch the activity.

"But we are a circle now," Baku laughed. "The Ballanan are no match for us. Let us enjoy this new planet until they come. Then we will relish their slaughter!"

"Shut up, Baku!" Umdala shouted. "This is my planet. I have everything exactly the way I want it to be. We summoned you to help us defeat the Ballanan, nothing else. I demand you leave my planet alone."

The other mages began to laugh. Keedu started, "Your planet! You've been hiding behind these weak creatures for too long. Now that we have a circle, it is time for us to rule." The other mages nodded in agreement and formed a circle around Umdala and Keedu.

"Keedu, we had a deal!" Umdala shouted. "I plan to keep you to it. I told you I would help convene the circle, but would then drop out. You promised the circle would strike out at the Ballanan and not destroy this planet." He waved his arms at the others in the circle. "Pick one of your own planets to destroy. You don't need the portal anymore. Get out of here and leave me alone!"

"I lied," Keedu laughed. "I don't know about the others, but my planet is horrible. The kindest creatures are the zongo and they are bloodthirsty savages. This planet is civilized with intelligent Beings who need our direction."

"This planet was not always as you see it today," Umdala said. "When I arrived twenty thousand of their years ago, they were barbarians too. But I have used my talents to build a planet that is perfect to protect me. I refuse to allow you fools to change that!"

"You refuse?" Baku laughed. "Brother, you are hardly in a position to tell the circle what to do, right boys?" The other mages hooted and laughed at Umdala. Keedu had stepped back and joined the group which now circled Umdala.

"Brothers!" Keedu shouted. "We must remember that Umdala is our host. I know where this discussion is leading, but it would be a terrible mistake to kill our own host." The other mages laughed and shouted, pointing gnarled fingers at Umdala. "I have another idea. Umdala has been changed by this planet and that is not good. I would not be surprised to find his genitalia have changed to that of a woman. Perhaps we should send him to be with a fellow woman? We have sensed an ice wizard. Reach into my mind and you will see for yourselves. I say we send Umdala to join her!" The mages shouted their approval and began to move around Umdala in a crazed dance.

"Brothers, have you forgotten the lesson of Orto Nong?" Umdala pleaded. "This planet will do the same to us if we try to destroy it. Please pay attention to me!"

The mages did not hear his words. They were absorbed into their chant and dance. They moved faster and faster around Umdala, who began to bleed from his ears and nose. Thousands of cuts appeared over his body, and he winced and screamed in pain. A funnel of black smoke rose and filled the center of the circle as the mages circled ever faster. Lightning crackled inside the room, and several books caught on fire. A final bolt of lightning shot through the mages and into the funnel cloud in a monstrous explosion. The mages collapsed to the floor and lay panting and gasping for air. The cloud dissipated, revealing that Umdala was gone.

Grand Master Golo Ung sat quietly at his breakfast table with Chief Priest Joco. "So, Joco, I hope you slept well."

"Yes, Grand Master, the accommodations were excellent," he replied. "Is Lance still here in the city?"

"No. He left to find his friends in the hidden lands," the Grand Master said. "It is unfortunate Nan-bo-Nan chose to take the other sentinel. Lance was quite upset, and I can't say I blame him."

"Surely Lance doesn't have the power to harm Nan-bo-Nan?" Joco asked.

"Of course not," Golo laughed. "But she would do better to keep Lance as a friend. I have foreseen the arrival of the Ballanan army. Nan-bo-Nan will need all the help she can get. I would send my own army to intercept them, but our weapons are feeble next to theirs. I just hope they spare our city."

"Do you think the lizard men will be able to kill Nan-bo-Nan, Grand Master?" Joco whispered. "I cannot imagine our planet without her protection."

"I don't know," he replied. "I pray she can protect us and save herself. She is not their enemy. Hopefully, she can convince them."

A soldier rushed in and up to the table. He was out of breath and panicking. "Grand Master, you must come with me. The lizard army is approaching and there is something else you must see."

"Relax, son," Golo said. "What can be this important?"

"Please, Grand Master, my sergeant has ordered me to get you," the soldier cried. "Please, you must come along."

"Very well, my son," Golo answered. The three men rushed out of the temple and toward the city gate. A line of priests and hundreds of citizens followed them through the narrow streets of Chang-A. The sky was clear blue without a cloud to be seen. A cool breeze that blew down from the mountains filled their lungs. As they ran through the gates out of the city, they noticed a large crowd was being held back by dozens of soldiers. When the Grand Master approached the troops, he demanded to know why he was summoned. A young officer with captain's insignia on his uniform pointed his hand back toward the city walls.

Umdala was crucified against the wall. Heavy spikes cut through his hands and feet. Thousands of small wounds oozed blood that stained his loincloth and the wall behind him. He was unconscious and his head hung down onto his chest, which rose slightly with each labored breath. "Who is God's name did such a thing?" Golo sighed.

"Grand Master, what is that thing?" Joco said.

"I don't know, Joco," he replied. "How could anyone do such a thing to another Being? Perhaps we should take him down."

As they contemplated the crucified figure, two flying ships shot through the sky over their heads. The ships circled the city and then hovered near the creature nailed to the city wall. They then extended landing pylons and touched down just twenty feet from the stunned crowd. Several Ballanan soldiers climbed out of the ships and approached the crowd. The soldiers held their spears out to protect the Grand Master, but he waved them off.

One Ballanan removed his helmet. His scaly green skin made him look even more sinister than

Joco and this team had recounted. His yellow eyes seemed to bore right through them. He pointed at the crucified figure and smiled at the crowd, saying something they could not understand. He laughed at his own stupidity and opened a small bag to extract several crystal fragments. He walked forward slowly and offered a stone fragment to the Grand Master. Golo considered the Ballanan's large scaly hand. He remembered what Lance and Joco had told him and gingerly took a small stone and motioned for others to do the same.

"Greetings, Ballanan warrior, I am Grand Master Golo Ung and this is my city of Chang-A. Why have you done this horrible thing to that creature?" Golo said.

"Me? I thought you did this. I am General Atar Nbele of the Ballanan Marines," the solider replied. "My forces are just now arriving here. We had nothing to do with the capture of the black mage, although we wish we had!" He turned to look at the mage again, and shook his head. "We have traveled very far to find and destroy the black mages, but I don't know if my own forces could have done this. How did you do this with your primitive weapons, Grand Master?"

"I told you we did not do this," Golo shuddered. "We could never do such a thing to an intelligent creature. This is barbaric."

"If you knew what these creatures did to my home world, you might think differently," Atar replied. "But I am very confused now. Didn't this animal control your planet? The black mages live only to destroy and manipulate for their own pleasure. You've never seen him before?"

"No, we have never seen this Being before," Golo said. "I have heard recently of black mages, but until today, I have never seen one."

"That cannot be true, old man," Atar laughed. "Our probes clearly showed a mage on your planet. If it was not this one, there must be another. Perhaps that other mage did this? But don't worry; we will protect you from them. We have spent many years trying to find the mages and we will not allow them to rule you as they did us."

"That is a lie!" Joco shouted. "You and your soldiers destroyed my temple and killed hundreds of villagers in the jungle! How can we believe that you are now our protector?"

"Ah, that was unfortunate," Atar said. "Our excitement at finding a mage planet got the best of our advance team. We expected to find rabid slaves of the mage trying to kill us. It wasn't until we encountered the Sentinel from Far Sun that we realized our error. You must let us rid your planet of the filthy mages and then we will do all we can to rebuild your city."

An icy breeze blew through the gathering and the temperature dropped twenty degrees instantly. A figure in a long, hooded white cloak moved through the line of soldiers and approached the Ballanan general. Nan-bo-Nan pulled off the hood and stood next to the Grand Master. Atar could feel her ice blue eyes piercing through him as the temperature continued to plummet. He felt himself shivering from the cold.

"Nan-bo-Nan, you should not be here," Golo said. "Things are particularly difficult right now, as you can see."

She smiled, leaned forward and kissed Golo on the cheek. "Don't worry, Golo, nothing bad can happen now." She turned to the general and extended her hand. "Welcome to my planet, General. I am Nan-bo-Nan. I fear I am the one your probes mistakenly identified as a black mage."

"You are not a black mage?" Atar asked. "Your ability to change the weather and appear suddenly makes me think otherwise."

Nan laughed. She pulled open her robe to expose her nude body, and then quickly closed it again. "That should prove I am not a mage. I am a woman as you could clearly see. Have you ever seen a female black mage?"

"Not that I can recall," Atar said, "although I have always assumed there must be both sexes if they are to procreate. And I have seen mages transform themselves into all sorts of creatures."

"That is true," she replied. "However, you know very little about black mages and ice wizards, General. A black mage would never masquerade as a female for fear the others would ridicule him."

"Nan-bo-Nan, did you do this to the mage?" Golo asked.

"Of course not, Golo," she smiled while stroking his face. "You should know me better than that. No, the only Beings capable of doing this are other black mages. A circle of mages has now formed on Sentinel Bill Marshall's home world, and I fear they banished this one for failing to agree with the rest. The mage is very weak and on the brink of death. He has lost much blood."

"Great!" the general laughed. "Then my soldiers can finish him off. One less mage to worry about."

"I'm very sorry, General," Nan said, "but I cannot allow that. I can sense goodness in this mage and I will nurse him back to health. Killing him in this condition would be murder."

"I don't think you understand, woman," Atar scowled. "I am not asking for your permission. I am telling you what I am going to do."

Nan laughed out loud. Clouds of fog rose from the ground and filled the air outside the city walls. The temperature dropped another fifty degrees and heavy snow dropped from newly formed clouds. The general reached for his blaster, but it was frozen into its holster. He turned to his aides, but found them frozen in place. The locals were huddled close to the ground and each other for warmth. As quickly as it started, the snow stopped. Three inches had already accumulated in the few seconds. The sky was clear and the fog quickly dissipated. Nan-bo-Nan and Umdala were gone.

Atar grabbed Golo, lifted him off the ground and held him up to his face. "Listen old man, where did they go? If you don't tell me, we will destroy your city and kill all of you."

Golo laughed heartily. "And you said you would protect us. That was all lies as Joco said."

"This is no time for argument. Your life is in my hands now," Atar replied.

"General, please release the Grand Master," Joco pleaded. "The lands north of here are the hidden lands, which are the home of Nan-bo-Nan. Our faith forbids us from entering there, but the legends tell us she lives on the highest mountains. She has a massive castle there made of ice. The Grand Master meant no disrespect."

Atar set Golo down. "I'm very sorry, Grand Master, it was not my intent to threaten you or your city. My mission is to find and destroy the mages, and Nan-bo-Nan infuriated me with her lies about not being one of them."

Golo took Atar's hand in his. "It is okay, my son. Anger is strong and can make us all do terrible things. If you feel your destiny is in the hidden lands, go there with my blessing. However, I know you are wrong about Nan-bo-Nan. She has always been a gracious friend of ours. She had never done intentional harm to any of our people. There was a time when we yearned to worship her as a god. But it was Nan-bo-Nan who came and told us not to. She is very powerful, but she is also just a woman. Go in peace." Golo kissed the general's hand and led his people back toward the city gate.

Atar surveyed the area. His army was coming into view as they marched toward the city. His aides were warming themselves as best they could. Since Nan-bo-Nan had left, the temperature had risen to seventy-five degrees and the warm sun shone brightly overhead.

Chapter 27

Bill sat silently on a chair next to Bonnie's chamber. The cuts on her body were healing quickly and her cheeks had a slight rose tint. He watched her breathe and wondered when he could hold her in his arms again. Bill could feel the brutal cold of the room on his face, but he was remarkably warm and comfortable in the body armor suit Nan-bo-Nan had given him. He put his hands on the glass case and sighed. His warm breath condensed on the glass and turned to frost. He sat back and closed his eyes, remembering the days before the earthquake, when he would wake very early and head outside to tend his sheep. After they were out in the pasture, he would come home and find Bonnie busily making breakfast, and the smell of fresh coffee would fill the room.

August sat on a large white couch in the main room of Nan's residence. She pulled a heavy blanket up to her neck to stay warm and held a thick book in her lap. Nan had given her the book when she first brought August to this place. The title was embossed in gold, and read "Tales of Bala Napor." Bala Napor was the home world of the mages and wizards, and this ancient tome was filled the stories of life on that planet long before the inhabitants were forced to flee the nova. The book was massive, with more than ten thousand pages. August had read from it each day and had barely scratched the surface. Today she started to read the story of Nelu Abar Odwee, the woman who led the movement to reunite the sexes. It had been a thousand generations since men and women had stopped procreating in the natural way. Nelu could see the separation was tearing apart the fabric of society. The sexes lived separately and many had migrated to new parts of the planet that only accepted one sex. The men had become more and more aggressive, while the women were non-violent and intellectual. Nelu knew this would only increase unless both sexes realized the problem and actively worked to change back to a normal society. She created a new country where men and women would live together and form loving families. The movement was gaining momentum until the nova was first foretold. That revelation led to widespread panic.

That period was now remembered as the Schism. The men felt they must find new home planets quickly, even if that meant destroying the indigent cultures. Their personal preservation was paramount. The women wanted to avoid damaging any such cultures and felt they could use their strengths to help those cultures develop. Within a few years, the new country's population dwindled and the government failed. Nelu Abar Odwee disappeared and was never seen again. The legend said she died from a broken heart. August wiped a tear from her face and closed the book.

Lance burst into the room with his blaster aimed at August. "Nan-bo-Nan, you should know better than to masquerade as my sentinel," he shouted. "Where are August and Bill?"

August stood up and held her hands over her head. "Lance, it's me. I'm the real August."

"Don't expect me to fall for more of your lies," Lance said. "I'm giving you one last chance to save yourself before I fire!"

"Bill!" she shouted. "I really need you *now!*"

"That's the oldest trick in the book, Nan-bo-Nan," Lance laughed as he aimed the blaster at her head.

"Bill!" she shouted again. "For God's sake, get out here now!"

A door opened on the far side of the room and a cloud of fog poured out. Lance turned to aim his blaster at the fog. The fog quickly dissipated and Bill stood in the room. "Whoa, Lance, put that damn thing down. That really is August. Nan-bo-Nan left here half an hour ago."

"Oh my God," Lance said as he clipped his blaster to his belt. "I'm sorry you two, but I thought I'd never see either of you alive again."

August rushed over to Lance and threw her arms around his neck. "It's okay, Lance. I'm just glad you found us. How did you get here so quickly?"

"Well, that's a good question, August," Lance pondered. "I have no idea. This was the first place I came to."

A second cloud of fog poured from the opening door behind Bill. After it faded, Nan-bo-Nan stood next to Bill. "I know how you got here Lance. I guided your flyer here. Welcome to my home, Sentinel."

"Enough of this," Lance shouted as he pointed his blaster at the ice wizard. "You've been manipulating all of us for a long time, and I'm sick of it, you bitch."

"Lance, put the gun down," Bill interjected as he moved between the two. "Nan is our friend, and we need her to stop the black mages. She is our only hope."

Nan laughed and pushed Bill aside. "Thanks for the gallantry, Bill, but it is not necessary. I have dealt with male posturing before. Remember that I am the sister of the mages." She walked up to Lance until his blaster was touching her chest. "Go ahead and shoot Lance. You know you won't be happy until you kill me and doom your planets to slavery to the mages. I dare you."

"Happy to oblige," Lance smirked and pulled the trigger. The blast tossed Nan back ten feet and into the ice wall, which cracked from the impact. Nan fell to the ground and did not move.

"What the hell do you think you're doing?" Bill shouted. "You've killed us all." He turned and rushed over to Nan who was laying face down. He kneeled next to her and turned her over gently. He put his ear close to her mouth to listen for breathing. Nan threw her arms around Bill and kissed his cheek. Bill pulled back in shock. Nan smiled when she saw the worry in his eyes. "You're okay?"

"Even better than that, Bill," she said. "My flying back and crashing to the floor was just for Lance's benefit." Bill helped Nan to her feet. "I felt he needed to act out his aggression or it would poison him. Now he feels satisfied that I have been punished. And me? That blast just added to my strength. It's the old conservation of energy thing. My body absorbed the energy of the blast. I feel fantastic!"

Lance stood with his mouth open watching Nan, but not really believing his eyes. The blaster was still in his hand, held limply at his side. August gently took the weapon away and set it on the table next to the book. "I don't understand, Nan-bo-Nan. How can you not be injured by the blast?"

"I'm human like you, Lance, but let's say I'm a bit more evolved," she replied. "And please call me Nan, it's much simpler. My species has been evolving for billions of years." She walked over to the couch, grabbed the blanket and put it around his shoulders, then kissed him on the cheek. "You'd better keep this on, Lance. Your core temperature is dropping fast. Your uniform is not designed for the temperature of my home. That's why I modified the other uniforms. In fact, Bill will show you a bedroom where you can take off your suit and stay under some warm blankets. Then I'll fix your suit too."

"My uniform is fine, Nan," Lance argued. "We can't stay anyway. Come on team, let's get back to the flyer."

"Sorry, Lance, I can't allow that," Nan said. The Ballanan army is heading in this direction. They'd shoot you down as soon as you came in range. Besides, didn't you come here to see me?"

"I don't know anymore," Lance replied slowly shaking his head from side to side. "I can't seem to think clearly."

"That's not good, Lance. You're mind is shutting down from the cold," Nan said. "Let's go now." She picked Lance up in her arms and carried him toward the bedroom door. "Bill, be a dear and open the door for me. August, come with me too. I need you to help me take his uniform off."

August and Nan quickly pulled off Lance's clothes and put him under the covers, where he continued shivering. August disrobed and climbed under the covers to help warm him up. Nan touched their foreheads and a surge of warmth moved through their bodies, and they fell asleep. Smiling contentedly, Nan took Bill's hand and led him out of the room and closed the door. "That should do it," she laughed as she led him back into the main room. "I'll fix the suit in a while, but I want to show you something special."

"Where did you go, Nan?" Bill asked as she led him toward the door to the room where Bonnie was recovering. "I was certain that Lance would shoot August, and she is human."

Nan opened the door and the cloud of fog poured over them. "She would have been fine, Bill. The new armor suits can withstand a lot more than a blaster. But I want to show you why I left. Follow me." They walked into the other room and Nan closed the door.

The fog quickly faded and Bill noticed there were two glass cases in the room now. In the second was a large man with dark, swarthy skin. He had large holes in his hands and feet and hundreds of wounds all over his body. A small white sheet covered his privates.

"Wow, who is that?" Bill gasped. "It looks like he was crucified. Who could have done this, Nan?"

"His brothers did this," Nan sighed. "Bill, this is a black mage."

"Are you going to give him to the Ballanan so they leave?" he asked.

Nan looked stunned. "Bill, honestly, I could never do that. He is my brother, as are all mages. Besides, I have felt great compassion in this mage. This is a great opportunity for me to rehabilitate a mage."

"I don't know about that," Bill frowned. "Aren't these the ones who enslaved the Ballanan and caused everything that's been happening to my family? Why does he deserve special treatment?"

"I know you don't understand, Bill," she replied. "My people have lived apart for so long that most have never known life in a real society. That is why I have become close to the people of this world. But they are not my kind. This mage is my kind. His blood and mine both originated on Bala Napor. If this mage can be reasoned with, perhaps there is a small chance that our race can regenerate and end our separation."

"Great! Mages and wizards working together to take over the universe," Bill scoffed. "What happens to the rest of the Beings in the universe?"

"You don't understand, Bill," Nan stated. "If the two genders of Bala Napor can come together, we would become peaceful again. Perhaps not as shrinking and submissive as I and the other ice wizards, but somewhere in the middle between our two natures. We would become like you. Is that a bad thing?"

"Even humans with too much power can do horrible things, Nan. The history of my planet is full of examples," he replied.

"Yes, but you evolved," she smiled. "Look at you now, traversing the universe trying to stop the Ballanan from attacking innocent worlds. And the differences between your species and mine are not that great. We've been around longer and have learned new things. Compare your own people to those of this planet. To them, you are magical, but in reality it is only your improved science and technology."

"You'll have a difficult time convincing the Ballanan to accept all of this, I think," Bill said.

"And Lance as well, I expect," she pouted and then smiled broadly. "But you have more important things to take care of right now."

"What do you mean, Nan?" he asked.

She pointed toward Bonnie's chamber. She was awake and looking at them. "I think it's time for you and your wife to have some time to discuss all of this.

"Mr. Secretary General, I must protest," Elder Paul Justice said. "We requested to meet with either the Security Council or General Assembly. I don't understand the purpose of this meeting."

"Elder Justice," Arthur Benedict replied, "we understand your concerns and have spoken at length with both the U.S. Ambassador and the president about your activities at the Marshall ranch in California; however, this is a global organization. Until we have more information and verification of your status, I cannot burden either of these groups with another meeting."

Elder Jane Virtue stood looking out the window on the New York skyline. Heavy, dark clouds continued to lie low in the sky, dumping heavy rain. Lightning and thunder filled the air. A few inky tornadoes slipped out of the clouds but did not reach the ground. "Mr. Secretary General, I understand your concern. You and the people of this planet can do whatever you think is appropriate, but we can tell you that this world is in grave danger. Despite my colleague's comments, I doubt even our worlds can help you now."

"One might almost read that as a threat, Elder," Arthur replied. "Believe me, the armies of this world are up for any challenge."

"They will be useless against the evil that has been launched in this city," she said. "But there was no threat intended. Our people want to help defend you, but until you understand the scope of the danger, I doubt you will prepare."

"That is why we are having this meeting, Elders," Arthur replied. "Tell me and I will decide whether we should escalate this to other resources."

One of the office windows shattered and sprayed the three with shards of glass. An inky black and very narrow funnel cloud poured through the opening and moved about the office, tossing the furniture, books, and papers about. The three covered their heads and crawled into corners of the room. The desk flew up and landed against the door, just as security tried to open it. Suddenly, it was quiet. The three looked up to see Keedu, standing in the middle of the room, laughing out loud.

"How did you get in here?" Arthur shouted. "Security!"

Keedu looked at the door and could see it moving slightly. He waved his hand and the door seemed to weld itself to the surrounding wall. "Good. That's gives us plenty of time," he began. "I am Keedu Mongala Zimu, but you may call me Keedu, or my lord if you prefer. I have decided to take the place of my brother Umdala, and this planet is now mine. You may be allowed to survive if you serve me faithfully, but be assured your lives will not be as free as they were under Umdala's reign."

"I am not afraid of you," Arthur said. "I demand you leave my office immediately. This is no way to begin a diplomatic discussion."

Keedu was doubled over in laughter. "That's very funny. Umdala always said humans have good senses of humor. I guess he was right. Too bad he has been exiled. But I understand how this may seem unreal and perhaps even a fantasy. Let me explain." He waved his arm and the Secretary General was gone. He turned his attention to the others. "I'm glad to see you are not as arrogant as that man," Keedu said. "Perhaps we can work together. What do you think?"

"I think you know why we cannot, mage," Jane spit.

"Oh yes, I didn't notice at first. You are the elders from Far Sun," Keedu smiled. "Well, you can leave now that I'm here. The people of Earth will not negotiate with you. I will not allow that. The Secretary General will use his influence to turn the armies here against you. I have sent him and several heads of state on a little journey. When they return, I know I will be able to count on their support."

"I don't believe a mage could do that," Paul chided.

"You're right, but a circle of mages can do that and a lot more," Keedu replied. "Thanks to one of you, the Cantu Bagwa has been taken off the planet. That allowed Umdala and me to form the circle. You can be assured that we will not allow her back either."

"You formed a circle?" Jane asked. "I should have known. The signs are so clear."

"Did you like the writing on the mirror in blood?" Keedu laughed. "That was Baku's idea. I thought it was a bit over the top. Elder, I have no desire to hurt either of you. But I have much work to do here with my brothers in the circle." He waved his arm and the two elders were gone. He looked at the door and the desk slid away and the opening returned. He opened the door and walked into a hail of bullets.

Arthur Benedict found himself alone in a deep jungle. He looked for any sign of civilization, but found nothing. He wondered where he might be and whether this was real or he had lost his mind completely. The foliage looked very different from any he had seen in his youth when he explored the Amazon rain forest. The trees seemed to climb impossibly high into the sky, allowing almost no light to reach the ground. He walked for what seemed to be hours until he was totally drained. He sat heavily on a stump and wondered what to do. Buzzing sounds were growing in volume, and he looked up to see what was happening. He saw a swarm of small birds flying over head. Then the birds dived down toward him. The swarm of vorrath circled his head. Several landed on him and he swatted at them. There were hundreds of them, flying inches from him now, and his mind reeled. Then they were on him, each driving its five-inch proboscis into his skin and sucking his blood. He screamed in agony and passed out.

When he awoke, he was sure he was dead. But he never imagined heaven or hell to be a cold, damp cave. He was tired, but could find no evidence of the vorrath stings on his body. He was lying in a shallow pool of water. Perhaps it had been a dream. But what was this place? He could see light ahead and hoped he could get out of the cold, wet, claustrophobic surroundings. His wet shoes made walking difficult as he kept slipping backward. After a few minutes, he decided to crawl on his hands and knees. He made good progress and entered a large, open room. There was an opening to the outside on the opposite side of the room, so he climbed back to his feet and hurried forward. He found the ground under his feet to be soft and spongy, which was nothing like the stone floor of a cave on Earth. He was approaching the entrance to the cave when he noticed the hissing sounds growing louder with each step. He turned to see thousands of red eyes glowing in the light from the entrance. The mass of zongo rushed forward, knocking him to the ground. Arthur struggled to get the spiders off of him, but there were too many. He could feel their fangs cutting into his body and their venom coursing through his veins. His breathing became labored and he struggled to move even a finger. So this is what death feels like, he thought as he slipped from consciousness.

Arthur was dreaming about his wife and children back home. The holiday season was approaching and he had no idea what gifts to get for anyone. His wife had been hinting at a necklace to match the diamond studs he bought her on their last anniversary. How would the arrival of Keedu affect his ability to care for his family? How odd to dream about the mage, he thought. Yet, he felt warm and comfortable as if lying under a heavy quilt like his grandmother used to make for him. He felt a sharp pain in his neck and opened his eyes. He was asleep at his desk in the UN building in New York. He knew he should not sleep like this because it always gave him a stiff neck. He looked around his office and the window was still broken out, although plywood had been put in place to cover the opening. Then he noticed Keedu, sitting on the couch with his feet up on the coffee table. "So, it was all a dream?" he squeaked. His voice was rough and hoarse.

"Not at all, Mr. Secretary General," Keedu smiled. "You actually visited my former planet and that of my brother, Baku. I suppose you understand why we prefer this world to either of them."

"So, Keedu, what do you want from me?" Arthur said as he struggled to stand. "I don't know whether to believe you or not, but that was the most horrible experience I could imagine. But I'm just a figurehead here. The UN has no real authority. We are only an organization to bring the different countries together."

"We want nothing else, Arthur, if I may call you that," Keedu smiled. "And please don't feel singled out in any way. While you didn't see them, the leaders of the countries in your Security Council had the same experience as you. Think of that journey as a minor example of the power we mages possess. Do you also see all the holes in this wall?" Keedu motioned to one of the walls. "After you left, I went to meet others and was greeted by an attack. But don't worry, I wasn't harmed. Such archaic weapons are an amusement, nothing else. And I did not punish them for that. A father doesn't punish his children for playing with toys."

"Thank you for not taking any lives, Mr. Keedu," Arthur replied. "What are your plans for us now? I don't see how a weak people like us can do anything."

"Just call me Keedu, Arthur," the mage opened. "We ask only for your respect and hospitality. Your planet entertained my brother Umdala for many centuries. He chose to treat you well and your people returned the favor. However, my other brothers and I are not as forgiving and gentle, although we will try to let you live your lives if you do what we ask. Keep us fed and entertained and help defend us from those who wish us harm. I believe that is the mission of your organization, isn't it? You help other citizens to lead decent lives. Now you have eleven more citizens, nothing else."

"We will do our best, Keedu," Arthur sighed. "Whatever happened to the two elders who were here with me?"

Keedu laughed. "I have no animosity with the people of Far Sun, although they do wish us harm. I simply returned them safely to their planet." Keedu walked over to the small credenza and removed two glasses and a bottle of Scotch whisky. He poured glasses for Arthur and himself. "Actually, Arthur, I do have a first favor to ask. Since the sentinels of Far Sun are against my brothers, I would like you to ask them to leave this planet. You no longer need their help to protect Earth. You have my brothers and me to do that now, my friend."

Chapter 29

Bonnie was lying next to her husband under the heavy blankets. She could feel the biting cold of the room on her face. The room was completely white, except for the large window wall that looked out on a magical mountain view with tall, craggy peaks and broad glaciers. She snuggled up to Bill and kissed him softly on the cheek. He opened his eyes and gazed back at her with incredible relief that she was safely with him again. "It's all over now, honey," he smiled. "Nan will help us find our way home with our family."

"I hope you're right, Bill. But I did notice that man in the other chamber. I remember him from Earth. It was he and the other mage who hurt me and used me to bring the other mages to them," she replied with tears welling in her eyes. "I was frozen in place but could hear and see everything. When they joined consciousnesses, my mind went with them. They were watching little Cybil being taken through the portal to Far Sun. They kept mentioning the words Cantu Bagwa, but I don't know what it means."

"I agree the mage is very dangerous. I warned Nan about him, but she is convinced there is good in him," he replied as he took her into his arms.

"There is one thing I do remember, honey," Bonnie began. "In the morning, the mages formed a circle around that mage. I think they called him Umdala. They started to dance and shout like madmen. After a few minutes, he was gone."

"I have seen the same thing in his mind, Bonnie," Nan said as she strode into the room. She was smiling and carrying a new suit for Bonnie. "I sensed you two were awake, and I wanted to bring this for Bonnie before she tries to get out of bed. As you might have noticed, I love cold weather."

"It would be nice if you'd knock before coming in, Nan," Bill snarled.

"I'm sorry, Bill, but by now you must realize that I sense everything happening on this planet," Nan replied. "If you two had been involved in something more intimate, shall we say, I would not have come in." She walked over and sat on the bed next to them. "Bonnie, as you may have guessed, it is very cold here. I have made special suits for the sentinels and you so you are comfortable here."

"Thank you, Nan," she replied. "But why do you like it so cold? You seem pretty much the same as us."

"Physiologically, we are closely related," Nan started. "I mean no disrespect, but imagine if you met a human from ten thousand years ago on your planet. The physical similarities would be strong, and the differences would be somewhat hidden, but enormous. It has been so long since the Schism and the Exodus from our home planet that there is no record of how we were back then. I imagine that was almost a billion of your years ago. Our brothers, the black mages pursued a course of domination of the planets they settled. We are all together now due to the period they ruled Orto Nong. We women decided to take a more discrete course. We chose not to have a strong influence on the native cultures or evolution. Over time, we became reclusive and moved to out-of-the-way locations. On most planets, that means deep in the oceans or on high mountains. Since we are not fish, the mountains became our homes. Over more generations, our bodies evolved more to make us what we are today. Our love of the cold gave us the moniker of ice wizards."

"Are there more ice wizards here?" Bonnie asked.

"No. I can sense several hundred on other planets in this area of the galaxy, but we choose to live alone. The peoples of our planets are like our children. To our brothers, their citizens are slaves. That is why we have stayed apart so long. Perhaps, just perhaps, there is a chance to change that now. The dream of the Eretz Domma may come true," Nan said as she glanced out the window at the pristine landscape.

"What is the Eretz Domma?" Bill asked. "There are so many new terms that I'm having a hard time remembering them all."

"Those terms are from our ancient language. Even we don't remember all of it, but certain key phrases have survived." Nan walked over to the window and looked about as if daydreaming. "The Eretz Domma is the divine union. It is the rejoining of male and female, which ended too long ago to remember. Our legends tell us the first couple to join again will have ultimate dominion over the entire universe. No black mage or ice wizard will be able to stop them. Even circles of ten or ten million mages will be powerless."

"That actually sounds terrifying, Nan," Bill said. "You make it sound like a good thing, but ultimate power in the universe is not good."

Nan laughed and walked back over to the bed and sat. "You're so funny Bill. You should also know ice wizards are much more powerful than mages. Their evil has weakened them. If I'm right that the mage in the other room has good in him, then maybe there is a chance for a positive Eretz Domma." She wiped a few tears from her face. "But there is no time to consider that now. The mage is very weak and his improvement is slow. He may not survive his injuries. Also, the Ballanan army will arrive in a couple of hours. I have sensed their flyers and led a couple in this direction. You two need to get dressed and be ready to join me on the field of battle in one hour."

"I don't know how we can fight ten thousand Ballanan warriors, Nan," he replied. "It seems more like suicide."

Nan laughed again. "You haven't been listening to anything I've said, have you?" She stood and walked to the door, then looked back. "Just get ready and come out for some coffee and biscuits. Lance is recovered, dressed, and waiting to see you." She smiled again and left, closing the door behind her.

"So what do we do now, Bill?" Bonnie asked as she snuggled up to him. "It's awfully cold out there and we do have an hour."

Bill kissed her lips and pulled her close to him, running his fingers across her cheek. "I've missed you so much, sweetheart. I'm sure Nan's war can wait a few minutes." He kissed her again and ran his hand down her body. "I love you, Bonnie."

Chapter 80

The Ballanan army had traveled for days across the hidden lands. Rolling grassy hills had turned to huge, bare mountains stretching up into the sky. Each soldier now wore two uniforms in order to keep warm, and the column had to stop every few hours to defrost their faces and feet. General Atar Nbele stood at the front of the army, insisting on facing the same dangers as they. He felt frozen to the core, but kept driving forward. Looking ahead, he could see the large ice palace halfway up a mountain on the opposite side of a wide glacier. This is exactly what his flight crews had told him, and he smiled and laughed. He turned to his commanders and said, "Okay men, we are almost there. Get everyone ready and let's march."

"General, the glacier may not support the weight of our tanks," Major Igua Nant urged. "The men are concerned about facing the mage without heavy weapons."

"Sir, the air temperature here continues to drop," Colonel Singa Ontopa said. "I don't think it is safe to user our flyers either. Their fuel lines are almost frozen solid already."

Atar scowled as he looked at his most senior advisors. "What do you want to do? Give up? This is the battle of our lives men. We must go forward and face the mage. Only God knows if our forces are strong enough to defeat her. But we will fight today. If our flyers cannot fly, we will leave them here, but the tanks will move forward. I will ride on the first tank to show the men not to be afraid."

Atar climbed on board the lead tank and signaled the army to move forward. He took the position of the tank commander, who was grateful not to drive onto the ice. There were few mountains and no glaciers on Orto Nong. Global warming brought on by massive development under mage rule had destroyed the natural balance, making most of the planet either dry, dusty plains, or dense jungle. No Ballanan had been exposed to mountain warfare and the bitter cold. As his tank first touched the ice with its treads, Atar could hear the ice compressing and cracking under him. Being a leader meant taking the same risks he would expose his troops to, so he knew his destiny was here on the ice.

The ice supported the tank and more followed until all the tanks were lumbering forward, followed by the foot soldiers. Colonel Ontopa had his flight crews remove the heavy weapons from the flyers and mount them as artillery pieces to support the attack. From this distance, their rounds would almost reach the opposite side of the glacier. He knew these would be a last line of defense, as the risk to disrupting the glacier was too high to fire for effect.

Portable bridges were used to cross several crevasses that cut deep into the ice. As the troops crossed, they could see torrents of icy water coursing along at the bottom of the glacier. For safety, all troops were connected by safety ropes to avoid slipping and falling to their deaths. It was early afternoon when the troops stopped halfway across the glacier. General

Nbele was growing concerned that night might fall before they could reach the other side. The temperature was bitterly cold and dropping as they moved toward the ice palace. Atar sat on the tank eating a field ration while his men tried to warm themselves as best they could. His confidence in the battle to come was waning by the moment; but he knew he must move forward to give his all, or he and his men would be marked as cowards. Now he was facing the bitter cold reality of the situation. He and his men were reaching their breaking point. He doubted they would be able to mount any meaningful attack in their current condition, which was horribly dangerous considering the formidable strength of a black mage. He heard a commotion in the middle of the encampment and jumped down to check it out. His men had formed a large circle and had their blasters leveled. He pushed through the line and saw Nan and the humans standing calmly in the middle. He laughed out loud and marched toward them, saying, "It's so good to see you again, mage. You've saved me the trouble of hunting you down."

"General, I already told you I'm no mage," Nan smiled.

"Our sensors tell us you are a mage, woman," Atar said. "And what have you done with the other mage? We were about to use him for target practice when you stole him away."

"He is safely inside my palace over there," she replied. "He is recovering from his wounds slowly."

"That's great news, mage," he shouted. "After we kill you, we can go after him. Thanks for letting me know." He turned and walked back toward his troops. "Okay men, it's time for target practice. Be ready to fire on my command."

"Atar, we are not your enemy," Nan's voice whispered in his ear. He spun around, but she was still standing with the others in the center of the circle. "I'm speaking directly to your mind. Please don't be confused. The enemies of Orto Nong died long ago at the hands of the Hopestone swords and the diseases that stone brought. The mages who were your enemy are dead and buried. It is time for your people to move on and stop chasing phantoms."

"You are real enough and the mage in your palace is real as well," he thought back. "That is enough enemy for us today. We are not cowards and we will not back down. Release the humans and let them come with us. They will come to no harm. You have my word."

"Don't be a fool, Atar," she thought. "These people are my friends. They need my help and yours as well. A circle of mages has formed on one of their planets. That is where the enemy is today. I need your men to go after them. I can protect you. You can win a glorious battle there, but not here. There will be no battle today."

Having reached the circle of soldiers, he spun around and shouted, "That's where you are wrong, Nan! There will be a battle today! Fire at will, men!" Thousands of blasters fired at once and the mass of energy balls shot through the air, exploding in a giant fire ball in the center of the circle. They fired again and again until their weapons were discharged. As the fire and smoke cleared, Atar could see Nan and the others standing inside a clear bubble which had absorbed all the energy of their weapons. Nan smiled, saying, "General, I told you there would be no battle today. Your forces are too weak to affect me. All of the energy of your attack has been absorbed into my body, making me even more powerful. Please be reasonable. I don't want to fight you or have to give you a lesson. Join with us and we will defeat the evil mages."

Atar signaled for several tanks to join the circle. He ordered them to fire on the group in the center. One by one they fired their rounds. The first round pierced the bubble, but Nan caught it out of the air. She held it close to her and it was absorbed into her body. She now stood ten feet tall. More and more rounds were fired, all with the same effect. When they stopped, Nan stood fifty feet tall in the middle of the circle, with a halo of energy surrounding her.

She spoke in a powerful voice that every Ballanan could hear to his soul. "You sincerely wish to die here to prove some point about your gallantry. That's such a shame." She waved her arm and a cyclone of frigid air descended on the Ballanan army. Within a few seconds, every soldier was frozen solid. She made a fist with her hand and pushed it forward as if throwing a punch. All of the soldiers shattered into tiny pieces on the ground, except General Nbele. She casually walked over to him and whispered in his ear, "Atar, is this the honor you want for your soldiers?" Tears rolled down his icy face, freezing into pellets as they fell to the ground at his feet. "I didn't think so." She waved both arms and the pieces reassembled into the soldiers, and they were alive and able to move again.

"Perhaps this is the honor your men would prefer?" she shouted again and the entire glaciers turned liquid. The tanks sank immediately with their crews desperately trying to escape. The soldiers cried for help as their heavy uniforms pulled them down into the frigid water. Nan and the humans were safely standing on top of the waves as was the general. "Is this the death you wished for them, Atar?" she shouted.

"For God's sake, at least let me die with them!" he screamed.

"No, such a horrible death is not right for honorable men such as these," she sighed. She raised her arms over her head and all of the soldiers and tanks rose out of the water, which refroze into the glacier. She nodded her head and all of the soldiers were alive again and very warm in their dry uniforms. The soldiers began to fall to their knees and worship Nan. Even the general fell to the ground and begged for mercy. She hurried over to Atar and helped him up on his feet, kissing him warmly on the lips. She turned to the other soldiers and shouted, "Stop groveling, I am not a god. I am just a person like each of you, although my technology is somewhat more advanced." She walked around the circle, helping soldiers get up and hugging them and reassuring them the lesson was over. Then she took Atar by the hand and led him to the center of the circle where he warmly greeted the others.

Nan was her normal height again and stood with them. She faced the army and said, "Please believe me. I did not enjoy that. I never had any intention of allowing any of you to die for this. You are all brave soldiers and we need your help. The mages who destroyed your world are dead. However, there are other mages who may do the same to other planets, including Earth, where my friends Bill and Bonnie are from. I will now return all of you to the jungle city so you can be near the portal. Tonight, each of you will dream about the circle of mages on Earth and the challenges you will face if you join us. If you prefer to return to Orto Nong, I will not begrudge you. Frankly, if I could stay here and be left alone, I would do so. Today, you have seen a small sample of what I can do. I swear on my life that I will use every ounce of myself to protect each and every one of you if you join us. We are on the verge of greatness, and our actions now may safeguard the universe for a very long time." Each Ballanan felt her warm lips kissing theirs. "Sleep well, comrades. Tomorrow is the beginning of our great adventure." She waved her arms and the Ballanan army was gone, leaving only General Atar Nbele with them.

"What is the meaning of this Nan?" he asked. "Can't I return with my men?"

"Of course, Atar, but I wanted to talk to you for a moment," she replied. "Your men will ask you about today and I hope you remind them I begged you to help us and not try to start a battle. None of the lessons would have happened if you had done that. You know that, right?"

"Of course, Nan. But we could not imagine your power or that you might be telling the truth. We have been so trained to think mages are bad that I reacted instinctively," he said.

"I know, Atar. But when you meet with your men, let them know again I will protect them to the utmost of my abilities. I am not a god, so it is likely many will die in a real war with the mages. Also, I want you and your commanders to repeat my message about returning home to Orto Nong. No one should feel compelled to give their life for me or Earth or anyone else. We all make our own choices. I know with the dedication and commitment of the Ballanan army, we can be victorious. But I don't want one soldier in that war who does not feel it is his destiny." She kissed him again and smiled at him. Then she touched his face with her hand and he disappeared.

"I don't know what to say," Bill said. "That was the most exciting and, at the same time, horrifying experience of my life."

Nan brushed his face with her hand. "Bill, sometimes people need a very clear picture of their options in order to make changes. The Ballanan have dedicated their lives to killing every creature they think might be a mage. Unfortunately, their drive is not matched with power or intelligence. Honestly, I could have killed them when they entered the stone temple, but by then I already knew my destiny required their assistance." She turned to Bonnie. "I hear you are a great cook. Let's go back to my home and you can help me make a nice dinner, what do you say?"

Chapter 31

The dinner had been wonderful. Everyone except Nan and Bill had retired for the night. Nan was grateful for the company as she rarely slept, although tonight it was apparent the intensity of today's action had taken a toll on her. Bill's mind was still reeling from what he had seen today. Ten thousand Ballanan warriors had died twice, but were now safely sleeping in their beds far away. He tried to imagine himself talking to a caveman from Earth's past to understand the difference in technology, but what he had seen was still magical.

"Nan, you look pretty tired," he said. "Perhaps you should get some sleep. I have so many questions, but I don't want to keep you up."

"Don't worry about me, Bill," she yawned. "I never sleep. Ask me your questions."

"I'm trying to understand the difference in your technology, but I have to admit it is not easy. Turning an entire glacier into a swimming pool and back again was unbelievable. And how did you reanimate them after they froze or drowned."

"You're over-thinking it, Bill," she laughed. "I certainly could have done most of that, but perhaps I just put those thoughts into everyone's minds. Did you consider that?"

"Frankly no. So even the barrage of blasters was not real?" he asked.

"Oh no, that part was very real," she answered. "But to me it felt wonderful. Energy is a gift which we cannot get enough of. The same is true for you, but your body is not equipped to handle massive bursts of it. The new uniform will help a lot, but my body has evolved until I can handle almost any energy surge. You probably won't believe this, but the biggest thrill for me is flying through a solar atmosphere. The power surge is amazing, although I'm not too crazy about the heat."

"That is hard to believe," he laughed. "I'm pretty sure my poor body would be vaporized before I got close. But there was one other thing, Nan. When you spoke to the General about Orto Nong, you spoke of a Hopestone. What is that? I've heard of Heartstones, like the two on Earth, but never the other."

She moved next to him on the couch and held his hand, resting her head on his shoulder. "You know Bill, I am a bit tired. But let me try to tell you. First of all, every planet only has one Heartstone. What you think is a second is the Hopestone. The Heartstone is always fairly close to the surface, because the people are supposed to find it when they are ready. It provides a safety valve for the physical universe as well as a portal for advanced societies to travel the stars. As the universe expands, it will be increasingly difficult to use space travel to get around. The portals make it simple. It's like God's shortcut. All of our societies are supposed to interact, just like we are now. The Hopestone is very different. It is buried deep in the planet and is not supposed to be found. It provides a different kind of connection to all of reality. All of our spirits are linked through our Hopestones."

"What about those black and clear stones you added to my suit?" Bill asked. I thought they came from the two Heartstones on Bala Napor."

"The black stones did, Bill," she replied in a very soft voice. "The clear ones are from the Hopestone. My planet was destroyed by a nova. We had no hope and did not want to leave it behind. After the last men had left the planet, we unearthed the Hopestone and broke it into pieces. The ice wizards are the guardians of the stone now. If the stone had been destroyed by the nova, none of us would have a spiritual connection and we would have descended into savagery like the black mages. The clear stones keep us safe and grounded in our faith. That's why I gave some to you. I only gave black stones to the others so we could communicate." Her eyes were closed and her breathing was becoming very deep.

"But why Nan?" Bill asked. "I don't understand. Why me?"

She opened her eyes and looked up at him. "It's because I love you, Bill." She reached up and kissed his lips. "I've never met anyone like you. You have such love and compassion inside of you. Plus you have incredible powers like I've never seen."

"I have incredible powers?" he asked. "I'm just a man, Nan."

"And I'm just a woman, Bill. You saw what I did today. When you discover the strength within you, you will be much stronger than me. How could I help falling in love with you?" She nestled her head against his chest and fell asleep.

Bill sat there a few minutes trying to understand what she had said. He was not a mage or a wizard, just a sheep rancher. He longed for those simple days, now gone forever. He lost the ranch and sold his sheep. Now he was infinitely far away on a strange planet with a beautiful wizard sleeping in his arms. There must be some other explanation, he thought. He stood slowly and set her head on a cushion. He took a heavy blanket and covered her with it. He smiled down at her, then leaned forward and kissed her cheek. "Good night, Nan," he whispered. She smiled but did not awaken.

He was walking toward the bedroom when a sharp pain shot through his head. He stumbled and turned back and sat on a chair opposite where Nan was sleeping. He closed his eyes and tried to clear his mind. Pushing the pain aside, he thought he could see Cybil sitting a few feet away from him. She was with her father Frank and Elder Jane Virtue.

"Elder, what happened to you?" Frank asked. "I thought you were meeting at the UN today."

"My God, Frank, we've made a terrible mistake," she mumbled with tears flowing down her cheeks. "Please forgive me, but we didn't know."

"Know what, Elder?" he demanded. "What are you hiding from me?"

"It's like I told you, Daddy," Cybil said. "I begged you not to take me here, but you refused. A black mage took grandma and used her to make a circle of mages on Earth."

"What are you talking about, Cybil?" he asked. "Elder, what's going on here?"

"Just listen to her, Frank. She is speaking the truth. I didn't believe it myself before, but I have seen a mage on Earth and your planet is now totally under his control," Jane replied.

"Don't be afraid, Elder," Cybil smiled. "Everything is going to be okay soon." She turned to her father. "Daddy, I am the Singer of Praises, the Cantu Bagwa. As long as I was on Earth, the mages could not form a circle. Now that I am here, they have done so, and will now rule Earth as slave masters until we take the planet back."

"I don't understand, honey," he said. "Whose praises do you sing and what happened to grandma?"

"Don't be silly, Daddy, it's just a title," she replied. "Grandma is safe now, though. She is with grandpa and the ice wizard."

"Ice wizard, what kind of nonsense is this Elder?" he shouted.

"Please be calm, Frank, this isn't helping any of us," Jane begged. "The talk of mages and wizards is the stuff of legends on this planet. We have never encountered any of them until my meeting at the UN today. According to the legends of Far Sun, the Singer of Praises is the physical embodiment of the Heartstone. That person is supposed to have the same power as the stone and can protect the planet from others using it for evil."

"Actually, the Cantu Bagwa is the master of the Heartstone and the Hopestone," Cybil interrupted. "Fortunately, the black mages don't know what a Hopestone is." She giggled. "They think it's just a second Heartstone. But it's not. It is linked to all the power in the universe. The Cantu Bagwa has all the power in the universe when she is on her planet. Elder, do you know who is the Cantu Bagwa for Far Sun?"

"No dear. We have an honorary title of Singer of Praises, but that person has no power that I know of," Jane replied. "Do you know who it is?"

Cybil giggled again. "Of course I do. I recognized her when I met her on Earth. She came to my house. Sentinel August Reason is the Cantu Bagwa of Far Sun."

"But she is lost too," Jane sighed. "So there is no hope for my planet either."

"Of course there is, Jane," Cybil said as she walked over and took the Elder's hands. She reached forward and kissed Jane on the cheek. "Daddy, you come over here too, and let's form a circle."

He stood and walked over to the others, taking one of each of their hands. "What's this all about, Cybil?"

"Please Daddy, take this seriously," his daughter chastised. "Just close your eyes and try to keep your minds clear. I am sensing someone reaching out to us right now. Someone who is more worried about us than we are about him. Open your minds and hearts." They stood silently for a minute. The air in the room became electrified and each could feel their hair standing on end. "Now open your eyes and say 'Hi' to Grandpa."

When they opened their eyes, a shimmery blob of energy floated between them. Gradually, it coalesced into a figure of light that looked like Bill Marshall. He smiled at them and caressed Cybil's face.

"Dad, where are you?" Frank asked. "How can you be here?"

"Frankly son, I have no idea," Bill laughed. "But you need to know that your mother and I are safe here with Nan-bo-Nan, the ice wizard. Elder, Lance, and August are here with me too. We are recruiting the Ballanan army to join us fighting the circle of mages. I'm not certain what's going to happen tomorrow, but please know that I love you all and will be with you soon." The image faded and the three stood silently, not certain what to think about the sudden appearance.

"That was amazing," Jane gasped. "Cybil, was that really Bill Marshall?"

"Or course, didn't you recognize him?" she laughed.

"How was that possible? Did you bring him here, Cybil?" Frank asked.

"I helped a little," she smiled. "But grandpa is a lot stronger than any of us know. After feeling him reach out to us, I knew immediately he had to be the Candu Mali Siwa."

"And what does that mean, honey?" Jane asked.

"I'm not really sure," Cybil said looking confused. "The words just came to me. Perhaps the ice wizard can translate. Well, I'm very tired, so I think I'll go to bed now." She kissed the two and walked to her bedroom.

Keedu sat straight up in bed. Rivers of sweat poured down his face and his bed was drenched. He was shivering and shaking uncontrollably. Baku burst into the room, sensing that something horrible was wrong with his friend. "What's wrong, Keedu?" he asked. "Your emotions woke me up from a sound sleep."

"You remember the Cantu Bagwa from this planet?" he questioned. "I saw her in my dream."

"So what? That little girl is on another planet. She is no threat to us," Baku laughed. "And here you are crying in your bed. What happened to you? Do I have to exile you along with your sister, Umdala?"

"Shut up, Baku!" he shouted. "I'm not afraid of the Cantu Bagwa as long as she's on another planet."

"Then what's the matter, old friend," he urged. "What happened to frighten you so much?"

"She was in a room on Far Sun with two others. I don't know what they were saying. After some time, they stood in a circle and held hands."

"That is frightening," Baku laughed.

"I told you to shut up!" Keedu snarled. "That wasn't it at all. After they broke their circle, she said three words that I did hear."

"What did she say?" Baku asked.

"She said Candu Mali Siwa," Keedu sighed.

"Oh my God," Baku said, sitting heavily on the bed. "But that is just a legend, Keedu. It's an old woman's tale from ancient history."

"I don't think so," Keedu continued. "There was powerful energy in that room. I could feel it from here. You don't think the Candu Mali Siwa is going to help these humans, do you?"

"Baku, I'm still hoping you dreamt the whole thing!" Baku laughed. "Let's not over-think this, old friend. You'll be fine in the morning. Get some sleep."

Chapter 82

Bill rose early and took a hot shower. The steam and heat revitalized him for another day. He closed his eyes and let the water wash over his face. He felt two hands reach around him and hold him tight. He turned to kiss his wife and found Nan instead. "Pasha, what are you doing here? For God's sake, Bonnie is asleep in the other room."

She looked into his eyes and kissed his forehead, saying, "Did you just call me Pasha? Thank you for that, Bill."

"I guess I did, but I don't know why," he said as he tried to escape from her hug. He felt her body tight against his and thought again for a moment about Tactic 87. He knew he had to keep his mind clear and broke her grip. "I don't think this is right, Nan."

Nan frowned and closed her eyes. Bill noticed her slender yet beautiful body with the rain of water flowing over her shoulders and down her chest. He felt himself losing control and turned to face the wall. "It's okay, Bill," she said finally. "Your sense of integrity and honor impresses me greatly, perhaps even more than my physical desire for you." She kissed his back and ran her hands down his sides. "I just wanted to thank you for helping me to sleep and covering me with the blanket last night. You are a true friend. By the way, Pasha is a very intimate term of endearment in our ancient language. It implies almost a holy connection between souls."

Bill turned to face her and looked into her icy blue eyes. "Then I meant it completely, Pasha. But you know my wife is in the other room, and I wouldn't dishonor her even if she was in another galaxy."

Nan smiled and kissed Bill on the lips, hugging him tightly one more time so he could feel her passion. "I have felt for some time my destiny is to be the Eretz Domma, but I thought I would explore our connection again just for fun. I told you last night I loved you, and that will never change. And now that I am your Pasha, I know your feelings are as strong and real as mine. I'll prepare the coffee." Bill was standing in the shower alone. He stood there for a moment and let the hot water run over his head. Then he turned off the water and dried off.

Nan stood naked in the room with the glass chamber. Umdala's crucifixion wounds were almost healed and the small cuts were completely gone. She leaned over the case and pressed her body against it, while her mind reached out to the mage. "Byu, can you hear me?" she thought.

"What? Who are you to reach out to me with my own name?" he thought. "Where am I? Is that you, Keedu?"

"No, Byu, it is me, Nandez Bonanifas Ziulu," she thought. "I am an ice wizard, and you are on my planet recovering from your injuries."

"I don't understand, Ulu," he replied. "Why am I here and who injured me so? I can feel the loss of blood and flesh, but don't remember."

"Let your mind touch mine, Umdala Paraka Byulani," she thought. "You are still quite weak, but my thoughts can help you remember."

"How can I trust you, Ulu?" he argued. "Perhaps you have done this to me. Let me go back to my friends."

"Calm down, Byu!" she shouted in her mind. "Remember that you were in a circle of twelve mages on Earth. How could a weak woman like me snatch you from there? Think man, think!"

"I do remember that," he thought. "And I remember them dancing around me and threatening to kill me. I begged them to leave my planet alone, but they just laughed and kept dancing about."

"Good, Byu, you are remembering now, please continue," she said, relieved.

"Keedu called me a woman and threatened to send me to an ice wizard where I would have the company of another female. I couldn't believe it was my own loyalty to Keedu that caused this to happen." Tears streamed out of Umdala's eyes and his body trembled. "Then I felt my body dissolving. I begged them to stop but they kept laughing at me."

"And then what happened, Byu?" Nan asked.

"I felt my body flying uncontrollably through space. I tried to change my course to the planets I passed, but I had no control. After what seemed to be hours, I began to fall through a heavy atmosphere. The skin on my back burned and blistered. I thought only about how I wished to be dead to make it stop. Then I crashed into a stone wall. I could feel my bones breaking. But I didn't slip down to the ground. I opened my eyes and saw myself glued to the wall several feet off the ground. As I looked forward I could see four massive spikes flying right at me. I prayed they would pierce my head and heart to end the torture, but they did not. Instead, they impaled my hands and feet. I wanted to shriek in pain, but passed out instead."

"And those are the friends you want me to send you back to?" Nan thought.

"No! Please don't Ulu," he begged. "Will I survive this?"

"Of course, Byu," she giggled. "It was a difficult recovery, but you are doing quite well now. I think you'll be able to leave the healing chamber in another day or two."

"Why have you done this, Ulu?" he asked. "Certainly, I don't deserve it."

"I disagree, Byu. I sense great compassion in you. I think you might help return our people to their rightful course, if you know what I mean," she replied.

"I don't think I'm worthy of the Eretz Domma, Ulu," he thought. "It's been too long for our people. Perhaps you should just kill me now. If my brothers reach out to me, I will likely turn against you."

"I don't think so, but that is a risk I am willing to take, Byu," she said. "But rest now so you can think with a clearer mind later, my love." She moved away from the chamber and her uniform appeared on her body. She smiled at the mage and wiped tears from her eyes.

Keedu sat silently in the chamber room in Umdala's residence. The other ten mages were chatting among themselves and arguing over which parts of Earth each would rule. He watched them bicker like children and hated them for their avarice and stupidity. Bola and Iglu were arm wrestling for India. Baku and the others were watching and laughing. "Bola, you are such a weakling!" Iglu laughed.

"You haven't beat me yet, Iglu!" Bola sneered. "You can have China if you like. There are almost as many people to torture there. We agreed to that last night over whisky, don't you remember?"

"I changed my mind," Iglu said. "I am stronger and I get my choice first!"

"Shut up and stop it all of you!" Keedu shouted as he stepped in to break up the fight. "I did not bring you here to play with this planet. This planet is nothing! We have important business and I demand this circle come to order!" The other mages stood looking shocked that Keedu would break up their fun.

"Brother, we meant no harm. It was just a bit of play," Iglu said.

"We don't have time for that anymore," Keedu replied. "The Ballanan army will come this way soon and we must be prepared."

"But we are a circle now, and this is not their home world," Baku argued. "They have no power against us. Why are you afraid?"

"I had a vision in my dreams last night," Keedu responded. "I saw the end of black mages. I saw our defeat here and across the universe."

"Our brother has foreseen the Candu Mali Siwa," Baku interjected. The mages looked stunned and sat in the circle. "But perhaps it was just a dream, brother?"

"We still need to take the appropriate steps," Keedu warned. "We must do everything we can to prevent the Candu Mali Siwa from coming here. Have all the Beings from Far Sun been exiled?"

"Yes, Lord Keedu," Baku answered. "I took care of it personally. Our sentinels at the portal key have orders to keep Far Sun from connecting. If it does, they have orders to kill anything that tries to pass through the portal."

"That is some good news," Keedu sighed. "Thank you, Baku. I knew I could count on you. If I may ask, please have them prevent Goola from attaching as well."

"Of course, Lord Keedu. Consider it done," Baku replied.

Bola had put his arm around Iglu's shoulders. "You can count on us too, Lord Keedu. Just tell us what we need to do."

"I appreciate it, boys. In fact I do have an assignment for you two," Keedu smiled. "As you know, the Cantu Bagwa has escaped to Far Sun. I need you two to go there and kill her. She is the greatest threat to us on this planet, but her powers are limited there."

"Killing the Cantu Bagwa is a big job, Lord Keedu," Iglu replied. "Do you think the two of us are enough?"

"Well, do what you can. If you can't kill her, do what you can to keep Far Sun from sending her back here. Kill a few thousand sentinels. That should slow them down," Keedu howled with laughter. The other mages began to laugh as well.

"Yes, Lord Keedu," both mages said. They melted into a cloud of black smoke which spun around the room and then shot out into space.

Bill woke Bonnie up and carried her to the bathroom where she could get ready for the day. He kissed her warmly and left to have the coffee that Nan had promised. As he entered the main room, he saw August lying on the floor sobbing inconsolably. He rushed over to her and lifted her up and set her on the couch. He sat next to her and put his arm around her shoulders. "August, what's wrong? What happened?"

At that moment, Nan emerged from the chamber room and rushed over to them. "What has happened, August?"

"I'm not sure," she said, wiping the tears from her face. "I was coming to get some coffee and a horrible feeling shot through my body. I was overcome with sorrow and collapsed to the floor. I have a feeling something horrible is happening on Far Sun."

Nan closed her eyes and thought about the planet, but felt nothing. "I feel like I'm being blocked or something. What about you Bill?"

Bill closed his eyes for a second and then opened them widely. "My God, Pasha, there are two mages on Far Sun. They are trying to find Cybil and are slaughtering everyone they can. We've got to do something!"

"Just relax you two," Nan urged. "Everything will be okay. Let me think for a second." While she paced back and forth, Lance and Bonnie joined the others. Bill told them about what was happening.

Nan sat on the couch next to Bill. "Bill, please hold my hand. I need your strength to help me see through the fog."

He took her hand and said, "Of course, Pasha."

After a few seconds, she opened her eyes, which welled with tears. "Okay, I am being blocked by someone, so I do not have the power to send you to Far Sun, but the Ballanan are waiting for you. I need to stay here with the black mage, but all four of you should go right away. Bill and August, please stand and join hands with the others." They stood and formed a circle. "Have a safe trip!" She nodded her head and the four were gone. She rose and went to pour a cup of coffee.

<h1 style="text-align:center">Chapter 33</h1>

The four appeared in the center square outside the steps to the stone temple. The Ballanan warriors were stunned by their miraculous appearance and moved back quickly to form a circle around them. Having heard the commotion, General Atar Nbele rushed out of his headquarters toward the square. He pushed his men aside and saw the four humans standing in the center. He frowned and hurried toward them. "Where is the ice wizard?" he said. "I was expecting her today."

"General, we need to get to Far Sun as soon as possible," Bill replied. "There are black mages there senselessly killing people."

"You can go, but you have to go alone," he said. "My superiors have not authorized us to leave here yet. They want someone to meet with our Council of Elders and plead the case."

"We don't have time for this," August pleaded. "The tragedy is still happening. I have to get back there now!"

"August, please calm down for a second," Bill urged. He took her hands in his. "August close your eyes and let my mind touch yours, please. This is important."

"My mind is a blank, Bill," she cried. "What do you see?"

"It's not good, August," he stammered. "Hundreds of sentinels are dead and the mages are moving quickly toward the safe house where Cybil is staying." He closed his eyes again and raised his head skyward. He was lost in thought.

"Bill, come on now. Stop wasting time!" Lance urged. "We've got to get there now."

Bill opened his eyes and looked at Lance. "I put a thought into the mages' minds about August. I could feel their panic. Do you know what that means?"

"I have no idea, Bill," Lance replied. "But we don't have time for guessing games."

Bill pulled August close to him and whispered in her ear, "August, you are the Cantu Bagwa for Far Sun."

"What does that mean?" she asked. "If I go there, they'll try to kill me too? I don't care, I have to go."

"Please listen to me, August," he whispered. "The mages cannot harm you if you are on Far Sun. You are the Soul of the Planet. The Heartstone and Hopestone serve you alone. My granddaughter Cybil is the Cantu Bagwa for Earth. She is on Far Sun and is helping you even now. Find her and protect her." He kissed her on the cheek. "Please remember the mages cannot harm you. They will try, but their powers are nothing compared to yours. Please believe me." He kissed her again and let her go, turning to the general. "General, please connect the portal to Far Sun and allow Lance and August to go through. Lance, please remember that August must go first, otherwise she cannot protect you. Once she is safely there, the mages will begin to lose their battle. Then connect to Orto Nong, and Bonnie and I will travel there to meet with your Council."

"I sort of told the Council the ice wizard would do that, Bill," Atar snarled. "They will be very disappointed."

"Perhaps, but that cannot be helped now," Bill said. "Let's hurry, there's no time to waste." The group ran from the square and began to ascend the steps to the temple entrance. The soldiers guarding the temple stepped aside to form a corridor for them to hurry through. They moved quickly through the temple and into the tunnel leading to the portal room. The guards were shocked to see General Nbele rush into their presence.

"Men, set the portal to Far Sun!" Atar shouted to them.

"I'll help with the settings," Lance said as he ran behind the control panel and began turning knobs and pressing keys. In a few seconds, the familiar hillside leading up to Lance's cottage appeared. It was a scene of carnage, with dozens of bodies lying on the ground and first responder teams trying to help the survivors. Lance turned to the Ballanan soldier and said, "Don't let these settings change until we're through." Then he ran back to August, who was overcome with emotion at the image on the other side of the portal. He turned and smiled at Bill and Bonnie. He kissed August on the cheek and picked her up in his arms, holding her tightly. Then he ran through the portal. When the general saw them on the other side, he ordered the guard to change the settings to Orto Nong.

After a minute, the portal was locked again. It was night on Orto Nong, but floodlights cast sharp shadows on the gun emplacements protecting the portal. General Nbele walked through the portal and talked to the commander on site. After a few minutes, he motioned for Bill and Bonnie to step through.

"Are you sure this is the right thing to do?" Bonnie asked as she held his hand.

"No, darling, I'm not. But it is the only thing we can do," he replied and kissed her lips. "But there is one problem. The uniform you're wearing is great for combat, but that is not your role here." He put his hands over her head and moved them down her sides. The tight body armor changed into flowing robes. "There, now you look like an elder from both Earth and Goola. Let's go, sweetie-pie." He took her hand and they walked slowly through the portal and onto Orto Nong.

"Something feels terribly wrong, Iglu," Bola said, as he stood outside the safe house. The bodies of fifty dead sentinels were strewn about them. "My mental connection to Lord Keedu is broken. I cannot feel our circle anymore."

"You idiot," Iglu laughed. "Keedu probably did that intentionally to keep us sharp. Obviously we have not killed enough sentinels yet."

"I'm not so sure, brother," Bola replied. "It's something else."

While they spoke, the door to the safe house opened and Cybil Marshall stepped out. The mages turned when they heard her mother screaming for her to come back inside. The little girl smiled at them.

"Cantu Bagwa, you are making our job too easy," Iglu laughed again. "Come on brother, it's time to do the job we were sent here for."

"Brother, I think we should reconsider," Bola said, cringing at the sight of the small child. "Iglu, she is the Cantu Bagwa. I feel that we are in over our heads."

"Bola, you are a moron. This child is the Cantu Bagwa of Earth, not this planet. She has no power here. Either join with me in killing her or I'll kill you too!" Iglu shouted.

"Perhaps your brother is right, Iglu Nasto Baloy," Cybil said. "You read about the powers of the Cantu Bagwa in an ancient text. How do you know it was right? Perhaps I will kill you where you stand!"

"The child is threatening us, Bola! You must fight with me now!" Iglu screamed as he pointed his arms at her. Streams of fire shot from his fingertips toward Cybil, who stood calmly. Bola joined and fired at her as well. The walls and door behind her were on fire and beginning to crumble. The child just stood there smiling at them.

"I'm trying as hard as I can, Iglu!" Bola cried. "It's doesn't seem to affect the girl. Perhaps we should flee."

"You run away and I will hunt you down and kill you if it is the last thing I do, brother," Iglu screamed back. They redoubled their efforts and the flames from their fingers became white hot. The door behind Cybil exploded in a ball of charred shards, revealing Frank and Cindy Marshall and Elder Jane Virtue cowering on the ground. "Well, if we can't kill her, we will kill her parents. Do it Bola!"

The mages focused their fire on the innocents in the room, but a light blue bubble of light covered them, absorbing the power of the flames. The bubble glowed white and its power surged through Cybil's body. She extended one finger and the two mages were knocked back and collapsed on the ground. Bola was panting hard and covered in burns and sweat. "We must flee, brother," he whimpered. "The battle is lost."

"Never, coward," Iglu said as he climbed to his feet. He withdrew his blade from its sheath and approached the child who remained standing and smiling. "Perhaps you can fight our energy blasts, but this blade will split you in half, Cantu Bagwa."

"Do your worst, mage. I am not afraid of you," Cybil said. "You are too weak to harm anyone else now, isn't that right, August?"

A voice behind Iglu said, "That's right Cybil. I am here now to save you." Iglu spun around to see the tall redhead standing ten feet from him, with one foot on Bola's chest, who was begging for mercy.

"Oh, good," Iglu grinned. "I thought I killed all the sentinels. It's nice to find another to make my day. And you are a pretty girl. Too bad I have to chop off you head." He walked toward her. "Perhaps if you release my cowardly brother, I shall make your death quick and somewhat less painful."

"You've overestimated yourself, Baloy," August sneered. "Do what you will, but you will be dead in a few seconds."

"Iglu, please stop," Bola implored. "This woman is the Cantu Bagwa of this planet, I can feel it. You cannot harm her."

"Frankly, I've had enough of these old legends. I am a black mage, the most powerful Being in the universe. Everything else is old wives' tales," Iglu laughed. He continued to walk up to August who did not flinch. He pulled back his arm and then thrust the blade into her chest. Iglu looked confused. He could see the hilt of his blade resting on her clothes, but she still stood looking perfectly well. He pulled his blade back, but only the hilt was there. "What have you done, sentinel?"

"Nothing yet, mage," August smiled. She pulled open her breastplate to show Iglu that she was not harmed. She then winked at Cybil who giggled. August snapped her fingers and Iglu froze in place. Gradually, his body turned to ash as if being consumed by fire from inside. She blew on the ashen figure and the cloud of ashes blew away in the breeze. She sat down on Bola's chest and looked him in the eye. "Now what am I to do with you?" she asked. "You did fire on the poor little girl, which was very bad."

"Cantu Bagwa, please show some mercy," he begged. "Iglu said he would kill me if I did not help him."

Cybil had walked over and stood next to August. "That is true, August, I heard the other say those words."

"Bola Untola Zimafar, that is a beautiful name," August said. "Are you a coward, a woman, or an idiot?"

"Probably all three, Cantu Bagwa," the mage replied. "I do not want to die. That I know for certain."

"Well, you and your friend killed too many sentinels to go unpunished," August argued.

"August, I have something for you that will lessen his crime," Cybil said.

August looked sternly at Bola and said, "Don't move if you want to live." She stood and walked a few steps away with Cybil. "What do you have, Cybil?"

Cybil cupped her hands together and then opened them to reveal a shimmery glass globe. "August, I was able to capture the souls of those who died here in this vessel," she said. "As the Cantu Bagwa, you can revive them."

"Cybil, you haven't been a Cantu Bagwa that long. How do you know so much?" August smiled and touched her head.

"You have to be open, August," she smiled back. "You already know all of this, but you just have to believe it. Now take the globe, kiss it, and then pray for the lives of those souls." August followed the orders. "Now, squeeze the globe between your hands until it breaks. Then open your hands and allow the spirits to float into the air."

August did as she was told and the bits of dust filled the air around them, and most flew away in the wind. While they watched, the dead bodies of the sentinels healed and they began to sit up and breathe again. "Wow! I did that?"

"You see, August, it's good to be the Cantu Bagwa!" Cybil laughed as she hugged August. "But now I need your help. We need to go to the portal and connect to Earth. Keep my family here, but I need to go through the portal."

"I don't know, honey," Frank said as he joined them. "It will be very dangerous there. The mages are in complete control."

Cybil hugged her father. "Daddy, didn't you see what just happened here? The mages have no power over me if I am on Earth." She turned her attention to August. "Where is my grandpa?"

"He and your grandmother went to Orto Nong to ask the Ballanan to help with the battle on Earth,"

August answered. "Do you need him on Earth? I can go there and get him."

Cybil shook her head. "August, you can never leave Far Sun while the mages are still powerful. They could come back at any time if you leave. I will be fine on Earth without my grandpa, and the Ballanan need him there now more than ever."

"I don't understand," August said.

"Of course you do, silly. Just accept that what you feel is true and all will be clear," Cybil said. "We need to go to the portal now before more humans are injured."

"But what about the mage?" August said as she pointed to Bola lying shivering and shaking on the ground.

"How about the zongo planet?" Cybil asked.

"Great idea," August laughed. She walked over to Bola who was on the verge of passing out from fear. "Zima, for some reason, I feel compassion for you, even though you have never felt that emotion. I am going to send you to your Lord Keedu's former planet. Be good, because Cybil and I will be keeping an eye on you. If you behave until after the war is won, I will try to find an ice wizard to take mercy on you and befriend you. Is that a deal?"

"Bless you Cantu Bagwa," he grinned. "Bless you both, please let me tell you how . . ."

"Enough," August said as she snapped her fingers. Bola was gone.

Chapter 34

Keedu and the other mages were walking along Fifth Avenue in Manhattan when Keedu suddenly doubled over in pain. The others formed a tight circle around him. "Lord Keedu, what is wrong?" Baku asked.

"Iglu is dead and Bola has been banished from Far Sun. It was the work of the Cantu Bagwa who has returned to that horrible planet," Keedu said as he tried to straighten up. "She also resurrected the sentinels they had been able to kill. The tide of this war is turning against us, brothers."

Ika replied, "Lord Keedu, without Iglu and Bola we do not have enough mages to form a circle. If the Cantu Bagwa from Earth returns here, all is lost!"

"Don't be a coward, Ika!" Baku scoffed. "Lord Keedu will have a solution, right sir?"

"Ika, even you should know that two mages could never handle a Cantu Bagwa," Keedu laughed. "I fear that nine may not be enough here either, however, we are still here and we can call all the other mages to our assistance before she arrives." Let's form a circle and begin the chant. Baku and Keedu raised their arms, and the cars and pedestrians were pushed back in all directions until the entire block was empty. The mages formed a tight circle and wrapped their arms around each other's shoulders and began to move around the circle and shout.

A strong wind poured down the street raising a cloud of dust and debris. The people on the street rushed for cover as trash cans and dumpsters began to fly around and crash into buildings. The mages were singing now and their voices became so loud that nearby windows began to shatter. Black clouds circled overhead and the winds sped up to almost hurricane force. Crooked fingers of black smoke began to shoot through the air and strike the ground around them. As each cloud cleared, a new mage appeared. The new mages began to form a second circle around the first, dancing in the opposite direction.

Within minutes, tens of thousands of mages filled the streets shouting and singing praises to Lord Keedu. And still they danced. The sound was so loud that the buildings themselves began to shake and vibrate with the sounds. Lightning shot through the mages and they laughed and sang all the more. Then, in one instant, the clouds cleared and the winds stopped. More thin fingers of black smoke shot through the air. When they landed, only the charred bones of dead mages lay in piles on the ground. Keedu shouted to get the group to stop. As they did, the smell of death was heavy in the air. Oali, one of the last mages to arrive safely stood over the bones of a dead mage. Keedu walked over to him and put his arm on his shoulder.

"Lord Keedu, these are the bones of my dearest friend," he cried. "We were very far from here, but came as quickly as we heard your call. What has happened here?"

"Oali, I am very sorry for your friend," Keedu said, rubbing his shoulders. "Only one thing could cause this, my brother. The Cantu Bagwa has returned, as I have foretold."

Moments before, August and Cybil stood next to the portal key on Far Sun. The key was set for maximum defense as the humans had orders to shoot when the Far Sun portal key attempted to connect. "August, I am afraid it is too dangerous to connect. You and Cybil will be easy targets for them," Lance said from the control panel.

"Don't be afraid, Lance," Cybil smiled. "No one can be harmed on this world while August is here, and I cannot be harmed on Earth. This is the way it must be." She turned to August and held her hands. "You need to focus your mind on a bubble of energy that will block the portal key, reaching right up to the line where it touches Earth. Then you need to try very hard to extend your bubble at least a few feet onto the other side. That will give me time to step through the portal and be safely on Earth. Do you understand?"

"Not really, Cybil. I'm still new at this," August replied. "But I will try."

"Trying isn't good enough, August," Cybil frowned. "Listen to me, you have the power! You saw what you did earlier to the mage and reviving your friends, right? Have faith in yourself, like I do. You are the most powerful Being on this planet. The stones serve you alone. If you know that and do this, then I can save Earth."

"But you helped me here, Cybil," August sighed, feeling hopeless. "There, you will be all alone, and you're just a small girl. Perhaps I should come with you?"

"All I did was protect my family and the souls of the murdered sentinels, August," the girl replied. "You did the rest. I could never have done that on this world. But I can on Earth. Let's do this now."

August stood in front of the portal, which was not connected to any planet. She closed her eyes and said a small prayer for strength. Then she opened her eyes and concentrated on the portal key. She thought about protecting Far Sun and Cybil Marshall. Soon she was surrounded by a bubble of bright blue light. She focused on the portal and extended the bubble forward until it touched the open portal. "Okay, Lance, make the connection to Earth!" she shouted. After a minute, the grassy hill that had been the cave on Bill Marshall's land appeared. It was late morning in California. Heavy machine guns opened fire on the portal opening. The bullets dissolved as they hit the blue bubble. The troops increased their rate of fire.

"August, now push your bubble through the portal!" Cybil shouted. "Concentrate harder, this is the most critical part. Don't ease off or bullets might make it through."

August pushed with her mind and the bubble pierced the portal. A single bullet flew through the portal and zipped inches from August's head. She gritted her teeth and focused more. The bubble pushed out ten feet beyond the edge of the Earth portal. "Okay, Cybil, I think it's ready. Be safe honey."

Cybil walked in front of the portal key and watched the cascade of bullets striking the bubble on the other side. She turned and smiled back at August and Lance and stepped through onto Earth. At that same moment, the first mage was incinerated when trying to land on Earth. The troops near the Earth portal had their orders, but were now faced with a small child standing twenty feet in front of them. A couple of the soldiers stopped firing, but the rest continued. Just as Cybil approached the edge of the bubble of light, she snapped her fingers and all the guns and bullets changed to water and fell to the ground, leaving puddles around the stunned troops. She turned back to the portal and shouted, "Okay, August, that's all I need. Thank you!" She turned and walked up the hill away from the portal key.

Cybil stopped and talked to the soldiers and forgave them. She kissed some on the cheek and took the hands of two of the soldiers who had first stopped firing. The three walked away from the portal. Halfway up the hill, two mages stood in their path. "Greetings, Nasta and Jumba, my name is Cybil," she smiled.

"Ah, so the Cantu Bagwa has returned," Nasta laughed. "That was quite a show. But even a mage baby can do such things. Let's see if you can protect your new friends." He pulled his long blade from the scabbard on his back and approached them. One of the soldiers moved his body in front of the child. "Brave for a dead man!" Nasta shouted. He swung his blade and it slashed through the neck of the stunned soldier.

"Good job, Nasta!" Jumba shouted. But Nasta did not respond and the soldier stood in his tracks. Jumba looked at Nasta whose horrified expression told the whole story. Nasta's head fell to the ground and body collapsed on top of it. "What did you do, you unholy bitch?"

Cybil laughed. "Jumba, for the Cantu Bagwa, that was simple. Just like this." She snapped her fingers and Jumba turned to water and fell into a pool where he had been standing. She kissed the two soldiers on the cheek and told them everything would now be okay, and asked them to go home to their families. When they were gone from sight, she nodded her head and disappeared.

"Keedu, did you feel that?" Baku asked, racked in pain. "Jumba and Nasta are dead! What do we do now?"

"Shut up, Baku and let me think," Keedu begged.

"I know what to do!" Ika laughed. "Until the Cantu Bagwa arrives, we must kill as many of her precious people as we can. Watch me, it's fun."

"Don't be a fool, Ika. You're just going to kill yourself," Keedu chided.

"Old wives' tales, Lord Keedu," Ika scoffed. "Just watch this." He walked over to a coffee shop a few feet away where dozens of people were hiding from the storm in the street. He ripped the doors off the building and grabbed a woman cowering near the door with her two small children. They all screamed as Ika grabbed her by the waist and shook the children loose. They cried and begged Ika for mercy. All he did was laugh at them. "Look at this, Lord Keedu. I have no fear!" He pulled his blade and drove it through the screaming woman's chest. He was shocked that her expression did not change and she kept screaming. He stumbled back a step. He looked down and saw an incision in his own chest of the same size as his blade. He slowly pulled the blade from her chest and dropped her to the ground. She scrambled to recover her crying children. Ika stumbled again and sat on the pavement. A gusher of blood poured from the wound on his chest and trickles of blood oozed out of his mouth. He looked at Keedu who was frowning at him. Then he fell back dead.

"So, I take it there is no intelligence requirement to be a black mage," said a small voice across the street. Keedu turned and saw Cybil standing on the sidewalk in front of the shivering woman. "The crazy part is that you warned him yourself." She turned to the woman and her children. She kissed each on the cheek and they disappeared. "I thought I should send them home. They've been through enough today."

"If it isn't the Cantu Bagwa, returned to Earth to get rid of my brothers?" Keedu laughed. "Ika was an idiot, I grant you that. But we are not all fools. You can see I have amassed a large army. I think you do not have the power to defeat us all." He waved his army to close in around the girl who found herself pinned among them in the middle of the street. "Who is going to help you, little girl?"

"Don't you read, Keedu?" she laughed. "The Heartstone and Hopestone are already helping me."

"Not more of those ice wizard romantic meanderings about a Hopestone. There is no such thing," Keedu replied. "Perhaps my men should exile you along with Bola. My spiders like fresh young meat."

"You have quite the sense of humor, Keedu," Cybil laughed. "I didn't know mages were capable of that. But the Hopestone is real. Please, let me show you." She snapped her fingers and they were gone, leaving the mages stunned and wondering what to do.

It was cold and very dark. Keedu felt his men were far away, but he was still on Earth. "Where are we, Cantu Bagwa?"

"You can call me Cybil, if you prefer," she offered, taking his hands. "And I shall call you Zimu, if I may. We are at the location of the Hopestone. I told you I would show you." She waved her arms over her head and the moon tripled in brightness, unveiling the rugged Australian outback.

"It is beautiful here, Cybil," he replied. "If you wish to call me Zimu, please promise only to do so when we are alone. Where are we?"

"Of course, Zimu, I promise," she giggled. "This is the center of the continent of Australia. We are standing on top of Uluru. It is a mountain sacred to the native population."

"Is this rock the Hopestone?" he said. "I was hoping for something more dramatic."

"No, this is just a marker. Here, hold my hands again." He took her hands and they sank into the mountain. Down and down they went into the crust. Keedu did not know how he was still alive buried in this rock, but held her hands tightly so as not to be left here to suffocate. After several miles, they stopped on a hard surface. Cybil exhaled and a pocket of fresh air appeared around them. After releasing herself from Keedu's deathgrip on her fingers, she waved her hand over the floor and the crystal beneath them glowed bright red. "Zimu, this is the Hopestone of Earth."

"This is unbelievable," Keedu gasped. "How big is this Heartstone?"

"The Hopestone is five hundred yards in diameter," she frowned. "I said Hopestone, not Heartstone. It is a single red diamond crystal."

"I don't understand the difference and I guess I don't really care," Keedu said. "It is a second portal through the universe that somehow got buried by plate tectonics or something. Can we leave now? My men still need to kill you."

Cybil laughed out loud. "You really are a funny mage, Zimu. If you understood this stone, perhaps the Schism could end and the mages could end their blood quest. This stone represents the souls of all the life on this planet. It gives us hope there is something more than our own pitifully short lives."

"Too bad, Cybil," Keedu scoffed. "If Bala Napor ever had a Hopestone, it was destroyed in the nova. If you're going to leave me here, please kill me instead. This place is too much like a grave to me."

Cybil kissed his hands. "Zimu, I could never leave you here. That would be horrible. And I won't harm you either, unless you try to harm us. You should know the ice wizards saved the Bala Napor Hopestone and they have pieces held for the day the Schism ends. If you touch the stone, perhaps you will find hope and love."

"I don't think that is my fate, Cybil, although I do appreciate the kindly words. We mages are not sweet and huggable though. We live only for power and blood. We can never change," Keedu said.

"I disagree, Zimu," Cybil said, squeezing his hands again. "But your fate is in your own hands, not mine. I am sorry for scaring you by putting you here twenty miles under the mountain. We can go now."

"Please!" he said. Before the sound came out of his mouth, they were standing in Manhattan again, surrounded by his men. "Thank you for the interesting experience, Cantu Bagwa. But that changes nothing."

"I didn't think it would, Keedu," Cybil smiled. "In a strange way, I respect your men for following you, even when there is no chance for success. Do what you want."

"You heard her, mages, let's show the Cantu Bagwa the power of a hundred thousand mages!" Keedu shouted as they all fired at her with white flame from their fingers. A massive white hot ball of plasma surrounded her tiny body. They doubled their effort and she fell to the ground covering her head with her hands. The edge of the plasma was within millimeters of her skin. The windows and facades of nearby buildings began to melt and a river of molten glass and metal poured down the street. Cybil's face was contorted with fear and effort as she pushed back with all of her might. "It's almost the end, boys! Turn up the heat," Keedu shouted again as the inner circle of mages moved forward to watch Cybil be incinerated by their fire.

Then Cybil looked up and laughed. Keedu couldn't believe his eyes. She stood and was smiling and shaking her index finger at him. She dropped her hands to her sides and closed her eyes. The mass of plasma shot into her body and an exploding fireball shot through her. As it cleared, Cybil was still standing and smiling. Her body was intensely bright white and the mages had to turn their heads to avoid blindness. She continued to laugh as she raised her hands up. All the mages were pulled up in the air inside a massive bright blue ball of energy. They struggled to move and escape but could not. Cybil began to spin the ball and toss it around the open space. The mages were tumbling around each other and crashing into the walls of the sphere. Finally, she let the ball fly a hundred feet in the air. Then it turned into water and the mages crashed to the ground and floundered around gasping for breath.

Cybil spoke into the minds of each mage at that moment, using their given names. "Zimu, this battle is lost for you. What you have seen is only the smallest part of my abilities. If you leave this place now and vow never to return, I will allow you safe passage. You can choose to fight here again and now, but there will be no mercy a second time." One by one, the mages shot up into the sky and escaped. Cybil walked over to Keedu, who was still trying to breathe. "Don't leave yet, Zimu," she said. "I need to show you one more thing." She helped him to his feet.

He looked down at her smiling face. "You have won the day, Cybil. I can't thank you enough for not killing more of my brothers. I will leave now."

"In a moment, Zimu," she giggled. "I have not killed any mage this day, not even Ika who deserves death for what he did."

"I know, Cybil," he panted. "They killed themselves by going against the Cantu Bagwa."

"That's not what I mean at all, Zimu," she frowned. "Just relax and listen for a minute. You can run away when I'm finished." Resigned, he sat on the curb and waited for her to speak her mind. "Here, I want you to hold this," she said as she cupped her hands. When she opened them, a small crystal globe was between them. She handed it to him.

"A gift for losing a battle," Zimu said. "Hm. That's a very strange custom here on Earth."

"There's that mage sense of humor again," she laughed. "Please just do what I said. Trust me, it's a good thing. Now kiss the globe and say a prayer for those who died today."

"That's not really our custom, Cybil," he chuckled.

"Just shut up and do it," she demanded. When he had, she said, "Now crush the globe between your hands and toss what's left into the air." A cloud of particles floated around them. As he watched, Ika's blood returned to his body and he coughed and sat up. Keedu looked around and saw sinew and flesh beginning to grow on the piles of charred bones. Within a few moments, those mages were standing around Cybil and Keedu.

"What is this, Cybil?" he asked. "Am I dreaming? What have you done?"

"Zimu, I told you earlier I did not kill any mage today," she reminded him. "Now you know I was telling the truth. Killing and murder are horrible things and the Cantu Bagwa must avoid them if possible. I have spoken with the souls of each of these men and they have sworn to stay far away from civilizations and other mages, especially you. Don't hold that against them. Their only other choice was to stay dead and have their souls released into Universal Consciousness. As you can see, they chose life." She turned to the others. "You have made your promise to me and to God. Leave now before you change your minds and make me kill you again."

Ika came over and touched Keedu on the shoulder. "Lord Keedu, I am sorry for my vile act before. I apologize for my stupidity. Live well, brother." He shot up into the sky and disappeared along with the others.

"Now what happens, Cybil," Keedu asked. "I'm sure you know the future, so save me some time."

"I'm not a seer, Zimu," she laughed. "I know you and your men will go to Goola to face Nan-bo-Nan and Umdala and to Orto Nong to try to destroy the Ballanan again. I sincerely hope you either change your mind or fail. But your personal destiny is in your hands. Here, take this." She handed him a small red stone.

"Ah, the Hopestone," he laughed. "You really think there is hope for me, Cybil."

"As long as there is life, there is hope, Zimu," she said kissing him on the cheek. "And as you just saw, often there is hope even after death. But don't press your luck."

"I think we can prevail in those places, Cybil," Keedu considered. "We do not have to face a formidable Cantu Bagwa such as you."

"Perhaps not, Zimu, but there are more powerful forces in the universe than me," she smiled. "But I'll let you find that out for yourself."

A large crowd of people had come out of the buildings and gathered around them. They looked ready to rip Keedu limb from limb. He watched their faces and said, "I think it's time for me to go, Cybil. This has been a humbling experience for an old man like me."

"Choose life, Zimu," she smiled. "Goodbye." He shot up into the sky in a pillar of black smoke and disappeared from Earth forever. The crowd erupted into cheers and thousands of people poured into the streets to relish in their freedom.

Chapter 35

Keedu found Baku and the others as they fled Earth. He called them together and told them he would lead them to their ultimate victory on Orto Nong. He then asked Baku to take a hundred mages to Goola and dispense with the ice wizard and the coward Umdala before they joined him on Orto Nong.

Bill and Bonnie Marshall were led into the Council chamber on Orto Nong to meet with the elders. As Atar Nbele had predicted, the elders were quite disappointed not to meet the ice wizard. The meeting was not going well. The twenty elders sat at a high bench looking down on the Earthlings, while a crowd of servant girls moved among the elders with drink and documents for their review.

"Elder Marshall, am I to understand you now do not wish us to send troops to Far Sun?" the Chief Elder, Molo Indigar asked. She was an old woman with long silver hair and a deeply wrinkled face. She motioned to her servant to bring her more water. The young girl rushed over, but in her haste to serve, she spilled water on the elder's papers. Molo slapped the girl across the face and she cried and moved away quickly. "It is so difficult to find girls who do this work well."

"Chief Elder, you are correct," Bonnie replied. "The situation has now changed dramatically. I have seen the defeat of the mages on Far Sun and Earth. Now, the remaining force is coming here. We strongly recommend that you bring as many soldiers back here to protect your citizens."

"Point of order, Chief Elder," a very old Elder sitting at the end of the bench said. "I understand the visitor's concern, but we have defeated the mages before with fewer troops than we have today."

"That is an excellent point, Alakar," Molo said. "Our Council Guards still carry the Heartstone swords from so long ago." She turned back to Bonnie. "Elder, we believe we have the resources to fend for ourselves. After all, we could have defeated Earth if not for the sentinels of Far Sun. And as you say, Earth has defeated the mages. Doesn't that mean a smaller force is coming here? What makes you think we are incapable of protecting ourselves?"

"Madam, that was not my precise point," Bonnie said.

Bill was shaking his head. He stood up and said, "Elders of Orto Nong, have you forgotten your history already?"

A Council Guard pulled his blade and grabbed Bill from behind, "How dare you address the Council, soldier? I should gut you with my blade. It has not tasted blood for a long time."

"Oiala, stop it and put that weapon away!" Molo shouted. "You must remember these people do not know our customs and are trying to help us. Let him speak." The guard put his sword away and took two steps back.

"Chief Elder, I meant no disrespect," Bill said. "When the black mages came here before, they ruled this planet with impunity for many generations. It was only the Hopestone that ultimately prevailed by creating diseases to weaken them and then cleaving itself into blades to allow the Ballanan to push them back into space. How many generations of slavery are you willing to endure a second time?"

Oiala was seething with hatred and his desire to slaughter the Earthlings here and now. Only the steely gaze of the Chief Elder kept him from lashing out. "It would seem you have no confidence in us, Sentinel. If we are so weak, how did Earth and Far Sun defeat them?" Molo asked.

"The Cantu Bagwas of those planets stopped the mages, Chief Elder," he replied coldly. "Where is your Cantu Bagwa, madam?"

"We do not have the same faith in legends as you, Bill Marshall," she laughed. "You are here, many light-years away from those planets. Do you expect us to believe your story?"

"It is the only hope, Chief Elder," he said. The Council were laughing among themselves and pointing at Bill, who stood silently, gazing into space.

"Are you well, Bill?" Molo asked.

"Please forgive me, Chief Elder," he replied. "I had a vision and saw that the mage army is very close now. There is no time now to bring your soldiers back from Goola." The elders laughed again, and Molo winked at Oiala.

The guard moved quickly and withdrew his blade again. He grabbed Bill by the shoulder and spun him around, thrusting the blade into his abdomen and twisting it. "Another fool pays for his insolence with his life," he laughed as Bill doubled over. Bonnie screamed and rushed to his side. The Chief Elder's servant girl did the same. General Atar Nbele jumped from his seat and grabbed Oiala and tossed him in the air. The guard crashed against the bench.

"Treason, General!" Molo shouted. "Kill him too, Oiala!"

The guard jumped to his feet and held out his sword menacingly. The General laughed. Oiala looked at his weapon and saw only the hilt in his hand. "What is this?" he gasped. He turned to see Bill standing upright with no marks on his body. Everyone in the room could see the blade inside his body moving about until it settled just under the skin over his sternum. "I don't understand. I killed you."

Tears poured down the cheeks of Bonnie and the servant girl who held tightly onto Bill. He kissed them both on the cheek and walked over to the stunned guard. He took the hilt of the sword from his hand and dropped it to the floor. Then he kissed the guard on the cheek. "Oiala, you have the capacity to be a great man. Today you acted as a spoiled child wanting his own way. If you expect to survive the mage attack, I strongly urge you to calm down and think rationally. In order to protect this planet, I needed a piece of the

Hopestone, which you have now provided. Thank you for that."

"Okay, I don't know what's going on here," Molo said. "What just happened here, Sentinel? Who exactly are you anyway? No man could do that."

The servant girl walked over to Bill and took his hand. She turned to the bench and said, "Elders, have you forgotten the sacred texts already? Bill is the Candu Mali Siwa. He is the Master of the Stones. Now our Hopestone serves him only." She kissed Bill's hand. "Candu Mali Siwa, will you protect us please? Our elders simply forgot the truth."

"Shut up, Alani, and fetch me more water!" Molo shouted at the girl. "The Council will now meet to decide what to do next. Clear the chamber!"

Bill knelt next to the small girl and kissed her forehead. "Alani, I don't know if I am who you think, but I will do all I can to help you." He stood again and faced the bench. "There is no time to discuss anything, Elders. The mages are here."

Light-years away, a hundred mages shot through the atmosphere of Goola and landed on a broad snowy field leading up to the ice palace of Nan-bo-Nan. Baku and the others were shivering in the frigid weather. He looked around at his brothers, most of whom he had never seen before. He frowned realizing that Keedu had kept the best warriors for himself. "Brothers, we will join Lord Keedu on Orto Nong soon. Umdala, the coward, is hiding in that palace with an ice wizard. We can leave this godforsaken ice ball when they are both dead."

Akul was one of the few mages Baku had seen before. He approached Baku and said, "Brother, I am not certain we are strong enough to take on an ice wizard. Perhaps Lord Keedu could send reinforcements."

"Akul, you are a little girl," Baku scoffed. "Lord Keedu never makes a mistake. If he sent us, he expects us to succeed. Let's go."

"With all due respect, Baku," the other replied. "Lord Keedu's plans on Far Sun and Earth did not turn out so well. Please reconsider."

"If we were not so small a force, I would strike you dead myself," Baku growled. "How dare you slander Lord Keedu like that?"

Akul bowed deeply, saying, "Please forgive my impertinence, Baku. It was only an opinion, sir."

"Keep your opinions to yourself from now on, Akul," Baku barked. "Let us proceed now before we all freeze to death. The group began to march toward the palace. The temperature seemed to drop with every step they took. The snow became deeper and deeper as well, until each step was a struggle.

A little snow shower blew around them and as the wind touched their ear-holes, they heard the voice of Nan-bo-Nan speak to each of them, saying, "Brothers, welcome to Goola and my home. I know you have come to destroy Umdala and me, but I cannot allow that. Leave now before I am forced to harm you. There is no disgrace is saving your own life."

Nan was standing at a large window looking down on the rag-tag group approaching. She smiled at them, knowing they were her brothers. She felt no fear. Any fool knows a hundred mages are no match for an ice wizard. Perhaps she would have a little fun with them for a while, though. "Nan, what are you doing?" Umdala said as he approached her from behind. His wounds were almost completely healed, although he wore bandages on his hands and feet.

"Byu, don't worry. I won't allow them to harm you," she said, smiling warmly at him. "I won't hurt them either, but I want to teach them a little lesson about attacking ice wizards."

"Can't you just send them away, Ulu?" Umdala urged.

"Those men are like children, Byu," she laughed. "They won't learn without a lesson. Please trust me on this. I swear I won't harm them." She turned back to the window and watched the mages approach. Resigned to his fate, Umdala fell into a chair and began to look through the large book on Bala Napor.

The mages were halfway up the snowy slope when the snow turned to liquid water and they tumbled down the rocky slope caught in the current. When they hit the glacier, it had also turned into a vast lake of almost freezing water. The mages struggled to stay afloat and gradually began to swim back to shore. Just as they reached the edge, the water froze solid trapping them in the ice. They screamed for mercy as their bodies began to freeze. Umdala could hear them shouting, and he felt anger rising inside of him. He put the book under his arm and walked over to the window to see what was happening. Several of the mages were turning blue from hypothermia. "Stop it Ulu!" he demanded.

The mages found themselves back on the shore and warm. Baku growled and ordered the rest to follow him again up the rocky slope. They quickly reached the point where they had slipped into the deluge and focused their attention on the palace. White hot flames shot from their hands toward the palace, only to be blocked by a clear field of frigid air forming a dome over the building. "We must get closer, men!" Baku shouted and the group stopped firing and continued their march upward.

"Is all of this necessary, Nan?" Umdala said.

She turned to look at him. "I guess I am no longer your Ulu, is that right, Byu?"

"No, Ulu. I am just upset about all of this. They are my brothers and you are torturing them," he complained.

She walked up to Umdala and put her arms around his neck, kissing him on the cheek. "Byu, these men exiled you from Earth and nailed you to a wall, leaving you for dead. Now what do you want me to do? They are my brothers too."

"I know all of that, Ulu," he sighed. "But the Schism was so long ago. Men and women have not lived together in thousands of generations. Look at us. I am bent and disfigured with no ears. You look like the women in this book still. We are too different now. I fear there can be no Eretz Domma anymore. Those dreams died long ago."

She kissed his lips and said, "Byu, you are wrong! There is hope because we are together. Give love a chance to change you. I love you, Byu." They could hear the mages laughing hysterically outside and returned to the window. The mages were standing at the edge of the dome of light.

"We can hear you in there," Baku laughed, "and frankly it sickens us. Umdala, you have failed Lord Keedu once, but perhaps there is retribution for you. Join us, old friend. This place is a needless distraction. We all need to go to Orto Nong and destroy the Ballanan scourge once and for all."

"It is you who are the fool, Baku!" Nan shouted. "You should not have come here, and your stupid brother Keedu will forever regret his visit to Orto Nong. Only death lies on these worlds. Flee now before I get angry!"

"Ooh, I'm so scared," Baku laughed. "Okay, men, let's fire point blank at this force screen so we can kill them both."

Before they could act, Nan raised her arms over her head. The mages flew up from the ground and shot up two hundred thousand feet in the air, where their bodies froze solid. She dropped her arms and they plummeted downward at terminal velocity. "Nan, stop this! I beg you!" Umdala urged as he stepped up behind her. "Don't do this."

"They should have known better than to attack me!" she screamed. Umdala took the heavy book and swung it with all his might against Nan's back. Her body smashed against the glass and she fell to the floor in a heap. Umdala raised his arms and slowed the falling mages and used his mind to gradually warm them. When they landed, they were stunned to be alive. "Why, Byu?" Nan groaned. "I told you I would not harm them."

The palace exploded in a massive ball of fire. Umdala and Nan flew through the air, landing in a pile of broken ice blocks. As the laughing mages approached, Umdala scrambled to his feet. He stood astride Nan and held out his arms to protect her from the approaching men. "That's enough, Baku!" he demanded. "You have your revenge, now get out of here!"

Baku was laughing as he approached with the others. He smiled at Umdala and threw his arms around him. "Brother, you have woken up in time!" he shouted with glee. "I will tell Lord Keedu that you deserve another chance."

"I want you to leave Nan alone and go," Umdala said. "I won't let you hurt her."

"Didn't you just smash her with all your might?" Baku asked. "Now you want to deprive us of the pleasure as well? That doesn't make any sense. If you like this animal, why did you attack her?"

"I don't know, brother," he sighed. "I just couldn't stand to see her hurting you anymore. But she is a good woman and deserves to live. Can't we leave it at that?"

"No, I'm afraid not, brother," Baku spat. "Lord Keedu was right. You are indeed a weakling. You have no right to consider yourself a mage, Umdala. Normally, I would have my men here kill you as well, but considering that you made our victory possible, I will let you escape alive. But go now before I change my mind."

Tears poured out of Umdala's eyes as he looked at Nan lying helpless on the ground below them. He could sense her internal injuries and knew the mages would finish her off as soon as he left. He could fight for her now, but then he would die along with her. "Nan, I am sorry, but I can no longer help you. I hope I can forgive myself one day."

Nan coughed up blood and whispered, "I understand, Byu. I forgive you." She passed out. The mages were still laughing at Umdala, but were ready to kill him soon. He shot away from the planet in a pillar of black smoke.

"Well, boys, it's time to make Lord Keedu proud," Baku laughed. "Let's have a little fun here. No need for magic now." He kicked her in the ribs and the rest joined in.

Chapter 36

The Elder Council building exploded as the army of mages shot at it. Bricks and wood beams filled the air, settling quickly to leave a cloud of dust and debris. When the air cleared, only a bright-blue dome of light was visible. The elders and several hundred soldiers were cowering inside. Keedu led his men forward. "What is this?" he asked. "I was not aware of a Cantu Bagwa on Orto Nong? Who is doing this?"

Bill Marshall stepped through the wall of the dome and walked toward the mages. "I am the one you are looking for, Keedu."

"That's Lord Keedu to you, human," the mage sneered. "My mind tells me there is no Cantu Bagwa on this planet. Are you a mage? You don't have the figure for an ice wizard."

"No Zimu, I am none of those," he laughed. "I am the Candu Mali Siwa."

"Oh, you're a comedian, I get it," he chuckled. "That is a legend fool. And the legend says that a mage must be the Candu Mali Siwa, and you are no mage."

"It's good that you can read, Zimu," Bill replied. "But not everything in the ancient texts should be taken so literally. But I am the Master of the Stones. There are domes like this one all over Orto Nong now to protect the people. You should run away while you can."

"Stop using my given name, human!" Keedu screamed. "You are not my friend. Who in heaven are you?"

"I'm sorry, Keedu," Bill said. "I meant no disrespect. I am Bill Marshall of Earth. I believe you met my granddaughter recently. Her name is Cybil."

"Ah, you are related to the Cantu Bagwa. Is that where you get these powers?" Keedu asked.

"No, I told you I am the Candu Mali Siwa," Bill scoffed. "Can't you remember anything?"

"Oh, I remember all right Bill," Keedu laughed. "I simply don't believe it." As he spoke, the hundred mages shot to the surface and materialized in front of Keedu. "Ah, Baku, what word do you bring from Goola?"

"Master, as you requested, we have killed the ice wizard and destroyed her palace," Baku said as he bowed.

"Excellent! And what of the coward Umdala?" Keedu asked.

"Lord Keedu, I gave him clemency. It was his action alone that enabled us to defeat the ice wizard. I thought it best to complete the important mission first. We can always hunt down Umdala after our victory here," Baku replied.

Keedu could see the look of seething hatred in Bill's eyes. "Baku, you have done well. Now join the rest while we kill this weak human." Keedu turned his attention to Bill Marshall. "Human, you seem bothered. Did you know the ice wizard?"

"You son of a bitch!" Bill shouted. "You'll be in hell soon enough. Attack me!"

Keedu laughed. "Bill, you are a single man. I have fifty thousand mages here. What chance do you have?"

"More like forty thousand by my count, mage," Bill said. "Even your hundred thousand couldn't defeat my granddaughter. What makes you think you can defeat me?"

"But Bill, you're forgetting that you are not the Cantu Bagwa," Keedu giggled. "Nice knowing you. Kill him men!"

The white flames shot at Bill and his bubble surrounded him just in time. He pushed with his mind but the bubble was shrinking. It wouldn't be long before it collapsed around him. He closed his eyes to increase his concentration and saw Nan standing in front of him. She smiled and said, "Use the stones, Pashna! They will protect you!" He felt the blade under his chest and concentrated on it. The blade glowed bright white and a blast of energy from it shot out of him and knocked the mages off their feet. They flew backward and landed in piles.

"Nice trick, Bill," Keedu said as he stood again. "But we're still here and will kill you none the less. Fire again, brothers!" The blast pushed on Bill, but did not come as close as before. The stone glowed but was fading. He closed his eyes again to focus and saw Cybil smiling at him. He could feel her lips touching his cheek and her voice whispered in his ears. "Use the stones, Grandpa. You are the Candu Mali Siwa. Trust yourself to know what to do." The mages were moving forward as their fire closed in about him. He opened his hand and a small stone pushed through his skin and sat on his palm. He threw the stone into the crowd of mages, who did not notice it fly over their heads.

When the stone touched the ground, it swelled and opened a portal through which a cloud of a million vorrath zoomed skyward. They flew through the mages and inserted their proboscises in their heads and hearts. Dozens of mages screamed and fell dead. The mages broke off their attack on Bill and fought off the vorrath. Bill opened his palm and the vorrath shot back into the stone which flew up and landed on it. It sank back into his skin.

The mages stood stunned by the carnage. Keedu looked about and said, "That's quite the parlor trick, Bill. But a few casualties in war are to be expected." He turned back to his troops to order them to fire as another stone emerged from Bill's skin. He threw it into the crowd of mages. When it opened, thousands of voracious zongo crawled out and into the mass of mages. The mages tried to get away, but hundreds were stung and lay dead from poison. The zongo then crawled back into the stone and it flew back into Bill's hand.

"Have you had enough, Zimu?" Bill laughed.

Keedu looked around at his men. Most were terrified but stood by their leader. At the edges of the group, he could see some mages escaping the planet with their lives. He turned back to Bill and scowled. "You miserable piece of crap! Your efforts have little effect, but I must applaud your ability to terrorize my men. None of this will save you. In fact, let me do this myself." He pulled his blade from its scabbard and walked toward Bill, who found another stone in his hand and threw it over Keedu's head. He noticed but did not care. "You die now, Candu Mali Siwa!" He held the blade high over his head, ready to strike.

As Keedu was about to swing the blade, he heard a commotion and loud growling behind him. He turned to see several thousand ulluba moving toward his men. The largest was right behind him. He turned to Bill again and saw he was smiling. The large ulluba was Buffy, still wearing the collar of Heartstones that August had made for her. "You know what to do Buffy," Bill said. The ulluba attacked the mages, biting out large chunks of flesh and ripping off arms and legs. Buffy jumped on Keedu's back and knocked him to the ground. She then bit off his right hand with the sword still in it. Then she and the others ran back into the stone, which faithfully returned to Bill's hand.

"We're not done here, Bill Marshall," Keedu spat. "I can still kill you with one hand. I still have thousands of loyal mages here today." Bill looked up and could see more and more mages shooting back into space.

"I was hoping you would say that Keedu," Bill laughed. "And I'm very glad that your friend Baku is still here too. So, you ordered Baku to carry out the execution of the ice wizard on Goola, is that right?"

"That bitch deserved to die," Keedu said with thin lines of blood trickling out of his mouth. "The Schism was too long ago. We are supreme and it's time the ice wizards accept that."

A large clear diamond pushed through Bill's hand. "I was expecting this stone. Do you know what this is, Zimu?"

"I don't know and I don't care," Keedu said as he sat back and rested. "Here, take this, I'll never need it." He tossed a small red stone toward Bill. "Do your worst, Candu Mali Siwa."

Bill tossed the stone behind Keedu. When it opened a blisteringly cold wind shot out and white light filled the battlefield. Two hundred ice wizards shot through the air firing blasts at the retreating mages. As each was struck, he froze solid and shattered into millions of pieces. Baku came over to Keedu and touched his shoulder. The two shot up in the air and disappeared into space. Bill sat on the ground exhausted. The domes over the cities disappeared and the council rushed out to help him.

When Bonnie reached him, she pulled Bill up to his feet and hugged him. She kissed his lips and he could feel tears on her cheeks. "Oh Bill, thank God you're safe."

"I think it's all over now, sweetheart," Bill sighed. "I have to tell you I was scared out of my mind at first, but then I saw Nan and Cybil in my mind. They told me what to do." His head fell down on his chest. "I can't believe she's dead."

"She's not dead, Candu Mali Siwa," one of the ice wizards said as she approached. "The mages have all been killed or escaped, Master." She bent down and picked up the red stone Keedu had tossed at Bill.

"Nan is alive?" he gasped.

"Yes, Bill, she still lives, but barely. I am Sonjee. Nan is a close friend. Our planets are close and I can still feel her spirit, although it is weakening. You must go to her."

"But what can I do?" he asked. "Can I help her?"

Sonjee laughed. "Bill, you are the Candu Mali Siwa. You can do anything. You are the master of the stones. They all do your bidding. You know how every ancient phrase in my language has two meanings? That's because our language split in two after the Schism. In the male dialect, Candu Mali Siwa means Stone Master of the Universe. In the female dialect, it means Fountain of Hope for the Universe. Bill, you give us all hope. Nan holds that hope in her heart that you will return."

Bonnie turned his head to hers and kissed his lips again. "Bill, you have to go. Please save her. Without her we would all be dead. Do you remember the ulluba that helped Zelda get Chachis to Lance's cottage? We thought it was Buffy, but it wasn't. It was Nan. She came through the portal with the other ulluba and waited to help our dogs. Chachis was almost dead, so Nan took most of the poison out of her so Lance would be able to revive her. If it wasn't for Nan, we all would have died that night at your sister's house. She saved our family!" Bonnie dropped her head. "Bill, darling, I know exactly what it means if you go. But that's okay. This is meant to be. Without that woman, we wouldn't be alive now. Who am I to deny her anything?"

"Okay, I understand." He turned to Sonjee and asked, "But how do I get there?"

"The Candu Mali Siwa already knows the answer to that," she laughed. "The stones will do anything you ask."

"Wait!" shouted Chief Elder Molo Indigar as she approached with the servant girl, Alani. "Bill Marshall, those mages have impregnated Alani. You must help her first."

Alani was trembling and soaked in her own tears. Her abdomen was swollen and filled with glowing light. "Elder, they did not touch me! It must be a horrible disease."

Bill took her in his arms and lifted her up. He kissed her cheek. "Please don't cry, Alani. You are not pregnant or diseased. You are the Cantu Bagwa of Orto Nong. Although you were unaware, your body had been safeguarding the souls of everyone who died here today. This is a great miracle!"

"Get those demons out of her or we will have no choice but to kill her!" Molo shouted.

"Shut up, Elder," Bill laughed. "The stones will not allow anything to harm Alani. She is the Soul of the Planet and you must treat her as such."

"I'm afraid, Candu Mali Siwa," the girl cried. "Please help me."

Bill kissed her again and sat her on the ground. He knelt next to her. "Don't be afraid, Cantu Bagwa. You are the most powerful force on this planet. Just do as I say." He took her hands in his. "Now, cup your hands like this over your stomach and remember the Ballanan who died today." She closed her eyes tight. "Okay, open your eyes and your hands." A glowing globe of light sat in her palm.

"What is that?" she asked.

"The souls of the Ballanan are now in your hands," Bill said. "Kiss the globe and pray for their spirits. Then crush the globe between your hands and toss the remains into the air." The bits flew through the sky and dead Ballanan all over the planet rose and walked again. Bill had her do the same for the vorrath, zongo and ulluba. Finally she created the globe with the souls of the mages and her abdomen was normal again.

"What do I do with this one, Bill?" she asked.

"That's a good question. I don't know," he replied. "What do you think, Sonjee?"

"Please give it to me, Bill," she said. "I don't know if they deserve to live or not, but we can think about it." Bill handed her the globe. She handed him the white diamond and the red stone. "Bill, here is our Hopestone. We don't need it to get to our homes. The red stone is from the Hopestone on Earth. Your granddaughter gave it to Keedu, knowing it would end up with you. Please squeeze them in your hand."

He squeezed them tight, and when he opened his palm, two identical rose diamonds sat there. "I know what these are for," he said as he let them slide into his skin. "One last thing. He reached through the skin of his chest and broke off a small piece of the Hopestone blade. He held it against Alani's chest and a thick gold necklace and pendant formed around it. "Alani, this stone and necklace mark you as the Cantu Bagwa. Never remove them. You and I are now connected through the stones. I will always watch over you. Please remember you are the Soul of Orto Nong. Nothing can harm you here, and it is your duty to protect this planet."

"I understand, Bill," she said, gently stroking the stone. "I won't let you down."

Bill kissed Bonnie again. "I'll see you at home soon, darling." She could still feel his breath on her face, but he was gone.

Chapter 37

The ice palace was gone. Bill stood at what had been the twenty-foot-tall ice doors that led into the entry way. Now there was nothing but broken bits of furniture and blocks of ice, many several feet square. He wondered how he would ever find her small body in this mess. He thought if he could fly, he might see her lying below. His body lifted off the ground and he drifted upward, not knowing how to stop. He tried to remember what Sonjee had told him, but his anxiety level was rising quickly. At seventy feet off the ground he saw bloody snow. Without thinking, he flew down and landed next to her. "Pasha, I have returned," he said. He checked to see if she was breathing. He saw her chest move very slowly. "Oh thank God! Pasha, can you hear me?"

"Bill, you returned for me," she whispered. "Now I can die happy."

"You're not dying today, Nan!" he shouted. "I'm here to save you."

"I think it's too late for that Pashna," she coughed. "Thank you for trying though. My whole body had been smashed. I can feel all my organs and bones broken. Only a miracle could help me now."

"Then one miracle is coming up!" he said. He put his hands over his face and prayed for strength. Then he touched her head and slowly slid his hands down her body. She cried and trembled with each inch his hands moved.

"Bill, please stop for the love of God," she cried. "My blood is boiling and my organs and bones are grinding together. Just let me go, Pashna."

"Not in a million year, Pasha," he said as he continued moving down her body. He could see her bones resetting and the blood was coming out of the snow and returning to her body. Her body had been covered with horrible bruises, but as his hands passed, they faded away. He could feel her femurs stitching together as his fingertips moved down her thighs. Her ankles had been broken and her feet were sideways when he reached them. Bill could hear the bones snapping back into place and she cried and moaned horribly. Then he was finished. "How are you, my darling?" he asked.

"Not bad, considering I was begging for death a few seconds ago," she whispered. "Please help me sit up, Bill." He helped her and sat next to her on the snow. "Thank you for this, Bill. Ten minutes ago, my greatest wish in this life was to die here in your arms. I begged God for that. Now I am happy to be alive. How did you do that, Pashna?"

"By now you know I am the Candu Mali Siwa, right?" he laughed.

"Oh, I forgot about that," she giggled. "How did the battle go on Orto Nong?"

"I'm sure Sonjee already told you," Bill smirked. "Your sisters saved us all."

"Pashna, you saved us all!" Nan said.

Bill laughed and put his arm around her shoulders, holding her tightly to him. "Bonnie told me how it was you, not Buffy the ulluba, who saved my dogs and led Lance to save my family. You saved us, Pasha. I will love you forever for that." He kissed her lips passionately. "Thank you."

"You are quite welcome, Candu Mali Siwa," she laughed. "But you should know we are not alone."

"I know," Bill replied. "I sensed the mage when I first arrived."

"Please don't harm him, Pashna. It is Umdala, the one I saved from crucifixion," Nan begged. "I know he was to blame for my injuries, but we are a conflicted race. Men and women have been apart so long. It was really my fault for saving him. I was so certain he and I would become the Eretz Domma."

Bill kissed her again and said, "No, he is not the one meant for you, Pasha." He held her tightly and whispered in her ear, "You and I are the Eretz Domma, Pasha."

She looked at him with a confused look on her face. "Bill, the ancient texts clearly say the Eretz Domma will end the Schism. That means the man must be a mage."

"Well, you can't believe everything you read, Nan. You said it yourself. Our races are practically identical, except you are more technologically advanced. None of us know the true ancient history of the universe. Perhaps all humanoid species are descendants of the original men and women. And why can't I help end the Schism too?" Bill stood and paced about. "What do we do about Umdala?"

She shrugged her shoulders. "I don't know anymore. I still feel the good in him. Perhaps he may yet find his own ice wizard."

"I hate leaving these things to chance," Bill frowned. "Perhaps we should take this matter into our own hands." He snapped his fingers and Umdala was standing in front of them, shaking in fear. "Umdala Paraka Byulani, you are charged with willfully attacking this beautiful woman and leading to her near death. How do you plead?"

"I'm so sorry, Ulu," he said to Nan. He turned to face Bill. "I am guilty as charged, Candu Mali Siwa. I throw myself on your mercy." He fell to the ground sobbing, groveling at Bill's feet for compassion.

"Nan, what do you think we should do?" Bill asked.

"Release the fool. He had his chance to be Eretz Domma. Let him go now and Keedu will catch up to him eventually and kill him for us," she giggled.

"Wow! That's pretty harsh, even for me, Pasha," Bill replied, looking startled. Bill touched Umdala's head with his fingers. "Okay, Umdala, now you have seen what happened on Orto Nong. Keedu and his army are finished, but we both know Keedu will be back. If I let you go, what would you do?"

"Please don't let me go, Candu Mali Siwa," he begged. "Other mages will find me quickly and kill me. I know I did this to myself, but I want to do the right thing."

Bill stood quietly and closed his eyes. Nan and Umdala both looked at him and wondered what was going on in his mind. In a flash of frost, Sonjee was standing there with them. She hugged Nan and kissed her cheeks. "Sister, I am so happy to see you recovering." She turned to Bill and asked, "How may I serve you Master?"

He kissed her cheeks. "Sonjee, please just call me Bill. I'm no person's master." He was blushing. "This mage is a quandary. He wants to reform but his actions almost killed my Pasha. He is personally responsible for most of the progress made on Earth over the last twenty thousand years, so I owe him a great debt of gratitude. What would you do?"

"Everyone deserves another chance, Bill," Sonjee said, now blushing herself. "But how do we make certain he doesn't revert to his hedonistic ways?"

"I won't, I swear it," Umdala cried.

"Well, I have one idea that might work," Bill smiled. He put his hands over Umdala's head and moved them down his body. By the time he reached his feet, the human version of Umdala, the one known to the employees of his companies stood before them. He walked around the mage to inspect his work. "Not bad if I do say so myself."

"You let him morph back into human shape?" Nan asked.

"Not exactly, Pasha," Bill laughed. "Umdala Paraka Byulani is dead. This is Robert Umdala, billionaire entrepreneur from Earth. He can never morph into his mage body again. The stones and I will make certain of that. Sonjee, if you agree, your new name is Sonya. You are his wife. Both of you will move to Earth and continue to run his companies. You and I can keep an eye on him there, if that's okay with you?"

Sonjee picked Umdala from the ground and looked at him in the eye. "I could do better, but he is handsome in this form. But I thought you and Nan were the Eretz Domma?"

"If the Eretz Domma is truly to end the Schism, there has to be more than one man-woman coupling. What would one couple do to end anything?" Bill walked over to Nan and kissed her again. "However, Sonya, I would prefer if you two wait a day or two before you become intimate. Then Nan and I will still be the original." Nan was blushing bright red.

"Come along, husband!" Sonjee demanded. They both disappeared in a cloud of frost.

"Pashna, I still do not understand," Nan started. "You are married. Bonnie is a wonderful person and I would never wish to harm her in anyway. Don't worry about me. I am still very weak and it will take years to rebuild my strength and this palace. The people here still need me. I can't expect you to leave your family for this."

Bill put his arms against his sides and gradually raised them. The walls of the ice palace grew quickly around them. By the time his hands met over his head, they were standing in the main room where they had spent so much time together. The palace was complete again. "A Candu Mali Siwa's work is never done," he laughed. He took her in his arms and carried her into the bedroom and set her gently down. Then he sat by her side. He opened his hand and the two pink diamonds appeared. "Pasha, these stones were created by joining the Hopestones of Earth and Bala Napor."

"They are so beautiful, Pashna," she said as she took one in her left hand and held it up to the light. "It is a single crystal! How did the stones join so perfectly?"

"You said the Candu Mali Siwa was the master of the stones, right? Well, I held them in my hand and they joined for me. They represent the eternal connection between you and me," he replied. The stone on his palm disappeared back into his skin. "Let me see that stone, Pasha." She handed it to him and he held her hand. He held the stone against her left ring finger and a gold setting materialized around it. "This ring is our bond, Pasha. The other stone will always be with me. The two will keep us connected for all time."

"Pashna, it is so perfect." She turned her head and said, "But I don't know. You will be so far away and I don't know when or if I'll ever see you."

"Pasha, this is all very strange for me too. You have always been an ice wizard. A few months ago, I was a sheep rancher and cheese maker. Now I am told

I am the Fountain of Hope for the Universe. Can you imagine the shock to my brain that title gave me? All I know is that without you, my family and I would have died when the Ballanan came to Earth looking for Umdala. You ask me if I love my wife, children and grandchild. The answer is yes, of course I do. But now I look where I am today and the gift that has been given to me to hold this role, and I am without words. It is just too miraculous. If I am to be guardian of hope for the universe, I can certainly keep you as my Pasha and Bonnie as my wife. Anything else would be a dishonor to you both. I love you Pasha, and I always will."

"And I love you Pashna," she whispered.

He pulled back the blankets and climbed in bed. He smiled and their clothes were gone. Bill kissed her lips and ran his hands down her body. She moaned and kissed his neck and chest. He kissed her breasts and her stomach. He ached for her. Soon they were making love. He watched her eyes and she looked at him with total love. "Pasha, thank you for loving me and helping me become the person I was meant to be."

"I love you, Pashna. I never could have imagined this moment." She moaned with pleasure. "You have saved me and my soul."

Chapter 38

The night was too quiet. Bill Marshall was accustomed to the sounds of crickets chirping outside his ranch house. The occasional hoot of a passing owl would normally remind him that nature is hard at work even in the middle of the night. Even when he was asleep, his ears were focused on the sounds of the local coyotes. He had lost more than one lamb to the intruders who were brazen enough to make their way into the barn. Tonight though, there was no sound outside. He could only hear Bonnie breathing deeply as she slept next to him.

Bill rolled over and looked at his alarm clock, which read 5:00 a.m. He climbed out of bed and walked over to the small window overlooking the front of the house. The portal key was quiet tonight, but the lights were on and several sentinels could be seen patrolling the area. It had taken a long time to get his farmhouse back on this land. The military resisted for some time, but no force can resist the Candu Mali Siwa for very long. He pulled on his jeans, boots, and a tee shirt and walked to the door of his room.

"What's wrong, honey?" Bonnie asked.

"Nothing, sweetheart, please go back to sleep," he replied. "I'm just going to check on the sentinels." He walked out of the room down the hall. The new house had more rooms since Frank, Cindy, and Cybil had moved in. There was a downstairs addition too for Wilbur, Eileen, and their kids. The lonely farmhouse was now a hub of family activity, which Bill adored. He opened the door to Cybil's room and saw her sitting up in bed with the covers over her head. "What are you up to, Cyb? It's only five o'clock."

She pulled the covers off and said, "Nothing, Grandpa. August and I are just helping Alani get accustomed to the job. You'd better hurry, you have company coming." She covered herself again and Bill closed the door and walked downstairs. He had no idea what company she was talking about. As he walked down, he could smell coffee and wondered who else could be up at this early hour.

Walking into the kitchen, he saw his son Frank pouring a fresh cup. "Welcome home, son," he said softly. Frank set down the cup and rushed over to hug his dad. "I guess you finished sentinel training early, huh?"

"That's right, Dad," he smiled. "I'm so excited about taking my place with the others." He turned to pour a cup for his father and handed it to him. "I'm hoping to do temporary duty on Goola. It will be years before they can man their own portal key. Have a seat Dad."

"I thought I'd go check on the sentinels, son," Bill smiled. "Why don't you walk with me?" The two men walked outside and felt the chill air of an early spring morning in East San Diego County. They walked slowly down the hill; taking sips of hot coffee and watching the mist fade as sunrise approached. When they reached the portal key, they could tell it was not locked on any location. "What's happening sentinel?"

"Nothing yet, Mr. Marshall," the young man said. "It's an honor to meet the Candu Mali Siwa, sir! I'm Joe Peterson, how do you do?" the man said as he stuck out his hand.

Bill shook it firmly, saying, "Just call me Bill, Joe. And this is my son, Frank."

"Hi Frank," Joe smiled. "I hear you got approved for the opening on Goola. Congratulations!"

"That is great news!" Frank exclaimed. "I hadn't heard yet."

"I didn't mean to ruin the surprise, Frank." At a tone from the key, Joe said, "Excuse me, but we're getting a connection request." He turned some controls and the grassy hill near Lance's home appeared. When the connection was complete, Lance Allright strode through the portal and stood next to them.

Bill and Frank both hugged Lance. "This must be the surprise visit Cybil was talking about. It's great to see you Lance!" Bill said. "How have you been?"

"I only have a moment, guys," Lance said. "When it happened, I couldn't wait to tell you, Bill."

"What is it? Don't keep us waiting!" Bill replied.

"Bill, August and I are engaged! Can you believe it?" Lance laughed. "I've never been so happy in my life!" The men embraced again.

"I'm so happy for you," Bill said. "I love you both."

"I've been crazy about her forever. Frankly, when we took our trip to Goola, I thought all was lost. I was so convinced it was August coming on to you, Bill. I was really pissed off until I found it was Nan-bo-Nan," Lance admitted.

"I thought the same thing, old friend," Bill said. "But the best man won."

"Thank you Bill. I've got to get back, though. I'm going to meet her parents today, and I can't be late. Take care and you will all be getting invitations to the wedding," Lance smiled. "You have to be there, even Cybil."

"I think the world can survive a few hours without her," Bill laughed.

"Bill, please invite Nan as well," Lance said. "I'm not sure how to do that or if it would hurt Bonnie. I don't want to do that either."

"Don't worry about it Lance. We will all be there!" Bill answered as Lance raced back through the portal and up the hill. He turned and waved at them and they waved back. The connection to Far Sun was broken. They turned to go back to the house and noticed a single figure in a long, white, hooded robe was standing halfway up the hill. As they came forward, Nan removed her hood and smiled at them.

Bill jogged ahead to reach her first and threw his arms around her and kissed her. "Pasha, what are you doing here?"

"I hate to be here with your family around," she replied. "But I have missed you and wanted to talk to you for a few minutes."

"Of course, you are always welcome here, Pasha. Do you want to come inside?" he asked as Frank approached.

"No, perhaps we can sit on that bench over there," she replied.

Frank joined them and went to welcome Nan. "Nan, it is our honor to have you here. Please come in." He leaned to kiss her cheek and she kissed his lips instead.

"Thank you Frank, but I just want to speak to Bill a little. I don't want to interrupt your family life," she said.

Frank took her hands in his and looked in her eyes. "Nan, we love you. You are the reason we are alive today. Thanks to you, my daughter is Cantu Bagwa of Earth, and my dad is the Candu Mali Siwa. I owe you my whole life." He kissed her cheeks and turned to Bill. "Dad, I'll see you inside." He walked away slowly.

Bill took Nan's hand and led her to the bench where they sat. "I've missed you too, Pasha. I have scheduled to spend next month with you if that's still okay."

She smiled. "Of course, Pashna. I remember that, but today I was just lonely and needed to see a happy face."

"You heard Frank. Why don't you stay with us a few days or weeks? I'm sure Goola can take care of itself for a little while," Bill urged.

"Thank you, Pashna, but I will wait my turn," she smiled shyly. "I just remembered a few things I forgot to tell you about being Candu Mali Siwa and the Eretz Domma."

"Okay, please tell me Pasha," he replied.

"First, the Candu Mali Siwa is almost immortal," she stated.

"Immortal? You mean I'll never die. I don't know about that. What about my family?" he asked.

"Well, almost immortal. No one knows how long one will live because the prophecy has never been fulfilled. But certainly you'll have a very long life," she answered. "Is that a problem?"

"I never imagined anything like that, but yes it is a problem," he said, with his face turning red with anger. "How am I supposed to sit here and watch my family die of old age?"

"Maybe not them, but others, yes," she replied. "Any one closely related to you becomes immortal too. When we became the Eretz Domma, that trait was passed to me. Bonnie and your son will also have this gift."

"I cannot imagine little Cybil growing old and dying before me," he said with his head in his hands.

"Oh, not her either, Bill. The Cantu Bagwa is immortal too," she remembered.

"I'm going to have to think about that one, Nan," he said. "This is too confusing. What other news do you have?"

"My sisters have determined that Keedu and Baku have left this galaxy. We believe they will try to rebuild a new army and find new tools to defeat you. Fortunately, that could take millions of years," she chuckled.

"Pasha, that would be more comforting if I knew I would be dead before then," he said, hugging her to him. "What do we do now?"

"Nothing, Bill. Even for an immortal a million years is a long time. We can worry about that when the time comes. You know, you are a bit of a worry wart, Bill Marshall," she laughed. "My sisters wanted me to give you these stones too." She opened a bag and showed hundreds of small diamonds of every hue. "These are the Heartstones and Hopestones from all of their worlds. If you possess these, you can watch over them as well, Pashna." He held out his hands and she poured the stones into his hands. He looked at them and imagined what those worlds were like. Slowly they slipped through his skin. Now he knew those worlds well.

"That was a gift of incomparable value, Pasha. Thank them for me," he requested. "I can see those planets in my mind now. We must visit them together, darling." He kissed her lips. "Anything else, my love?"

"Our babies are doing well, Pashna. They are all very healthy and growing quickly," she smiled shyly.

"Our babies? Why didn't you tell me sooner, Pasha?" he replied. He put his hand on her belly.

"I wanted some time to pass, my love," she said. "As I told you then, I wasn't sure our species could bear children, but you were right. My sisters visit me often and they can sense these things very well. My womb holds our two daughters and one son."

Bill held her tightly and kissed her again. "This is a miracle! Triplets! I am so happy. Wait until I tell Bonnie."

"Bill, please don't do that," she urged. "This transition is difficult enough for her. If you tell her I am pregnant, everything could come apart. Trust me here. I'm begging you not to say anything at this time, okay?"

"Of course, Pasha, if that is what you think is best," he sighed.

She turned her body to face him and put her hands on his knees. "Bill Marshall, the day the Ballanan attacked your world changed everything. The same happened on Goola as well. Billions of lives changed forever in an instant. Every action occurred for a reason, and we were just doing as we were meant to do. Now, a year later, three new children will be born. Never in the history of the universe has there been an Eretz Domma or a Candu Mali Siwa. Now there are both here and they are the same. They are you, Bill Marshall. God has his eye on you, me, Bonnie, Cybil, Frank, Cindy, August, Lance, and many others. We are here to accomplish great things together."

"I would have thought the defeat of the black mages was a major goal, Pasha," he said with his head bowed. He raised his head and looked in her eyes. "You think that was just the beginning, don't you?"

"Bill, you have only been the Candu Mali Siwa for a few weeks. Now I have told you that you will live forever. Do you think God would let a man accomplish good one day and then give him dominion over the universe forever?" she asked. "Seriously, do you believe that, Pashna?"

"Nan, you must remember I learned about being immortal less than five minutes ago. That's a lot to internalize. But of course, God would never do that." He stood and looked at his farmhouse and then back at the portal key. "Yes, Pasha, we have a lot more work to do." He pulled her to her feet and kissed her. "And you know, Pasha, I can't wait for the next adventure."

About the Author

Karl J. Morgan

Karl Morgan has enjoyed fantasy books, movies and television since he was a young boy watching remarkable programs like the Addams Family, Munsters, Twilight Zone, and Outer Limits. In college, the author followed a broad curriculum which included astronomy, Eastern religions and mythology. More recently, he has been obsessed with books about cosmology and quantum mechanics.

The blending of fantasy with his love for science fiction and fact provides a broad palette of stories to tell and reminds us that with everything mankind has learned the world is still a magical and mysterious place.

It is that sense of magic and mystery that brings Karl to tell the story of Bill Marshall, a rancher whose life is changed forever by an earthquake that opens a portal through space, unleashing dark and sinister forces intent on destroying all life on Earth. Sentinel Lance Allright arrives at the right moment to stop the attack. Bill and Lance then need to discover why Earth was attacked and restore balance in the universe.

Karl lives in San Diego with his wife, Aida and their beloved puppies. Their two grown children have fled the nest and started their own adventures in life.

To read more about Karl and his projects, please visit: website (blog): http://www.karljmorgan.com/ facebook: www.facebook.com/karlmorganauthor, and twitter: @karljmorgan.

Remembrances: Choose to Be Happy and Embrace the Possibilities
ISBN: 978-0-9826461-9-9

The Dave Brewster Series

The Dave Brewster Series: Showdown Over Neptune
(Book 1)
ISBN: 978-0-9860270-0-0

The Dave Brewster Series: Second Predaxian War
(Book 2)
ISBN: 978-0-9860270-1-7

The Dave Brewster Series: The Hive
(Book 3)
ISBN: 978-0-9860270-2-4

The Dave Brewster Series: Tears of Gallia
(Book 4)
ISBN: 978-0-9860270-4-8

Heartstone

Heartstone: The Time Walker
(Book 2)
ISBN 978-0-9860270-5-5